CW01501639

Nicky, maybe this one's Paris...

Love ya!

Original Sin

(The Alexandra Jones Series #2)

Samantha Towle

Contents

Your journey never ends. Life has a way of changing things in incredible ways.

Alexander Volkov

Chapter 1: Six Months Later

"Nathan?"

"Hey." His deep voice comes from behind me like a warm breeze in the cold darkness.

Coming up close, his fingers ever so lightly skim down my bare arms. He's hardly touching me, but it feels electric, intense. He slides his hands into mine, entwining our fingers, and brings both our arms to wrap around my chest. Shivering with goose-bumps of absolute delight, I never want to let him go again.

Closing my eyes, I rest my head back against his shoulder and just breathe him in. I can smell him so clearly I can literally taste him on my tongue.

"I missed you," I say.

The longing is so completely evident in my voice it's almost palpable. I want him to know how hard it's been without him. I'm never going to let him go again. Ever.

"I missed you too." His voice comes in my ear, just a whisper; raspy, warm, doing inexplicable things to me. I've never felt as relieved and happy as I do now, here in his arms.

He brushes his lips over my neck. Heat burns under my skin. When I feel the hint of his tongue on me, I all but combust. Freeing a hand from mine, Nathan slides his hand down.

Inching up my vest with his fingers, he smoothes his palm across my stomach. I feel a shudder deep within. Then fingers moving downwards, he hooks a couple into the elastic of my knickers, tugging on them he turns me around to face him.

Looking up at him, I feel like I haven't seen him in forever. He still looks as beautiful as I remember. His bright green eyes are smouldering down at me like there's a fire burning behind them, lighting them to such extremities they're almost glowing.

I run my hands up his firm chest, nails scratching over the fabric of his T-shirt. More than anything, I just need to feel him.

Nathan draws me closer to him by the fingers firmly hooked in the elastic of my knickers. He leans down and puts his mouth on mine.

I am melting into nothing.

His kiss is gentle, soft. He's kissing me the exact same way he did the first time he kissed me in Dalby Forest and it's making my legs so very weak, it's taking all my strength just to keep vertical.

I wrap my arms around his neck. He runs his tongue between my lips, sucking my bottom lip into his mouth. Murmuring a warm delicious sound that vibrates through me, pulsing down ... down. I can feel myself slipping further and further into him, and I love the feeling.

Beep ... beep ...

"Nathan?" Startled, breathless, I break our kiss.

"Time to go," he whispers, releasing me, he steps back.

Panic seers through me, gripping me, covering all other feelings. "No, I'm not ready! You can't go!" I reach for him, but he's moved too far from my grasp and he's slipping further and further away.

I want to run to him but my feet are fixed to the floor, like someone glued them there while I wasn't looking.

I spin my head wildly, looking for something, anything to help me move. I can't lose him. Not again. And then something catches my attention, coming from my right. A glow. Shimmering, sparkling, and it's moving toward me.

"Sol?" I gasp, as he materialises before my eyes.

"Hey Alex." His voice. I thought I'd never hear it again. Yet here he is talking to me.

My heart breaks. I can't believe he's here. He looks exactly as I remember. No blood. No death. Just Sol, stood here smiling at me, with his trademark cheeky glint sparkling in his eyes.

Pain aches through my chest. There are so many things I want to say to him. I need to tell him I'm sorry.

How so very sorry I am.

Something breaks inside me. I feel hot wet tears on my cheeks.

"Don't cry," says Sol. "I hate to see you cry."

In an instant he's standing before me.

I want to grab him, hug him, hold him tight to me and never let him go.

He reaches a hand to my face and dries the tears from my cheeks. His touch is golden on my skin.

"I'm so sorry," I choke. "I didn't know Jin was there and …"

"Ssh, it wasn't your fault. I want to talk to you, about everything, but I can't. I haven't got long." His voice suddenly sounds reedy. "It's taken me a really long time to get through to you and I don't know if and when I can get back, so you have to listen to me carefully."

He sounds so serious. My heart starts to pump hard against my chest.

Beep … beep …

I can hear the sound again.

Tearing my eyes from Sol, I glance back to where Nathan was, but he's gone. Like he was never there. Just a darkness where he once stood. A really big part of me wants to follow Nathan into the darkness, to find him. But I'm torn. I don't want to leave Sol, not now I have him here with me, and so very real.

"Alex." Sol takes hold of my chin forcing my eyes to his. "You're waking up. I just need you to hang on for a bit longer. I have to tell you something." Pausing, he shakes his head. "There are so many things I want to tell you," he breathes. "But there's no time, and this is important."

I'm trying to stay, trying to keep my focus on him. I can sense his importance, his urgency, but there's a strong lure of something pulling me away from him. My eyes start to drift again.

"Alex." He hardens my name, grabbing my focus. "Listen to me. You need to pay attention today. Keep your eyes wide open. Everything's not as it first seems. I know he's coming for you, and he's not–"

His head snaps to his left like he hears something. Something I don't hear.

"Sol?"

He looks quickly back to me.

In his green eyes I can see him contemplating something, like he's making the most important decision of his life.

Then taking my face in his hands, he leans close, and kisses me hard on the lips.

I open my eyes to the sound of my beeping alarm, alone in my bedroom. With a sigh, I reach over and slam my hand on it, hearing the crack as I break yet another alarm clock. I roll onto my back, sighing. Putting my hand to my face, I feel my cheeks are wet.

This isn't unusual. I cry a lot in my sleep. I won't let myself cry while I'm awake so I think it's my body's way of coping, you know, its natural way of dealing.

Pulling the duvet over my head, I close my eyes and rake up an old picture of Nathan in my mind. Just as I do every morning, and have done for the last six months.

Nathan is a constant in my mind, alongside everyone else I've lost. But thinking of him … them, is the only thing that keeps me going, gets me through this lonely bleak existence I have the pleasure of calling a life.

I spend all my time inanely fighting against my feelings of mourning the person I used to be. Mourning the life and people I've lost … Carrie. Sol. Jack. Erin … Nathan.

I miss Nathan so much it's hard to breathe at times. Like there's a physical ache in my chest that will never ever go away.

I'm trying really hard to move on. Move on from the life that used to belong to me. Move on from Nathan. Honestly I am.

It's just not going so well.

Mostly, I feel like I'm floating face side up in the ocean, heading to nowhere in particular, but knowing I never can reach the shore. Because if I do, then it's all over for me.

I spend all my time in my head, living in the past, dreaming of a future that can never be mine. So far, it's the only way I've found that has come anywhere close to helping combat some of the loneliness which threatens to strip me to pieces.

Every day, I wake, and paper over the cracks with floating memories, knowing it's not a permanent fix, but all I've got for now, until I somehow find a way to fill those holes permanently.

Throwing the duvet back off my head I flip myself over and growl the anger and frustration out into my pillow.

Eventually, I drag myself out of bed, go into the living room and switch on the TV. It comes to life with the early morning news.

The news reader is gabbling away in Italian. I understand little of what she's talking about, I just like the background noise. Silence and me do not go well together. The people in that little box over there are the closest to company that I have in my life now.

Trudging into the kitchen I empty dark roast local blend into the coffee machine, fill it with water from the jug, and set it going. I'm going to need a strong coffee to get me through my full day of serving it. Because that's my life now; well for the moment it is anyway, until it's time for me to move on again.

But for now, I'm living in Italy, working in a little café called Piaz, as a Barista.

It's not ideal, but it's better than the alternative offered to me. I could be with the Originals.

Chapter 2: Barista

"Barista, un cappuccino, per favore."

I brush the stray tendrils of my hair back off my clammy forehead, heated by the steam pouring out of the coffee machine I'm standing in front of, and turn my head slightly to acknowledge the deep male voice coming from behind me.

"Sì, certo," I reply, not really taking notice of him. "Grazie."

Out of my peripheral I can see he's still lingering at the counter.

I press the button on the coffee machine, setting it going, dry my damp and sweaty hands on my apron, and turn to him to see what else he wants.

He blindsides me a little. Mainly, because he's so striking.

Seriously good looking. And when I say seriously good looking I don't mean he's pretty. I mean this guy is incredibly good looking in the sculpted sense.

I know the general thinking is that all Italian men are beautiful, and I'm sure there are many beautiful men out there somewhere in Italy, I just haven't happened to come across them yet. Well, not until now that is.

Mostly, it's fat, greasy balding men, I have to serve coffee to all day long. Not that it matters either way to me. Nothing is of interest to me anymore. Especially not men.

But I do have to say this guy here is something altogether different. He is silver screen material. And he screams money and taste. All clean lines and crisp white shirt rolled up at the sleeves showing dark tanned forearms. Designer hangs off his clothes.

His hair is as black as the coffee I pour all day long and he eyes are inky to match. I'd say he's about thirty. And boy, he is tall. I'd give him six and a half feet. And I just know for a fact that he's all rock hard pecs underneath that white business shirt of his. He looks like a movie star or one of those aftershave models you see on the billboards. You know the type that cause you to rubberneck as you drive past. I wonder if he is a model? Or maybe even an actor?

He's the complete and utter contrast of Nathan. Nathan's all dirty blonde hair, piercing green eyes and ripped jeans. He's rough, ready, and very *very* edgy. My perfect.

I used to think I liked the clean shaven smooth type, like Mr Movie Star here. Eddie was the same. But that was until I met Nathan. He changed my world.

The thought brings a sad smile to my lips which I very quickly remove, plastering on a fake one.

"C'è qualcos'altro che posso ottenere?" I finally ask, realising I've been stood staring at him for what would be considered an unreasonable amount of time.

He's probably used to women staring at him, but still, I feel a blush start to rise in my cheeks.

A grin edges his lips, lifting his eyes. "No, solo il cappuccino."

"Prendete posto, io porterò sopra," I say, adding my best serving smile.

His black eyes linger on me for a moment, then he nods and heads over to an empty table by the window.

I told Mr Handsome, 'To take a seat, I'll bring it over.'

I'm not fluent in Italian. That's near on about the extent of my Italian vocabulary. I bought a phrase book and have been teaching myself the basics since my arrival.

I did the same when I was in France and Switzerland. It helps me get around, helps me get jobs like this one. I'm becoming bilingual, with a severe lack of fluency in any language.

I'll just be a collection of polite quotes in all languages soon enough. I don't stay in any particular town for long. I just wander the country, living and working in different towns until I reach the end, then I move to a different country. It's what I've done since I left Nathan, just work in an endless stream of cafés and bars, moving across Europe, heading to nowhere in particular.

It's hard to believe it's been six months since I left him sleeping in that hotel room.

I miss him.

A lot.

I thought this ache for him would have dulled by now. But it hasn't. Not an iota.

And it's not that I want to forget about Nathan, or any of them for that matter, because I don't, I just want to reach a functioning non-torture level. Which I thought I would have by now. But I haven't. It's all still as raw and painful as it was the day I left.

It's like I have this deep gaping void in my chest and no way to fill it.

But this is just life for me now. I know this. And no, I'm not throwing myself a pity party, even though sometimes I might want to. I want to become positive and move on.

And I'm sure it will happen, real soon.

I've just got to keep trying, and I will at some point figure out a way to stop pining for a future that will never be mine.

But for right now, I'll focus on keeping myself alive. I only have me to rely on. And for my own safety, as well as the worlds, I have to keep my identity hidden. I can't drop the ball.

That's why I don't stop moving. Ever.

The night I left Nathan sleeping in that hotel room in Scotland, I managed to hitch a ride with a woman who was heading home from work late. She dropped me in the town centre.

I wandered around all night, thinking about Nathan, wondering if he'd woken yet and knew I was gone. Then when dawn broke I got the first train heading to London. I didn't want to take the ferry over to France, Nathan would probably expect I would and that would be the first place he'd go looking, so I took the Eurostar.

I was nervous using the passport Craig procured for me, but there was no problem whatsoever, and the next thing I knew I was seated on the Eurostar heading to France, with absolutely no idea of what I would do when I got there.

When I arrived in Paris a few hours later, I checked into a cheap hotel near the station. Once I was safely in my room, I put my bag down, sat down on the edge of the bed, and cried. For what seemed like hours and hours.

When the tears ran out, I forced myself to think logically about my situation. The two things I knew I needed over everything else, was money and blood.

Just not necessarily in that order.

And I needed to move regularly, to not stay in the same place for too long, just like Nathan had said, but most importantly I needed to be aware of who and what was around me at all times. Risking discovery by another of my kind isn't an option.

So the next morning I paid for a few more nights stay at the hotel and went looking for a job. Any job. After two days I got one working as a waitress in a coffee shop. I stayed for two weeks, earning enough money to move me on to another town.

I moved through France for a couple of months, working in endless streams of cafés and bars, places which paid cash in hand with no questions asked.

I got myself supplies to make hunting easier; plastic bottles and a draining tube. I hunted at night in forests, stocking up on enough blood to last me a week.

After two months I moved from France to Switzerland, and continued on doing the same. After two and a half months in Switzerland, I moved to Italy.

I've been here for about six weeks. I've stayed in a couple of places so far, but now I find myself in Sassano in Western Italy, working here in Piaz.

It pays okay and the owner Joe Fonzarelli is nice. I've had the urge to call him The Fonz a few times, but he looks nothing like Fonzie and more like one of those fat balding types I mentioned.

But Joe's a nice guy, and the one bed apartment I'm currently renting belongs to him. Joe and his wife Carol own a few apartments which they rent out. I have it on a two month lease, which isn't ideal but is the best I could get, plus it's just down the road from the café.

I like it here. It's quiet. And it's a big enough place so that people don't ask questions, but not big enough to pose any risk of bumping into anything unwanted. I get to keep myself to myself and that suits me just fine.

The coffee machine starts to beep at me, breaking my reverie.

I make Handsome's cappuccino, put it onto a tray, and carry it over to his table.

He looks up from the book he's reading when I approach; Red Dragon by Thomas Harris, he's certainly got good taste in books. He puts his bookmark in, a receipt.

Funny, I do that too. I always use the receipt from the store I bought the book from as my bookmark. Not that I read much nowadays, actually come to think of it I haven't picked a book up since before the attack.

Putting his book down on the table he smiles at me, showing me a set of perfect white teeth. It's a nice smile. Not perfect, like his face, his lip crooks up more to the right, creating a dimple in his cheek.

I take the cup from the tray and place it on the table in front of him.

"Grazie," he says. For a deep voice, it's incredibly smooth.

"Godere." I turn away, taking the tray with me

"You're English?" he says in perfect English, but with an accent which I can't place.

He's obviously not Italian as I first thought.

I stop and turn back. "Yes," I nod.

It's not unusual for a customer to want to talk to me, especially if they're English, but I ensure I keep to the basic pleasantries.

I have to be careful with every stranger I speak to because there could always be that possibility that one day, one of them may have seen my picture in the paper and recognise me as that girl who went missing all those months ago when walking home from a night out with her best friend.

"Your accent. A dead give-away," he smiles.

"Ah right," I say. I take a tiny step back.

"Whereabouts in England are you from?"

"All over. I moved a lot."

He smiles again. Lips pressed together this time. "I lived in England for a while, Cornwall. It's a nice place."

I smile.

I don't want to make conversation. I don't have real conversations with people anymore. I just have polite interaction. But for some reason this guy seemingly wants to have a conversation with me. I know for certain he's not supernatural. He's human. I can always tell straight away, thankfully.

Maybe he's just lonely. But then, I can't imagine a guy who looks like he does being lonely for any significant period of time.

"But not as nice as here," he continues. "In my opinion of course." He winks.

"Yes. It is lovely here." I take another little step back.

"Sorry, I'm keeping you from your work." He gestures with his open hand. "I'm sure you're busy."

He casts a glance around the empty café. I see the smile in his eyes. He's taking the mick. There's only one other customer in the café at the moment and I'm fairly sure he fell asleep a while ago.

Releasing a little laugh I shake my head. "No, not really. But I should get back to pretending to work, just in case my boss turns up."

Now that's utter bollocks as I know for a fact Joe's not coming in today. But Handsome here doesn't know that. If Joe were coming in today then Celine, the other girl who works here, wouldn't have disappeared out back for a smoke twenty minutes ago. Actually, scrap that, she still would have even if Joe was here, she's a bit like that.

"I'm Zeff by the way," he holds out his hand for me to take.

Odd name.

"Sarah." That's the name on the passport Craig got for me - Sarah Tolliver.

It took some getting used to, but I'm there now. I sometimes wonder who Sarah Tolliver was, or if she was even real at all. For job and rental purposes I use Carrie's surname though, Ross. So currently, I'm Sarah Ross. I do that simply because, if for the slim chance Nathan is still looking for me, then he'll be looking for Sarah Tolliver.

Ensuring she can't be found by him.

Gingerly, I slip my hand into Zeff's to shake.

The sensation slams into my hand and flies up my arm the instant I make contact with him. It's like a magnetic, electrical charge. Literally, like someone has used one those defibrillators on me, jolting me, the charge rippling through my whole body. I'm half expecting someone to shout, 'Clear!' before zapping me again.

I snatch my hand back from his.

I see the element of surprise in his eyes, but I don't care, I'm instantly suspicious. My arm feels weird, numb, and my whole body is tingling.

Reaching out my senses I try to sense anything off about him. But there's nothing. He's just a regular human being.

Then my head starts to clear, and I start to think I might have overreacted a tad. Maybe it was just a static shock or something. But he doesn't seem to have had any reaction. Apart from the look on his face at me snatching my hand away, that is.

Feeling a flush creeping up my neck, I force an awkward smile and clasp the tray to my chest, gripping my hand around it to quell the sensation and bring my arm back to life.

"Well, it was really nice to meet you, Sarah." He picks his book up, "And thanks for the cappuccino."

"Nice to meet you." Turning, I head back behind the counter to dispose of the tray.

Celine comes back in soon after, reeking of cigarette smoke, so taking the chance to escape I leave her to keep cover of the café.

I head into the back to load the dishwasher with today's dirty cups and set it going. By the time I've finished and come back out, that Zeff guy is gone.

The rest of my shift passes by uneventfully. I get my bag, say good-bye to Celine, leaving her to lock up, and head back to my apartment.

Celine is okay, when she's not been brash. She's from California and is backpacking around Europe with her friends. She thinks I'm doing the same, but solo. I also get the impression she thinks it's quite tragic that I'm travelling alone. It is. Just not for the reasons she thinks.

Celine and her friends are doing what I am, moving around doing bar and waitressing jobs to give them money as they travel. Except mine is a little different. Well, a lot different.

As I walk toward my apartment, I notice the sky is coming in a little dark, earlier than normal. Crossing the street, I come up to the little complex of apartments where I live. Opening the gate, I walk across the courtyard, reaching the main door. I enter the security code in on the keypad and the door buzzes open.

There are only two floors; ground and first, I'm on the first so I take the stairs. Reaching my apartment, I unlock the door. Letting myself in, I turn the light on and cross through the open plan living room, dumping my rucksack on the kitchen counter.

I always have this rucksack with me, I don't go anywhere without it. It contains my passport and all the money I possess. It also has the newspaper cutting picture of Carrie and me. The one from the newspaper Nathan gave to me that first day when I'd woke to find out she was gone and I'd been changed into this monster.

It's the only photo I have of her. I ensure I always have those three things with me over everything else. I also carry around a tube for draining blood into bottles from the animals; and yes, it really is as gross as it sounds... and a silver blade for protection.

It was one of the first things I acquired after I left Nathan. So far I haven't needed to use it. I also carry around in my rucksack a spare set of clothes, for if I ever need to leave in a hurry, which in my case could be a big possibility. But thankfully, I haven't had to so far.

But I know one day, if not soon, it will happen, and I want to be as prepared as possible. I travel light. It makes moving all the more easier.

Going over to the fridge I get a bottle of blood out. Looking at the contents I see I'm down to a couple of days worth, max. I need to go hunting.

I very quickly learnt how to hunt since I didn't have Nathan taking care of me anymore. In the beginning I hated it, well I can't say I particularly love it now, but I'm accustomed to it.

Finishing the blood I go in my bedroom, change out of my work clothes, and put on my hunting clothes. Black jeans, a black long-sleeved sweater, and the Converse trainers Nathan bought me. They're looking old and battered but I can't bear to part with them.

I leave my hair tied in the ponytail it's been in all day. My hair is still brown, I decided to keep it this colour. It was just easier to carry on dyeing it than trying to get it back to my natural shade, and I quickly got used to it.

And with the slight tan I've got from constantly being in summer climes, the dark hair almost suits me. I didn't keep cutting it short though; I hated not having long hair so I let it grow. It's grown quite a bit, reaching to my shoulders now.

Getting myself ready to go hunting, I put the cleaned plastic bottles into my rucksack, ready for refilling. I double check I've included the tube I use to filter the blood out of the animals into the bottles. I also check my passport, money, picture, and clothes, are all there.

Last thing, I put my little handheld spade in and a pack of wet wipes. With everything ready, I set off, heading for the woods on the outskirts of town.

Chapter 3: The Hunter, the Hunted

I take a left at the top of the street my apartment building is on, walking away from the centre of town, uphill, heading straight for the wooded area surrounding it.

One of the reasons I like this place is because it has a great backdrop with a vast woodland area. Much bigger than the forest at the back of Nathan's farm. Nathan would love it here.

As I head out of town the streetlights become fewer, but it doesn't bother me as I can see just as well in the dark. Another side effect of being a Vârcolac, keen eyesight – well keen is putting it mildly – extraordinary is probably better suited.

When I reach the top of the steep incline, just outside of the woods, I stand for a moment, breathing in the cool crisp evening air. Letting my senses widen; I hear and smell.

These other things inside me just seem to know when there are others around – other 'beings'. I have to check there's no one in the forest. I would be surprised if a normal person were here at this time, but I need to make sure there are no supernaturals around.

Nope, all clear.

Making sure my backpack is secured, I walk down the little incline, knowing my way pretty well. I've hunted here twice already since I arrived. I tread over the hard mud and broken twigs, cracking them underfoot, bracing myself for the woodland.

The forest seems surprisingly well lit tonight. Glancing up I spy the moon, bright and full, huge in fact. It looks beautiful.

Taking a ten minute leisurely walk, I penetrate deeper into the forest. When I find a good spot, with plenty of roaming woodland creatures, I put the rucksack down beside a tree and retrieve the items I need.

I always hunt in the form I am in now, except with my fangs out. I now know how to protract and retract them as required. I haven't shifted into my wolf form yet. I have the urge inside me to do so, but I'm not just ready to face that side of myself yet.

And to be honest, I daren't.

I never got around to asking Nathan, to talk me through how I do it, and I know it might sound stupid, but I'm worried that if I shift while I am on my own, then I might not be able to get back to my human form as I won't know how to, then I'll be stuck as a wolf.

With everything I need ready, I begin the hunt.

After I've buried all the little bunnies I just killed, I clean the draining tube and spade with wet wipes, then spruce up myself the same way.

Packing the rucksack, I deposit the mud and bloodstained wipes into the front pocket to dispose of at home. I don't want to leave any evidence lying around, and I couldn't litter here anyway, it's too beautiful a place. I pull the zip closed and stand from the crouched position.

I feel it.

The hairs on the back of my neck prickle, every sense going on high alert.

There's someone, or *something* here. I stretch my senses out as far as I can. I hear him. He's light on his feet and is moving toward me – quickly.

A vampire.

Oh God. I've never encountered a vampire before. They hate my kind and will hate me even more. Or be curious. Either way it's not good. I need to get out of here, **now**.

If I know he's here, then he definitely knows I am.

Slinging the backpack on I sprint through the trees, with one direction in mind. The road. I need to get into population, then get myself the hell out of this town.

How did I not know there was a vampire living here?

This is bad.

Vampires don't know I exist. Well they do now. So not only will I have the Originals after me, also vampires.

Fuck.

Why do things have to go from bad to ridiculously worse?

Weaving through the trees I jump lithely over fallen bracken. My backpack is banging heavily against my back. I could do without it but it has everything I need to get me out of here, and quick, so there's no way I can ditch it.

I'm listening hard. I can hear him moving but can't pinpoint his exact location.

Keep moving, Alex. Just keep moving.

He jumps out from the thick stand of trees about thirty feet in front of me, skidding me to a halt. My heart whams into my ribcage.

He's not much bigger than me. Short dark hair and eyes to match. And he looks young. Twenty max. But I also know that even though he might look young and frail he's probably way stronger and far older than I am.

He raises an eyebrow.

"Now this is interesting," he says, in a European accent, maybe German, I'm not sure. He tilts his head. "I thought my senses were off for a moment back there. But looky here, I've got myself a lady Vârcolac."

I can't speak, I'm crippled with fear.

"What to do," he muses, tapping a finger against his lips. "Do I kill you myself ... or do I have a little fun with you first, then take you to Elijah? I'm sure he'd be *very* interested to meet you."

I inch a step backwards.

He raises an eyebrow.

"Y-you take me." My voice stammers. I try to garner control. "And the Originals will come after you – Matthias and Isaiah," I add their names on hoping it will make some difference.

Okay, it's bullshit, they have no clue where I am – with very good reason. But it's the only card I've got to play.

He folds his arms across his chest and narrows his gaze.

"Don't lie to me little girl. If Isaiah or Matthias had their hold on you they would not for one second let you out of their sight, let alone running around the forest late at night hunting animals. And if I didn't already know that fact, then it would have been the speed up in rate of that pretty little heart of yours. If you're going to lie honey, lie better. Get control of those human emotions you're so desperately and pathetically clinging to."

I see realisation flicker across his eyes. "Do they know of your existence?"

"Yes." Well I couldn't exactly say no. And I have a feeling either way I answered wouldn't work out well for me anyhow.

Loosening his arms, he scratches his cheek. "So I have something that Isaiah and Matthias want."

This seems to please and excite him. Me, not so much.

"This is going to be so much more fun than I first anticipated," he says.

I need my blade. It's in the pocket inside the rucksack, with my money and passport. If I could just get my hand in the bag without him noticing, then I might just stand a chance.

Taking another slight step back, I try to put more distance between him and me in the hope that he won't see as I try to slide my hand up my back. I can feel the zip.

Fuck! It's zipped up. Of course it is; nothing's ever easy for me. He smiles, quirking his lip. I leave my hand where it is on the zipper.

"So it's just you and me honey, and boy are we going to have some fun before I take you home to my family," he says.

Oh God.

I have two options. Fight or run. And that would be fight without my blade as it seems there is no way I can get it without taking my rucksack off, unzipping it, and getting it out. I have a feeling by that point he'd probably be kicking the crap out of me.

And then suddenly out of nowhere I get angry and pissed off.

Severely pissed off.

I'm tired of running. I'm tired in general to be quite honest. I've been running since the day I was changed. I've lost everything I've ever cared about. What else do I have to lose?

Nothing.

So I decide to do one of the stupidest things I've quite possibly ever done. I run at him full speed, using every bit of strength I have behind me.

I see the surprise register on his face, before he runs at me too. We crash into each other like a pair of bulldozers.

But he's the stronger of us two. He slams his hand flat against my chest, taking the wind out of me, knocking me backwards off my feet, and drives me down to the ground with one hand. I feel and hear the bones in my back crack.

Pain shoots up through my chest and my lungs start to burn. My head spins out of control, stars dancing before my eyes.

He's on top of me now, pinning me. Striving to battle through the agony, I struggle, trying to shift my weight and get out from underneath him, but he's strong – fuck is he strong – and I'm injured. I can barely move myself, let alone get him off me.

The plastic bottles in my rucksack are crushing beneath me, the impact having already shattered them. The smell of blood is wafting all around, and all I can keep thinking is my picture of Carrie is going to get ruined from the blood leaking out of the bottles.

I shove the thought aside, needing to focus on getting myself out of this. I'm all legs and arms, desperately kicking, hitting, trying anything I can to get free.

He's calm and collected, like he does this on a regular basis. He probably does.

I need to focus.

Think, Alex. *Think*. What will hurt him? He's a guy. I know one thing that hurts them.

So going with sheer desperation, that or stupidity, I go for the most sensitive part on a man and just hope it hurts a vampire the same. I clench my fist and punch him hard in the nuts before he even sees it coming.

His eyes go wide, veins splintering into the whites of his evil eyes, mouth tight in a grimace, his hands instantly going to his groin. He groans in pain and rolls off me, dropping to his side.

Not wasting a second, I scramble up onto my knees, then to my feet. Okay, I'm done fighting, now I'm running.

I'm fifty feet and still moving when he tackles me from behind. I feel like I'm being taken down by a three hundred pound man. The pain in my ribs intensifies.

Face down in the dirt, I have a flashback of the night I was attacked and turned into this monster. The shock of it loses me my momentum and gives him the advantage. He flips me over onto my back in one easy move, sitting on my chest, he pins my arms by my side with his legs, leaving his arms free for whatever use he wants. And no matter how much I fight beneath him, there's no give now. It seems he was going easy on me before, now he's putting real effort in, and I don't stand a chance.

I start screaming as loud as I can, out of fear and frustration.

The sound grates up out of my throat, my breath giving out on me. I know it won't achieve anything, no one can hear or help me, but I just can't do nothing. I could beg, but somehow I don't think begging is going to save me. And I get the distinct impression he's not the remorseful sort.

Especially when he laughs, and says, "I love a screamer. Keep it going honey."

I clamp my mouth shut.

He's looking down at me with real hunger. I'm surprised my blood would be of any interest to him, but from the look he's casting over me it seems I'm the very best on offer.

"Honestly, if you're going to kill me, just hurry up and get on with it because I can't bear to look at your ugly face a second longer," I say, through panted breath, my heart pounding painfully against my chest.

He laughs. Putting his hand over his heart, he says, "Ouch! That hurt honey." A sly grin. "And I never said I was going to kill you. I'm just going to have some fun with you first. You're a fighter. I like that. It gets me going."

His eyes drift to my mouth. He lifts his hand to it and runs his finger over my fangs; they came out as soon as I smelled the blood leaking out of my bag.

I bite his finger, hard, but not hard enough to bite it off, unfortunately. I get a sharp taste of his blood in my mouth. It's odd. Tangy, sharp, but nice. Very different to animal, and something altogether different to human I'm guessing. At least I'm still clean then.

He doesn't react to the pain. He just laughs again and puts his finger in his mouth, sucking the blood off. Then he removes it, holding it up in front of my face, and I watch in horror as it heals in a matter of seconds.

They heal a lot quicker than we do. I didn't know that. Shit.

I attempt to wriggle free again, but I'm going nowhere. Even though he's a small guy, I feel like I've got a truck sat on me.

"Honey, when are you going to realise I'm going nowhere … and neither are you," he smirks.

My heart is hammering in my chest. It hurts, so much. Adrenaline is flooding my body and mind. The word, panicking, just doesn't even cut it.

"Now, I've had Vârcolac before," he says in an easy tone. "It's not so bad. It was a man of course. And not anywhere as near pretty as you are." He runs the tip of his tongue along his top lip. "And well, you honey, you smell as sweet as sugar, and I'm sure you taste just as good."

Oh God.

My heart leaps into my throat. Every fibre of me going into blind frenzy as I see him release his fangs. The panic quickly rears my body into action. I start fighting for my freedom again, kicking and yelling for help, but he's unmoving.

He tilts his head back, cricking his neck, like his readying himself for a fight. Then in one swift move he plunges his teeth straight into my neck.

I scream. One single, piercing, painful scream.

It echoes around the empty forest and bounces right back at me.

Blood. There's blood everywhere. Swimming in my vision. Roaring in my ears. Trickling down my neck, soaking into the earth below.

His body tenses around me, clamping down harder, his knees tightening into me, the pain in my chest screaming a silent bellow as his hands pin my shoulders down to the hard ground.

I'm completely immobilised and tied to his will. He's sucking on my neck, harder and harder.

He's draining me.

He's not going to stop. He's going to bleed me dry. This is it. I'm going to die. I'm actually going to die here in this forest, at the hands of a vampire.

Of all the things I thought might kill me, I never ever considered it would be a vampire. I just assumed I'd die either old and alone, or if the Originals had me ... well ... when I could no longer give them what they so desire anymore.

I can feel my body weakening. Emptying. I'm dying.

I thought I'd feel relief when I knew I was going to die.

End what I've become.

End all of the pain and suffering.

But I don't. I just feel panicked. I don't want to die. I don't want to die and never see Nathan again.

I'm so tired. The pain's starting to drift away. My eyes pull down heavy. I search my mind for Nathan. I need to see him. Just one last time before I go.

Nathan. I wish you were here. I miss you so much.

Everything is going dark. So dark and empty. And I feel cold. So very cold.

'*Fight, don't let him win. Don't die like this. You've come too far to die now.*'

I hear the words clear in my mind, like someone has just spoken them to me, but I don't have the energy to process them.

I hear a growl, then a snap. The vampire's weight eases off me. And then I'm light, floating, off toward what I can only hope is Heaven.

Please not Hell. I've endured enough Hell.

Chapter 4: Déjà vu

I feel off. Unbalanced.

Memories start to flicker and stir. I become conscious of the sound of wood crackling on an open fire and the warm glow of heat on my skin. When I open my eyes, blinking through my haze, they settle on the hearth hosting the fire.

I'm laid on a sofa. A leather sofa. My body feels weak and my chest and neck are absolutely killing me.

The vampire, he bit me. I thought I was going to die. My hand instinctively goes to my neck. There's gauze on it. I can still feel the wound beneath. How long have I been out? It can't be long because I haven't healed yet.

Where am I?

"You lost a lot of blood, so the heal will take a bit longer than if you were at full strength."

The smooth deep voice that comes from behind me whips me up into a sitting position. And there I see sat on a leather chair, to my right, is the guy who was in Piaz earlier.

Zeff.

I remember his name because it is so unique.

My hand goes to my ribs, the pain my quick movement caused is aching its way through me. Still, I'm on instant alert, ready to protect myself if necessary.

I didn't sense him here.

Why not?

Maybe it's because I was out of it, and still kind of am. I open my mouth to speak but nothing comes out.

Before I get another chance to try, wordlessly, Zeff gets to his feet, walks past me, and crosses the open plan room to the kitchen at the other side.

He's still dressed in the clothes I saw him earlier, except there are blood marks staining his white shirt.

My blood?

My whole body may be riddled with fear but I'm already planning my escape out of here.

I already know exactly where everything is in this place. Most importantly, where all the exits are.

There are two.

The kitchen where Zeff currently is, is situated to my left, and that's where the back door is. Dining area behind me, with a hallway, presumably leading to the bedrooms. The front door to my right. My eyes lock with it for a long moment.

Bringing my eyes back front and centre, I give things another once over to see if I'm missing anything.

This place is nice. Plush. The living area I'm in has a huge black leather sofa, which I'm currently on, two leather armchairs either side of me, and the fireplace in front of me. Which is distracting.

Cosy and homely. Actually this whole place is homely, showered with expensive taste. The fireplace is set in a black marble surround with a deep hearth.

There are candles on the mantel and an old looking portrait of a stag hanging above it. There's a window seat adjacent to the fireplace on my left, a bookshelf beside it filled with books, surrounded by huge bay windows; the dark night the only thing currently visible through them.

I wonder what time it is, and how long I was out for?

And how I'm even here?

And who the hell is he, really?

He must have saved me from the vampire because I was as good as dead. The last thing I remember is that vampire draining me and how tired I was, how I felt like I was dying. But how could he have saved me from it – he's human.

And more importantly, *why* did he save me?

He must think I'm human, that'll be why he saved me.

Zeff opens the refrigerator door and gets something out. My eyes snap in his direction the instant I smell it. He doesn't need to turn around for me to know what's in his hand, but when he does, I see he's carrying a large glass of blood.

I'm stunned. He knows what I am. The blood's obviously not for him. And he can't think I'm a vampire, unless they feed on each other, which I highly doubt, so he must know I'm a Vârcolac. Or maybe he doesn't even know they exist? I didn't until I was turned into one. Maybe he just knows I'm not human – somehow. And also knows I'm a blood drinker.

Yet still he saved me. Go figure.

My mouth is flooded with hunger. I can feel the fangs pricking my bottom lip. I press my lips together, concealing them.

I watch his confident stride, listening to his heart beating, his intake of breath, as he walks toward me. His heartbeat is normal, he's breathing even. He's calm, not a trace of fear on him.

He isn't afraid of me. He knows what I am and he isn't afraid of me. And right now, I can't decide if that makes him brave or stupid. Not that he needs to be afraid of me, of course, I'm about as dangerous as those bunnies I kill, well as long as I've been fed that is, but he doesn't know that.

"You're going to need this," he says, standing over me, holding out the glass for me to take.

His voice is warm and husky, like melted chocolate, and ridiculously pleasant on my ears considering my current situation.

"You're going to need to feed to build up your strength and help heal those cracked ribs of yours."

Eyes wide, I tentatively reach out my hand and take the glass from him. Then I watch as he sits back down in his seat.

Suspicion has started to cloud my vision.

"You probably don't need me to tell you this," he continues. "But it is animal blood ... rabbit, and it's fresh."

My suspicion deepens further. Not just over the blood, but of this whole situation. It must show on my face and he reads it wrong, because he adds, "I'm a hunter. I shot them and drained them for you after I was sure you were okay."

I want to ask how long I've been out, but I don't because I have a far more pertinent question to ask, "Y–you know what I am?" I'm stumbling. I sound nervous, but I can't help it.

He meets my eyes with his black ones, and nods, "Yes."

"You know *exactly* what I am?"

"If you mean, do I know you're a Vârcolac? Then again – yes."

A dark shade of horror trickles through me. I look down at the glass in my hand. Then back up at him.

"How do you know? And how do you know I feed on animal blood and not human?"

I don't know quite why I just said that last bit. All I do know is there's a myriad of questions building in my mind, and it doesn't seem to be showing signs of slowing anytime soon.

I see consideration in his eyes. "I saw you hunting animals, stock piling."

He smiles, as though this is somehow amusing to him. Also, he answers my last question not my first, I note.

"Why didn't I sense you there?"

"I was keeping my distance. I know how it works. How *you* work."

"What were you doing in the woods so late?" I'm appearing calm, but my heart is hammering its way through my chest. It's doing nothing to help the rib pain.

The vampire was right, I have no control over my emotions and I'm relieved Zeff can't hear my heart, which is trying its best to give me away right now.

"I was following you," he says.

A chill slivers down my spine.

I lick my dry lips. "And why would you do that?"

"Because I knew what you were the second I met you in the coffee shop. I've spent long enough around the supernatural to know one when I see one." His dark eyes are coursing through me in the oddest way. I shift in my seat, clasping the glass of blood close to my stomach. The smell is calming me. A little. "I know you're not supposed to exist. I was curious. So I followed you."

"And why exactly do you spend time with the supernatural?"

I'm confused and worried. Okay, so worried is putting it mildly. Shitting myself probably just about covers it.

He pushes his tongue between his super white teeth. "Well, maybe spend time around them is the wrong term, more like … study them." Pause. "I'm a vampire hunter."

Holy hell.

I swallow down my fear, discreetly. "You were there to hunt me?"

"Not specifically." Leaning back in his chair, he stretches his long legs out and directs his look at me. "I hunt vampires. With you I was just – like I said – curious. I've never come across a female Vârcolac before. As far as I knew, you don't exist."

"So you don't hunt Vârcolacs?" I ask, dodging his unasked question.

A smile. "Oh, I never said that."

Those words freeze me cold. My hand trembles around the glass, shaking the contents. I put my other hand around it, steadying my hand and the glass.

"Anything that tries to make me its next meal," he continues, "then yeah, I'll kill it." He pauses. "With vampires, it's just … personal."

Am I afraid? Yes. Completely and totally fucking terrified.

I might be stronger than he is but I'm no fighter, and I'm especially not a killer. I think my poor showing with that vampire earlier proved that.

Well, that and the current hole in my neck and broken ribs. It takes me all my time to kill bunnies, and I can only just about manage that because it's better than killing a person.

Thing is, yes, I am stronger than Zeff, but I don't know his capabilities. I don't know a single thing about him. He might be human, but he killed that vampire, somehow.

I'm not really sure what his intentions are with me. He saved me, so I'm going to take a guess and say he's not out to hurt me. But what he actually is out for, well, I guess I'm going to have to wait to find out.

Now my hands have slowed down the shake, I move the glass away from my stomach and rest it against my thigh. His eyes follow it.

"Why is it personal with vampires?" I ask.

His eyes flicker back up to mine. There's something about the way he looks at me in this moment. Almost like he knows me. It's the oddest thing. Or maybe I'm reading it wrong and it's just suspicion and caution in his gaze.

Can't blame him for that, and it was a pretty direct question, one which could easily be misinterpreted. So I add, "Not that I have any issues with you killing vampires. Kill away, kill as many as you like – kill them all as far as I'm concerned. And actually while you're at it, have at Vârcolacs too – just not me, of course."

"Of course," he laughs.

It's deep and throaty, and it runs softly over my skin. It makes me feel odd.

Zeff pushes his hand through his black hair and his expression turns serious. "Vampires killed my parents." His tone is blank, even. "So I kill as many of them as I can, until I can get to the one who took their lives, so I can take his."

"Oh," I pause. "I'm sorry about your parents."

I certainly know how it feels to lose your parents. Your whole family for that matter. I send a shield down over my heart before I can start to feel maudlin.

"It was a long time ago." His tone is dismissive. Especially for someone hell bent on revenge.

"So that vampire," I ask, "was he one on your kill list?"

Something flickers in his eyes. If he was, he doesn't let on because he shakes his head and says, "No. I didn't know he was even here."

"You knew him?"

"Of him." He doesn't elaborate further. I don't push it. "Did he say anything to you before he attacked you?" Zeff asks.

I crawl back into my mind, trying to remember. "Erm, just that he was considering whether to kill me or take me to Elijah, I think he meant the head vampire. I'm guessing he decided to just kill me."

I see his eyes flicker in recognition to the name, Elijah. That, and something more.

"Or he just couldn't stop feeding," he says. "Sometimes they lose control. Surprising though, it's usually only the younger vampires that have little to no control. Maybe there's something about your blood that pushed him over the edge."

Contemplation passes over his face, but it's gone as quickly as it appeared.

"He was old?" I inquire.

"Very."

There's something in his tone that crawls across my skin and I shiver at the involuntary memory of the dirty fangs in my neck, draining me, his body pinning me to that cold floor.

As it flickers through my mind, I have to ask, "You did kill him, didn't you?"

He smiles. There's an edge to it. "Sure I did."

"How?" I'm curious.

I'm a Vârcolac and I couldn't take the fucker down.

He sits up straighter in his chair. "I shot him with a silver bullet, clear through his heart." He shrugs.

"Silver bullet?"

He gives me a suspicious look. "You do know what can kill you, don't you?"

I feel a rush of anger. "Of course I do. I just didn't know it could kill vampires too." In the limited discussion I had with Nathan about these things he never specified on that. But then, I never asked.

"Silver kills vamps, were's and vârcolac's."

I glare at him, biting the inside of my cheek. "Thanks for clearing that up."

Silence hits the room like a drunk stumbling in late to the party and I start to feel severely uncomfortable again, and not just with the pain in my ribs and neck.

When am I going to heal?

I can't remember a time I felt as beat up as this. Actually, I've never been beat up, apart from the attack which turned me into this monster, but thankfully I've never had a memory resurface of that.

Staring into the fire, I take a drink of blood hoping it will help, also unable to stave my hunger off any longer. I start to feel better the instant it washes down my throat, running through me like a healer.

I'm having a real sense of déjà vu here. This situation reminds me a lot of the first time I woke up in Nathan's room. Except it's not. And there wasn't a fireplace. And of course, he's not Nathan. He's nowhere close. No one ever will be.

I feel a pang for Nathan in my chest so hard it almost takes my breath away.

Putting the glass to my lips again, I try to pull my mind away from him. Now is not the time to get my Nathan head on.

I drain the contents. My fangs return home. I feel cleaner. Better. Then with a lot of effort, I get to my feet. I need to get out of here. And when I say here, I don't just mean this house, I mean this town.

That vampire might be dead but there could be more of them here, anywhere, lurking, just waiting to get me. I can't risk wasting any more time.

The blood will start to work soon. I'll feel better in a minute I'm sure of it. I just need to get moving.

Putting my empty glass on the wooden side table next to the sofa, I say to Zeff, "Thank you for all your help … for saving me."

He smiles a heart-warming smile. "Anytime."

I turn away, and my head goes light, stumbling I grip hold of the sofa arm to steady myself.

Zeff is at my side in an instant, his hand on my elbow. "You should sit back down. You lost a lot of blood. Give it a few hours and you'll be back to normal. But until then you're going to need to take it easy. Rest here until you're better, then I'll drive you home."

I shake his hand off, "No. Really, I need to go."

Eyes scanning the room, I look for my rucksack.

"Where's my rucksack?" I ask, voice edgy, alarmed that I can't locate it.

"It's in the kitchen. I'll go fetch it." He crosses the room and retrieves my rucksack from behind the kitchen counter. Carrying it back to me, I can see it looks like it's seen better days.

"I cleaned it up the best I could," he says, handing it to me. "But I had to throw your bottles away. They were all broken. Your tube and spade were okay, they're still in there, as is the flick blade." I see the ghost of a grin over his lips. "The wipes I binned and your clothes I put on to wash, they were soaked in blood. I did manage to save most of your money, it's in your bag."

I can feel my heart pumping hard against my chest. "There was a picture – a newspaper cutting … "

He shakes his head. "I'm sorry, it was ruined. I had to throw it away."

I bite my lip as tears burn the backs of my eyes. The only photo I had of Carrie, gone.

I see Zeff's lips turn down at the corners and I get the distinct impression he's got more bad news for me. "Your passport, it was also ruined. I'm sorry."

"What?!" I gasp.

A sinking feeling starts to shove my heart down into my stomach, ramming it down even further, when I actually see my passport which Zeff has just reached in and pulled out of my rucksack.

"Oh no!" I groan, taking it from his hand.

I examine it, flicking through the messed up pages. I drop my bag to the floor, despairing as I scour the pages, looking for some hope in them which is clearly not there. It's completely ruined. Blood staining every page.

I'm completely fucked. Out of the few possessions I own, which are very little believe me, this was the most important one of all. And it's ruined. I could have lost any of those other things, all replaceable, but not this.

I can't be restricted to one country; I need to constantly keep moving around. And as stupid as it sounds, it was also the last thing Nathan gave me. The one last remaining thing I had from him.

Oh God. How the hell am I going to get out of Italy now? It's not like I can just start crossing state border lines.

Or, could I?

No, not if I want to end up in prison, which wouldn't end well. There's not exactly an endless supply of animal blood in prison, and an orange jumpsuit really wouldn't suit me.

Seeing my obvious despair, Zeff says, "You can get a new passport through the British Embassy, I'm sure it wouldn't take long. Just don't tell them how the old one got destroyed."

He smiles, obviously trying to lighten the mood, not understanding my real and actual problem.

But I'm barely listening to him anyway.

I'm scanning my mind trying to come up with ideas and just coming up blank. This is hopeless.

I'm on the verge of letting those tears out. I can't breathe. I'm going to have a panic attack. I sink back down onto the edge of the sofa, putting hands on my knees. Leaning forward, I attempt to inhale deep calming breaths.

"Are you okay?" Zeff crouches down in front of me. "It's not that bad, it's only a passport, it's replaceable."

Lifting my head, I shake it. "It's not replaceable." I bite my lip. "It wasn't actually my passport … what I mean is it wasn't a real one. It was a fake."

I cast a glance at him to catch his expression, but it doesn't change from his current, concerned one. "And I can't apply for a new one, because … well … I can't."

A tear leaks from my eye. I brush it away.

I shouldn't have told him that. I don't know why I even did. He could tell someone. The police or anyone. Crap.

Oh God. Oh God. Oh God.

No, calm down. He doesn't know my real name, only the one that was printed on the passport if he checked it, or could still read it. He doesn't know anything about me. Except for that I'm a Vârcolac. The only female Vârcolac. Shit.

This is so much worse than I realised. It takes until now that I start cataloguing it all for me to realise. Sometimes I wonder how I manage to make it through the days. Seriously.

I need to get out of here and figure out what to do next. A thought appears in my mind. I could ring Craig and ask him to send me a new passport. I still have his card with his number on, back at the apartment.

No, that wouldn't work, because I'd have to give him a postal address and he'd tell Nathan where I am.

I could ask him not too.

But then I'm putting him in an awkward position and that's not fair. And would I listen if I were him? Nope. I would without a doubt tell Nathan where I am if I were Craig. Guys may like to deny it but they are just like us women in that respect.

Nathan might not even care where I am anymore, so it could be a moot point, but I can't take the risk.

Okay, so that's that out of the window. Now what?

Nothing. I have absolutely nothing. Maybe if I just start moving something will magically appear in my head.

Okay, so not highly likely, but here's hoping.

I reach down to retrieve my bag, when Zeff says, "I know someone who could get you a fake passport. Might take a week or so and it'll cost, but I'm pretty sure I can get you one."

My hope lifts. "Pretty sure?"

He smiles. "Definitely sure."

I could kiss him. I won't though.

"How much?" I ask.

"I'd say, maybe a thousand euros." He shrugs.

And my hope wilts as quickly as it rose. I shake my head disconsolately. "I don't have that much money. You saw everything I have."

"No money in the bank?"

I shake my head.

He drums his fingers over his lips. "Let me talk to my guy," he says kindly. "I might be able to get it cheaper. Either way, we'll figure something out."

Suspicion casts its cloud over me again. "Why are you helping me?"

"Cause I'm a sucker for a pretty face," he grins.

I blow out a sigh.

Ignoring his wit, I say, "Look I don't mean to sound rude or ungrateful, but you know what I am. And you're a hunter. It doesn't make sense that you saved me from that vampire, let alone that you would want to help me further."

Standing up, he moves away from me and sits on the chair arm, opposite. "Does it need to make sense?"

"Yes."

"Why?"

"Because it just does." *Because I have to be suspicious of everyone. It's how I survived this long.* I don't say that last bit though.

"I killed a vampire – a regular occurrence for me. It just so happened to help save you in the process. From where I'm stood you don't appear to be the murdering kind, you haven't done anything to me, and you seem to have enough problems to deal with right now. I'm generally a nice guy, you need a passport, and right now I'm the only one who can help you with that, and I'm just not the type of guy who can ignore a girl in distress."

"But I'm not just a girl, am I?" There's a challenge in my tone. I don't even know why.

He folds his arms across his chest. "Well I wouldn't exactly say you're a threat. You hunt rabbits to feed on and then dig them little rabbit sized graves to bury them in afterwards."

Shit, he saw that. My cheeks flame red hot.

"And don't worry, bunny girl," he adds as an afterthought. "I gave those ones a funeral after I'd finished draining them."

Smirking, he tilts his head in the direction of the empty, bloodstained glass.

If my face was red before, it's now reached mass spectrum. I've honestly got no come back.

"So do you want my help or not?" he asks in a neutral tone.

I take a moment to consider my options. I don't really have many. I can chase my own arse around Italy, but in the long run I need a passport, and he's my only key to that.

"Yes. Thank you. But the vampires … I can't stay here in this town."

"He was alone. There are no more here."

"How can you be sure?"

He smiles, "I can't be fully, but what other option do you have right now?"

Well that hasn't exactly appeased my fears, but he is right. For the time being I'm stuck here until I get that passport. I'm just going to have to be on constant alert if I'm going to last this week out.

With a sigh, I get to my feet and put my rucksack over my shoulder, wincing at the pain it causes in my ribs.

Zeff stands too. Putting a hand in his trousers pocket, he pulls out a car key. "Come on, Bunny, I'll give you a ride home."

My eyes widen with annoyance.

"Don't call me that," I say with an edge.

Zeff has already started to walk away, heading for the door, and looking over his shoulder at me, he gives me a nod, a cheeky glint reflecting out of his eyes. "Sure thing, Bunny."

Chapter 5: Bitch

On the ride home Zeff tells me he'll be in touch about the passport tomorrow. He's going to speak to his friend first thing and let me know the cost and time-scale.

He reiterated that I shouldn't worry about any more vampires turning up. That vampire was alone and as far as he knew no more of them are here, and he was dead so no one else knows about me.

But he hadn't known that vampire was here in the first place so that doesn't exactly appease me in any way. Not that I said that to him.

Even still, I don't really have much of a choice. I'm stuck here until Zeff gets me the passport, and I need to keep working to earn the money to pay for it.

Can I trust him?

I'm not entirely sure. But I really haven't got any other option. Except for getting in touch with Craig, and I know what that will lead to, so I can't. I need to keep Nathan safe. That's the whole point of this. And safe is far *far* away from me.

After Zeff drops me off at my flat, I go straight to take a shower. But not before I take a look at the bite that vampire has so generously bestowed on me.

I pull the gauze off that Zeff applied to find it's still in the healing process. By the looks of it, he sure did take a chunk out of me. A shudder charges through me.

I thank God every single day that I am not like that dirty bloodsucker. Thankful that Nathan was the one who found me and made sure I stayed on the right path. The only path.

If I'd been left alone who knows what would have happened to me. And sure drinking animal blood is gross – not to me anymore it isn't of course – but in general it's considered disgusting, and anyway, you know what I mean, and it sure beats eating people. Or other supernatural beings for that matter.

Carefully I remove my dirtied top, my ribs still sore. Looking down I see a big purple bruise over my ribcage. I glance at the scar below it. I have two bitemarks on me now. Well, at least the one on my neck will go, even if it is taking its sweet time. That one I've got forever.

Then without warning a memory of me in bed with Nathan, him kissing my scar, looking up at me with those beautiful green eyes of his, flashes so vivid in my mind it nearly knocks me off my feet.

I grip the edge of the sink for support. Deep breaths, Alex. Deep breaths. It will get easier. You will get over him.

After my shower I put my pyjamas on and climb into bed, close my eyes and think of happy things, okay Nathan, because I can't get him out of my head, until I drift off to sleep.

But I don't sleep well because my dreams are filled with vampires and hunters.

The first thing I do when I wake, is get out of bed and check my neck has healed. I can't exactly go to work with a wound like that on my neck. I could wear a scarf I suppose, but thankfully it's healed. Gone, like it was never there, and so has the bruising on my ribs.

I take a shower, brush my teeth and dress for work. Sitting on the stool at the breakfast bar I drink a cup of coffee, eat my toast, and drink a bottle of blood.

I'm going to have to go hunting again tonight after my less than successful night last night. Not a prospect I'm exactly relishing, and I'm going to have to get some more bottles to replace the ones I lost. Those poor little bunnies lost their lives for nothing. I hate that fucking vampire. I hope he's gone straight to Hell.

Rinsing the empty bottle out in the sink, I grab my rucksack off the side and head for work.

I'm just ending what has been a very long day when Zeff shows up at the café. He's wearing a pair of dark grey trousers and a white button down shirt, with the sleeves rolled up. Pretty much the same attire as yesterday. But certainly not the same clothes. I imagine he's the kind of guy who has a shirt for every day of the year.

He always looks so smart, so well groomed, screaming of money. The complete opposite of Nathan.

I do find his appearance surprising now I know he's a hunter. I just have an image of what a hunter would look like, and it's not him. I mean, the clothes he wears are not exactly hunting clothes. He dresses like a businessman.

Maybe it's his disguise. You know like Superman and Clark Kent.

"Hey, Bunny," he drawls, approaching the counter, that same twinkle in his eye as last night. I get the distinct impression he's enjoying winding me up.

With a sigh I ignore his comment, and ask in a lowered voice, "Any news on the passport?"

Leaning forward, I rest my arms up on the high counter.

He nods. "All good. I'll tell you about it soon. What time are you finished here?"

I cast a glance at the clock on the wall. "In fifteen minutes."

"Okay, pour me a coffee and I'll wait for you to get off. We can go and grab a bite to eat and I'll fill you in on the passport stuff."

Feeling dubious about it, I hesitate. I don't want to seem ungrateful but the last thing I want to do is eat dinner with Zeff. I barely know him for starters, and yes I know he saved my life and is helping me get a passport, blah blah, but to be honest, it just feels kind of … odd. Everything about this feels odd.

I know him killing a vampire to save my life would be considered 'odd' to most people, well pretty much everyone, but to me, unfortunately, that is fast becoming the norm. Going out for dinner, well, that's now my 'odd'.

He sees my hesitation. With his black eyebrow raised and irony in his voice he says, "You do eat don't you? I know rabbit is more your taste, but I was thinking something simpler."

"Sure I eat – it's just …"

Smirk. "Just what?"

"Just … I don't think it's a good idea."

"It's not a good idea to eat, or to eat with me?"

Bracing myself with a deep breath, I say, "You."

If I hurt his feelings it doesn't show. He lets out a short laugh and places his hands on the counter top, linking them together.

I move back.

"I'm not asking you out on a date, Bunny. I just happen to be hungry and I thought I could talk to you about the passport while I did that. You know, two birds one stone. But don't worry, it's not a big deal." Then he pauses, "Actually, thinking about it, do you need to …" He gives a quick glance around, and leans in closer, lowering his voice, "Stock up?"

I nod.

Continuing in a quiet voice, knowing I'll hear him loud and clear, says, "The woods surrounding my lodge are great for hunting. They'll be safe for you. I can pick you up later so you can hunt and I'll fill you in then."

And then I just feel like a prize bitch. It practically comes up and slaps me in the face. Zeff is being nice to me. Going out of his way for me, constantly, and I can't even accept his invitation to eat a simple meal with him while him updates me on the thing he's kindly going out of his way to help me out with.

God, I'm such a bitch at times.

"You know what," I say, quickly changing tact. "I am kind of hungry. Dinner would be great." I give the clock another glance. "And my times nearly up now. Will you wait for me in your car?"

I hope I don't come off as sounding rude, I just don't want him hanging in here any longer than necessary. Celine has been eyeing him curiously for the last few minutes while we've been talking.

Zeff is the kind of guy who attracts attention from females, and quite probably males too, and I don't want her talking to him. I'm sure he wouldn't say anything about me, especially with him being a hunter himself. But Celine has got a pretty face, huge cleavage, and legs that go on forever, and men can lose all sense when around those things.

And Celine is also incredibly nosey. She knows the bare minimum about me, well the lies I told her, and I don't want that to change anytime soon.

Zeff gives me a smile. "Sure. See you in five."

"Wait." I turn to the coffee machine and fill a to-go cup, and press a lid on it. "On the house," I say handing it over.

"Thanks," he smiles.

The second he's left the café Celine totters over in her crazy heels for a job where you're on your feet all day.

"Wasn't he in here the other day?" she questions.

I shrug, a noncommittal response.

"Now that is one hot piece of ass," she continues, eyes watching him through the window as he crosses the road and climbs in his car.

Celine doesn't mince her words. I don't know if it's the American in her, or just her.

A small part of me does envy her straightforwardness though. I used to be like her, not as brash, but somewhere close. But now I have to keep all my doors tightly sealed shut. I can't be the person I used to be.

"Can't say I noticed," I utter, turning away to wipe the coffee machine down.

She laughs, "Yeah, sure you haven't. Do you know him?"

"Kind of. We just met recently." *He saved me from a hungry vampire.*

"You dating him?"

I stop wiping and cast a glance at her over my shoulder, "No."

She quirks her eyebrow at me. "You intending to?"

"No."

She purses her lips, smiling. "Well if you're crazy enough to not wanna tap that hot tamale then I sure am gonna."

With a giggle and a wink she waltzes off into the back, her heels clicking like an annoying tune, against the floor.

Ignoring her comment I finish cleaning up the coffee machine, grab my rucksack from under the counter, and make my way out to Zeff's shiny black BMW X5.

Chapter 6: A Slice

It turns out dinner is pizza, and it's the best pizza I have ever tasted. Seriously. I'm honestly considering a marriage proposal to the chef.

And no matter how much I may hate to admit it, I'm actually enjoying having dinner with Zeff. It's been so long since I've sat down and eaten a meal with someone – so long since I've had a real conversation with someone. And he knows exactly what I am. There's no hiding, no pretence, well apart from the fact my real name is Alex Jones, I'm on the run and am technically dead to pretty much everyone who knew and loved me. But yeah, apart from that, it's great.

"So it'll be a week for the passport and your friend can do it for seven hundred euros?" I echo the words just spoken by Zeff.

I pick up another slice of pizza and take a bite. Oh God, this pizza really is heaven; heaven with a capital H.

"That's what he said."

I swallow down my mouthful, put the half-eaten slice back on the plate and lean back in my seat. "Does he take payment in instalments?" I add a little laugh at the end, but it just comes out sounding weak.

Finished with his own pizza, he wipes his mouth with a paper napkin. The guy really does eat quickly; I'm only half into mine. I'd be surprised if his stomach has had time to digest it. He chuckles and throws his screwed up napkin onto his empty plate. "How much are you short?"

I do a quick count in my head. "Not so much short, this week's earnings at the café, coupled with the money I already have will cover it, it's just … I never travel without a set four hundred euros on me. It'd mean staying on another couple of weeks to earn the money to travel."

"That so bad?"

I pull a face, letting him know exactly how bad that thought is. I don't want to be here for this week, let alone two more. I want to get as far away from this place as possible.

"So I'll give it to you."

"And why would you do that?" That came out sounding more like an accusation than a question.

He leans back in his chair and folds his arms across his chest. Contemplating me from across the table, he compresses his lips together.

"I'm sorry. That sounded … look I don't mean to sound ungrateful." I lay my palms flat out on the table. "And thanks all the same for the offer, but I can't take your money. I'll figure something out."

"Fair enough." He nods. "Just know the offer's there if you change your mind."

"I won't change my mind. Just tell your friend to go ahead with the passport, I'll have his money for him … and then I'm out of here no matter what," I add on quietly at the end. I lean forward in my seat and set about my pizza again.

I'll figure something out. I always do. I've got myself this far, I can and will keep going.

Zeff pulls a sleek black iPhone from his trouser pocket, dials, and puts the phone to his ear.

"It's Zeff … go ahead with that thing we spoke about earlier … sure … okay … I'll be in touch later." He disconnects the call and places his phone on the table beside his water glass.

Catching my eye, he says, "He needs a photo. One of those passport booth ones." His voice sounds slightly stilted.

"I'll get one done tomorrow."

"And he wants a deposit up front. Three hundred euros."

"I'll give that to you tomorrow with the photo."

He leans back in his chair. I take a drink of water from my glass, washing my pizza down, then grab another slice.

Zeff is tapping his fingernail against the screen on his phone. The sound is kind of annoying. I look at him. He's face is impassive but he's glancing around the restaurant. Looking everywhere, but me, basically.

He's clearly pissed off about something. I can see it in his moving eyes. Scanning my memory I recall what I've said in the last few minutes.

It must have upset him when I rejected his offer of money. Probably the, 'I won't change my mind', pissy attitude that sealed it.

I didn't figure him for the sensitive kind. But even so, he doesn't deserve it from me. In the two short days I've known Zeff, he's saved me from a vampire, patched me up, fed me, and has been nothing but nice to me. And I've bitten his head off at every turn, and all because of my own issues. Yet again, I've been nothing shy of a bitch to him.

I put my pizza back down on the plate, suddenly losing my appetite, and let out a long breath. "Look, Zeff, I'm sorry I've been a complete bitch to you since we met ... well, basically since you saved me from – you know what."

He swivels dark eyes to meet my gaze, "I wouldn't say you've been a *complete* bitch." A smile starts to filter its way onto his lips.

"Only a partial bitch?" I raise an eyebrow.

He lets out a laugh. It eases the tension right out of the air.

I smile at him.

He leans forward, elbows resting on the table, and looks me straight in the eye. "Look, all I see is a nice girl who's had a seemingly shitty time of things." His voice is low, deep. "So, I think I can afford her a couple of bitch moments."

He shrugs, lightly. His voice, the low tone, the words, I don't know maybe all three combined, have this odd effect on me. I don't even know why, or how to even explain it, because it's not like he's said something profoundly deep which will change the course of my life forever. It was just something small. Kind. And those two short sentences he's just spoken have reached into me, like a healing hand, and soothed that raw wounded part of me. Easing the pain, even if for a short while.

For a moment I can't stop staring at him. His eyes lock and widen in my gaze. Awakening, I blink myself free.

Shifting in my seat I pick my pizza up and put it straight back down. I suddenly don't know what to do with my hands. I'm like a recent quitter of cigarettes who's going through that 'no clue what to do with my hands' phase. I just keep picking up things on the table; the pepper shaker, my knife, the napkin, and putting them straight back down.

I can see Zeff eyeing me curiously. I force my hands onto my lap, binding them together.

"Thanks," I finally say. My voice has gone hoarse. I cough my clogged throat clear, then take a sip of water.

His eyes are still on me.

I'm not sure what to do. I just feel really awkward. The moment's gone from shitty, to light, to ridiculously intense in the space of ten seconds. It's like having a conversation with Nathan.

Nathan.

Oh no. I'm already wide open, so when that familiar pang of longing for him hits, it stabs me hard in the chest, rocking me to my core. And I'm right back to square one.

I'm losing my breath. I can't breathe. I can feel blood rushing to my head, ringing in my ears, making me hot.

I stand abruptly. My chair scrapes loudly against the hard floor. Zeff's dark eyes follow me up, with an expected element of surprise. I know just exactly how weird I'm acting right now. And also what he must be thinking.

That I'm odd. And a bit nuts. He wouldn't be far wrong. But I also don't care at this very moment, either.

"I need to use the bathroom." I thumb awkwardly over my shoulder, practically tripping over my own feet as I hightail it to the ladies room.

I splash cold water over my face from the tap as I try to regain some composure. What the hell was that all about? A kind word from a nice guy and I'm shot all over the place like a rogue bullet.

Not that I'm not well aware I'm already slightly crazy, but I am now starting to believe I've lost my shit completely. I just wish I was past this; past Nathan. I'm driving myself nuts.

Sometimes I feel like he's in my head, to the point of haunting me. If I didn't know better I would think he is a ghost, because I see him everywhere and in everything.

I've been pretty sure on a decent sized handful of occasions that I've seen him in the street, or when passing by a shop window, seeing his reflection clearly in it.

I know it's just because he is in my head constantly but it doesn't make it any easier.

When I left that night, I did it believing that I could live without him, in the knowledge that he was safe and alive. Turns out I actually can't live without him, period.

Just knowing he's out there, living his life, is way more difficult than I ever anticipated. I want him to be happy, sure I do, that's the reason I walked away. But that doesn't mean the thought of him happy, without me, doesn't make me feel like complete and utter crap.

After six months of no contact with Nathan, any normal person would be over him, or at least have had it lessen their feelings for him to a huge degree. But no, not me. I still feel exactly the same about him as I did back then. I'm still completely and ridiculously in love with him. Or maybe now, I'm just in love with the idea of him. I don't know.

All I do know is, mentally, I'm still stuck in that hotel room with my hand on the door handle, teetering between the room with Nathan in it, and the big bad world without him. I know I somehow managed to get my skinny ass physically out of that room. Now I just need to get my heart to follow too.

If I were an outsider looking in at me, I'd think I was seriously pathetic and would have slapped myself stupid by now. I need the sense beaten into me until it sticks.

Splashing cold water on my face again, I wash away my thoughts. Grabbing paper towels out of the unit beside the sink, I dry my face. Allowing myself a few deep cleansing breaths, I dump the paper towels in the bin and exit the bathroom, heading back to Zeff.

A waiter is standing at our table with a card machine in his hand; a different guy from the one who served us I note, and Zeff is currently paying the bill.

He looks up as I approach, "You okay?"

Briefly meeting his eyes, I nod. "Yes."

Then I notice our table has been cleared. They've taken the half a pizza I had left. Gutted. But then again I don't think I could have finished it with the way my stomach is churning over. Still, a doggie bag would have been awesome, you know, so I could eat it later.

"The remainder of your pizza is being boxed up," Zeff says, almost if as reading my mind.

"Oh, great, thanks." That actually raises a smile from me.

"We can head over to my lodge now if you want to get started on that … thing?" he says, as I sit back in my seat.

I know he was just trying to be discreet in front of the waiter, but the way he said it makes it sound like an innuendo. Which it is, kind of, but not the type the waiter clearly thinks it is, because from the looks he's casting between me and Zeff, I take it he speaks English, and well.

So yes, I'm pretty sure he thinks Zeff and me are off to have sex after this. I mean, really, as if Zeff would be so open about it if we were actually going to, or maybe that's the kind of clientele they're used to in here. And even though it's not true, I can feel my cheeks starting to burn.

I'm getting that guilty feeling thing happening, you know the one where you know you're not guilty of something but you can't help but worry people will think you are, so your face goes bright red, incorrectly incriminating you. Yep, that's what's happening right now.

And now Zeff has latched onto it, because I can see the amusement spreading across his features.

I pick my water up and take a sip trying to cool my face, using it to hide behind.

Zeff takes his credit card back from the waiter.

"So," he says to me, in an even tone, "have you got everything you need with you for the … *party*?"

"Huh?" I utter, my lip stuck on the glass.

He's looking at me evenly, "You know." The waiter is lingering near the table, in the pretence of doing something on the card reader, blatantly listening in. "The things you need to get started - the rubber tubing … wet wipes … oh yeah, and the spade."

I choke on the little bit of water in my mouth. The waiter snorts. I glare at him. He quickly walks off.

I stare at Zeff, "What did you say that for?"

"What?" he shrugs, feigning innocence, a smile playing on his lips in innocence.

I shake my head, clearly pissed off.

"You shouldn't have said that. He could take what you said seriously. I can't have people finding out what I am," I hiss over the table.

"Come on Bunny, I was just playing. He thought we were hooking up for something kinky and I was just winding him up, nothing more. Don't worry."

"More like winding me up," I snap. "And I do worry." I lean forward. "Because I have to. All the time." I sit back, shaking my head, adding, "That was a wanker's trick you just pulled then."

And yes, a waiter has just come with my pizza box as I said the word, wanker. A different waiter this time. And at least this one has the courtesy to pretend he didn't hear, or maybe honestly doesn't speak English.

Zeff starts to laugh.

My face is bright red. "It's not funny," I say, clearly hacked off.

"It kind of is."

"Fuck off." I pull a stern face at him.

"Lighten up, Bunny. It won't hurt you to laugh every once in a while. It might actually make you feel better."

"I'm just fine as I am."

I stand up.

"Are you coming or not?" I huff, grabbing my pizza box and rucksack, I turn and stalk off toward the exit.

I'm sure Zeff's current and sole purpose in life is to wind me up. He is beyond annoying at times.

"Sorry," comes his deep voice in my ear, "I was just having some fun."

"At my expense."

"No." He touches my arm stopping me.

His voice sounds really intense. I don't like the feeling it gives me.

"Whatever. It doesn't matter," I reply, shaking him off. I continue toward the door. "And I do laugh," I add, glancing up at him. "When there's something worth laughing about."

"Guess I'm just going to have to find out what exactly it is that makes you laugh then." He stares down at me with dark eyes.

I shift uncomfortably and clasp the pizza box to my chest like a shield.

When we get in his car I reach into my bag for money. "I need to pay you for my half of dinner."

He waves me away. "Dinner's on me. You need your money for the passport."

"No really, I want to pay my way."

"Bunny," he gives me a stern look. "Just let me pay for dinner, okay? You're not breaking any feminist rule by doing so."

I screw my face up. "I'm not a feminist." I drop my bag back down in the foot well. "I just like to pay my way is all. I'm not a leech."

"I got that for sure," he chuckles.

He turns the engine on and I glance sideways at him.

"You're a funny guy, you know," the words are out before I can stop them.

"Was that you paying me a compliment, Bunny?" he puts his hand to his heart, feigning cardiac arrest.

I purse my lips. "Um, no not really. But you can take it that way if like, as I need to ask a favour … or two."

"Shoot."

I glance down at my work clothes. "Would it be okay if you take me home first before going to your lodge? I need to change out of my work clothes. I want to keep the spare set in my bag clean."

"Sure … and favour number two?" he asks, putting his hand behind my seat, so he can turn to see clear as he reverses out of the parking spot.

"I need to go to the supermarket."

"For?"

"Water bottles."

Swinging the car around, he shifts into first, giving me a curious look with his eyes on their way back to the windscreen.

"To empty out and fill up with blood," I explain.

"Ah, sure, right. No probs," he smiles. "To the supermarket it is."

I settle back into my seat, resisting the urge to finish this pizza off, my appetite returning. I need to save my hunger for hunting.

Chapter 7: New Horizon

Walking up the porch steps to the lodge I knock on the door, putting my now full backpack down on the wooden floor.

Zeff was right, these woods are brilliant for hunting. I got everything I needed, enough blood bottled up to keep me going for a good while.

He swings the door open.

He changed his clothes while I was out hunting. He's wearing sweats and a running vest, and looks really different. I've only ever seen him in his smarts; shirts and trousers.

The casual relaxed look suits him. And I was right; he is as toned and muscular as I thought he would be under his shirts. His skin really is a lovely colour; the shade of caramel.

"You should have just let yourself in," he says with a warm smile.

"I didn't want to intrude."

"So you're all done?" he says.

"Yeah. I just thought I'd stop by and let you know I was going."

He leans his shoulder against the door frame. Giving me a funny expression, his eyes set on my face, he tilts his head to the side as if contemplating me.

It's making me feel a little uncomfortable to be honest. I shift on my feet. I'm just about to ask him 'what?', when he takes a step through the doorway, closer to me, and reaches his hand up to my face. He rubs his thumb across my cheek.

The instant his skin makes contact with mine a sensation jolts through me. Like a current zapping through me from touching an exposed wire. I feel shocked. Literally. Physically.

It's the exact same feeling I had in the café when he shook my hand. I feel wired. Like there's a magnetic charge pulsing through me. And in some ways it's so familiar, like

I've always experienced this sensation, like he's always been touching me.

I take a huge step back, a whoosh of air leaving my lungs.

"Blood." He holds his thumb up showing the evidence, obviously seeing my reaction.

But my reaction is not for the reason he thinks. It's not because I'm cautious of being touched by a man.

It's because the guy is able to physically shock me every time he touches me.

It's weird. And kind of worrying.

It certainly wasn't just a static shock like I tried to make myself believe the first time it happened. But I do get the distinct impression he doesn't get the same reaction when we make contact. I can tell from the way his heart rate stays steady. There's no fluctuation in it at all.

And it certainly isn't an emotional reaction like I would get every time Nathan would touch me. This is physical. Like he has high voltage electricity running through him.

I just don't understand why. And it's not something I can exactly come out and ask him either.

'Um, Zeff, do you run at a high charge by any chance ... you know like do you have electricity flowing through your veins? Well, basically are you sort of some superhuman freak?'

Yeah, I can't ask him that. I know how it feels to be a freak; I don't want to make anyone else feel like I do.

The only thing I can do is to just keep my distance, to avoid contact, equalling no more weird shocks. I'll be gone soon enough so it'll be irrelevant anyway.

Letting my mind click back into play with my mouth, I say, "Oh, right." But it comes out sounding a little shrill.

I lift my hand to my cheek rubbing roughly at it, trying to erase the sensation that he's left spinning under my skin.

"The guest bathroom is first door on the right if you want to clean up?" He tilts his head in the direction of the hallway, just off the dining room.

Moving back he allows me space to pass. Giving him a wide berth, I scurry off to find the bathroom so I can clean up my bloodstained face.

When I've finished using his fancy bathroom, I come back out into the living area.

No Zeff.

I scan around for him but can't seem to get a read on him. I'm sure he won't have just left. I head toward the still open front door.

When I step through the doorway onto the porch, I see Zeff is sitting on the swing chair, to my right. It was weird that I couldn't pick up on his whereabouts. Maybe I'm just a little off my game at the moment. Probably all those shocks he keeps giving me.

He glances up, smiling that crooked dimply smile of his. The sun is dipping behind the horizon and it's casting a clandestine shadow behind him. It's really kind of beautiful. The view I mean, not him. Obviously. Not that he's ugly, but – oh God, you know what I mean.

I really want to get back to my apartment and get the blood I've just acquired into the fridge, but I feel like I should go and sit with him for a while; it would be rude not to. Especially also since I can smell freshly brewed coffee, and he might have made one for me. Or is that me just hoping?

Twisting my hands together in front of me, I wander over and take a seat on the swing chair next to him, but leaving an audible gap between us. As I sit down, the chair moves backwards. Zeff steadies it, pressing his bare foot down to the floor.

"I made you a cup of coffee," he says, reaching over and lifting a steaming cup off the table beside the swing chair. "I put cream in, no sugar – that okay?"

Exactly how I take it. Lucky guess?

"Yeah, that's great, thanks." I take it from him but make sure not to touch his hand.

You'd think because I serve coffee all day long, I'd be sick of it, but I'm not. More of an addict than I ever used to be, and I can never say no to a cup nowadays. Especially not one that smells as awesome as this does.

"It's probably not as good as the Joe you make at the café, but I did my best," he gives me a cheeky wink.

"I'm sure it'll be fine," I take a sip.

Wow, this tastes as good as it smells. Definitely better than the stuff I serve at the café. Quite possibly the nicest coffee I've ever tasted.

"This is really good," I mumble, as the heat of it runs through me, the hit of caffeine doing its job to the fullest. "Way better than the stuff at the café,"

"Ah, now I know you're just taking the mick, Bunny," he murmurs, in that drawling way of his.

I stare at him wide eyed and annoyed. He smiles, a naughty glint in his dark eyes. It annoys me even further but I refuse to rise to the bait. I've already bit once today at one of his apparent 'jokes', so I'm not being pulled in again. But I really do wish he'd stop calling me Bunny. Maybe if I just ignore it, he'll eventually get bored and stop.

Zeff takes a sip of his own coffee and looks ahead, straight out over the horizon. I follow his gaze.

The view is amazing from up here. It's the first time I've stopped to appreciate it. It's uphill all the way to Zeff's lodge, so it gives a fantastic panoramic view of the town below. And even though on a hilltop, the lodge somehow still manages to stay completely secluded.

I could sit here all day and just stare at this view. It's incredibly relaxing, so serene, so peaceful. I close my eyes for a moment and just soak it up.

I can see why Zeff likes living here. This is a place I would be more than happy to spend the rest of my days in, if I had the luxury of being able to stay in one place at a time that is. Maybe one day, but for now, moving is what keeps me safe.

Exhaling out a light breath, I open my eyes, back to reality.

Zeff rests his foot up on his other knee and sits his coffee cup against his solid thigh. He has nice feet for a man. Actually, scrap that thought. That was a really weird thing to think.

"So ... can I ask who or what it is you're running from?" His tone is low.

I turn to look at him. He's not looking at me, but when he feels my stare he twists and meets my eyes.

I guess I shouldn't be surprised he asked. I'm just surprised he hasn't already, or at the very least figured out, who it is I'm running from. Being what I am, I'd just assumed he'd know all about the Originals, him being a hunter, but obviously not.

I look away, back to the view, and take a deep breath. "Have you heard of the Originals?"

"Yes." His tone is a little clipped. It surprises me.

"Well ... I'm kind of what could be called a precious commodity to them ... because I'm the only female of my kind in existence."

There's a slight pause. Not a really long one, just long enough to make it noticeable.

"Hmm. Right." He brings his cup to his lips and takes a drink. Swallowing, he asks, "So are they the ones who turned you?"

"No."

"Who then?"

A chill rolls over my skin. I wrap my hands around my cup, bringing it to rest against my chest. I really don't want to talk about this.

Keep it to the bare minimum, you can't let him know too many details – you still barely know him... to trust him.

A deep breath. "I don't know. I was out with my friend and we were walking home after a night out and well ... we were attacked." There's absolutely no tone to my voice. I had to numb myself just to get those few sentences out.

I feel a wave of anger pulse from out of him. It's a really weird sensation and it practically coats itself onto my skin like a slick of hot black oil. It's the oddest thing.

"Sorry," he says. He sounds like he genuinely means it.

But I'm just trying to wrap my head around the sensation of anger I just felt come from out of him and why I currently feel like I'm still wearing his anger like a steaming hot all-in-one suit.

What is it with him? Physically shocking me, and now projecting his emotions onto me. How is he doing it?

I slide my gaze toward him. I can see his eyes are fixed and focused ahead. His face appears impassive, but I can tell his mind is working furiously behind those dark unfathomable eyes.

Maybe he's just one of those intuitive sensitive people, and I'm somehow tuning into his reactions to things. At least I hope that's what it is.

And maybe that's something I can do, you know, *feel* certain people's feelings and energies. Sounds very 'new age' but who knows what I can do. I barely have a clue as to what I'm capable of. I've never bothered to learn. Maybe it's time I change that.

I wonder if he felt angry, because what happened to me reminded him of what happened to his parents. It would make sense as to the level of anger I can still feel emanating out of him like heat licking off a bonfire.

I move my hot coffee away from my body, resting the cup on my leg.

And now I just feel bad for him, even though I feel like I'm currently sitting on top of a bonfire, because I know how hard it is to lose your parents period; mine a car accident, but to lose them to a murdering vampire must be horrendous.

"Don't be. It was a long time ago," I finally utter, trying to put a close on the conversation.

But that's a lie because it doesn't feel like a long time ago. It still feels like it only happened yesterday. It's raw and painful, but I shrug it off because I don't want to talk about it with him. I don't want to talk about it with anyone.

But, as it seems, he's not giving up. "What happened to your friend?" His voice sounds a lot calmer than his body is saying.

I suck my cheek in, biting down on it. "She died." Blank and dull is all my voice can manage right now.

"And how did you survive?"

He's not getting it. I don't want to … can't talk about this. But I can't just ignore him either, so I utter, "Someone –" *Nathan.* I pause, collecting myself. "Someone saved me. But was too late to save my friend."

This catches his attention. He turns his head to look at me, curiosity peeking through his eyes. "A hunter?"

"No. Just a guy." *My guy. The only guy.*

"Did the Vârcolac get away?"

"No." I shake my head.

"Good," he murmurs, low. "And you survived the change." It's not question.

I nod.

"And you don't know how you survived?"

I shake my head, no. Putting my cup to my lips, I take a sip, then cradling it in both my hands, I rest it against my chest again, feeling cooler now his anger had seemingly subsided.

"What happens if the Original's find you?"

I'm starting to get fidgety. I really don't like this line of questioning. "Then my life is over."

"They'd kill you?"

"No," I say in a clipped voice. "The Original's believe I can create newborns for them. Immortal newborn Vârcolac's just like them. They want to build an army to help them eradicate the vampires."

He lets out a small laugh. It annoys me, but I say nothing, instead just slide him a look, which he doesn't see anyway.

He drums his fingers loudly against the arm rest. "And you could bear them an army big enough to kill all vampires?"

"No. But I could give them a good head start."

"Hmm." He puts his thumb and forefinger to his lips, pressing down on them, thoughtfully. "Guess I can see why you're running then," he exhales out, nodding, moving his hand up to his hair and pushing his fingers though it.

"Yep." I take another sip of my coffee, hoping, praying, that's the end of his line of questioning.

"So you're just going to spend the rest of your life on the run?"

I guess he's curiosity isn't quenched, just yet.

I let out a light sigh. "It's the only way I get to keep my life."

"Doesn't sound like much of a life."

He says it almost as though he was thinking it but didn't mean to say it. It's confirmed when I see the realisation flicker in his dark eyes, spreading like wildfire throughout his perfect features. "Sorry, that sounded – "

"It's fine." I cut him off with a wave of my hand. Anything to stop this conversation. My head is buzzing. The pain throbbing downwards, careening straight for my heart.

He's stays silent for a moment then …

"So the guy, the one who saved you, what happened to him?"

Not Nathan. Carrie was bad enough, but not Nathan as well. I can't talk about him. I'm afraid if I speak an actual real word about him, make Nathan real in my conversation, in my mind, then the floodgates will open and I'll never be able to close them again. And I won't be able to stop myself from running straight back to the farm, to him.

I bite down on my bottom lip and try to give an easy shrug. "He's living his life, I guess."

"You running from him too?"

His words slam into my chest with the force of a bulldozer. I stand abruptly. My movement so jerky and quick I slosh my coffee everywhere, all over my hand and clothes. "Shit," I mutter.

The hot liquid is burning my hand and has seeped straight through my T-shirt and jeans burning the skin on my stomach and legs, but the pain doesn't stop me moving.

Unfocused and flustered, I slam the cup down on the nearest surface I can find; the floor, and make for the door to grab my rucksack, so I can get the hell out of here.

"Are you okay?" Zeff asks, obviously concerned. I hear him put his cup down and get to his feet.

"I'm fine. I just need to get going – I just remembered I've – got this thing I need to do." I bend down to grab my rucksack.

"I was asking too many questions?" Zeff's soft voice comes from behind me.

My back stiffens. I straighten up, swinging the rucksack over my shoulder, I turn around to face him. "I just ..." My mouth has gone dry, tacky. I look at the floor and lift my shoulders. "I guess there are just some things I don't want to talk about."

I look up through my eyelashes to see his reaction. Looking down, he nods, slightly. It does something strange to me. And I feel almost guilty for reacting the way I just did.

"I get that," he says. "Sorry I was being intrusive."

Shifting from foot to foot, I nervously pick at my bag strap as I lift my shoulders, "Sorry I spilt coffee everywhere."

I gesture behind him at the massive coffee stain on the cushion seat of his swing chair.

He looks over his shoulder at it, then back to me. "I think there's more coffee on you than my cushions." He releases a smile... that slightly crooked smile of his, again. And that one single smile somehow manages to break all of my nervous resolve.

Glancing down at my mess, I wipe my hand down my damp top. "I really should get going, though." I walk toward the steps.

He follows me. "I'll drive you home."

Home. I don't have a home. "No it's fine, I can walk."

"I'll drive you," he says in a no-argument voice. "Let me just go grab my car keys."

I pause on the steps and wait there until he remerges, shoes on his feet, car keys in his hand. I follow him over to his car and climb in the passenger seat, dropping my bag into the foot well.

"So," he says, his voice back to that easy way of his, "I was thinking … while you're waiting for the passport to arrive, before you up sticks and leave, why don't I give you some lessons in fighting … or self-defence at the very least," he adds when he sees my expression.

"I don't need lessons in fighting." I fold my arms across my chest. "I know how to take care of myself."

"Oh yeah, sure, I got that from the other night," he says with a wry chuckle.

He's taking the piss. I hate that.

He turns the engine on and the radio bursts to life. As if on cue, a Killers song is playing. I have a vivid flash back of being in Nathan's car with him driving beside me. Then I get a sudden, unexpected whiff of his scent, blindsiding me. It makes me ache all over.

Wrapping my arms around myself, I try to ignore the song and the memories it's provoking.

I say, a little too defensively, "I am strong. I could kick your arse."

I can't believe I just said that. I sound so childish.

But I feel like I need to make him understand that I'm not defenceless. I'm not the same person I was six months ago. But really why should it matter what he thinks? He didn't know me back then, and he doesn't know me now. Not really. And honestly, why do I even care what he thinks, his opinion is irrelevant. He's irrelevant.

He laughs.

"You are strong, and I've no doubt you could 'kick my arse'," he mimics my Yorkshire accent to perfection. It grates on my aching skin. "But the things that are coming after you are a hell of a lot stronger than you are, and are way older. You've got the equipment Bunny, but if you don't know how to use it then you're just going into a fight blind."

"I'm not planning on getting into any more fights."

He gives me a look. "You might not be planning on it, but it sounds to me like they definitely are."

God, this song is driving me crazy. I'm starting to feel uncomfortable in my own skin. My eyes keep flicking to the stereo. I want to punch it to silent. Clenching and unclenching my fists, I will this feeling to go away.

"Okay, fine. And what – you know how to fight?" I grit my teeth together, trying to get past my inner demons.

He grins, "As it just so happens, I do."

And then I don't know why but I can't contain my emotions any longer, and a raw empty pain suddenly bursts out of me.

"Why are you doing this?!" I reach over and angrily twist the dial on the stereo, turning the song off, leaving us in a less than blissful silence. "Why are you always trying to help me?! From the second I met you it's all you do – help, help, help!! It's driving me crazy!"

And at this exact moment, I'm not actually sure if I'm yelling at Zeff, or Nathan.

Zeff looks from me, to the stereo, and back to me again. There's intricate darkness in his eyes and I can't get a clear read on him. But by the way he keeps clenching and unclenching his jaw; I going to take it he's a tad annoyed.

"Wow. Okay," he mutters.

And then I just feel horrible. And a little hollow. And also completely irrational and stupid for my outburst. I'm just a nasty cow. I never realised how much so until just recently.

I turn to him and the expression on his face actually pains me. "I'm really sorry."

I don't say that often. It's hurt me to just do it then, but he doesn't deserve what I said. "I didn't mean that – you're not driving me crazy. I'm driving me crazy. I shouldn't have taken it out on you." I sigh. "Look, I've just gone through some really huge changes recently, and I'm kind of trying to learn how to do things alone. I'm learning how to be alone for the first time in my life, and you being all nice and kind to me, and constantly helping, is … well, hindering that."

And it's also incredibly sweet if I bothered to look at it that way, which I now am of course.

Ugh, I'm a horrible person.

"Not that I don't appreciate your kindness, because I do. I really do, I'm just … "

"Look, from where I'm sitting, you're already doing everything alone," he picks up, obviously sensing I'm running out of words. His eyes drift to mine. "I'm just offering you a little extra help, that's all."

I look away. "I'm not doing well." I shake my head, wringing my hands in my lap.

"You're not giving yourself enough credit, Bunny. You're surviving, and that's what counts."

I slide my focus over to his.

"Accepting help from people doesn't make you weak, it makes you strong," he adds in a low voice.

"That's kind of insightful for a Thursday night." I give a weak smile.

"That's me – insightful and full of wisdom." Nodding, he taps his forehead with his finger, his eyes smiling at me. "And I'm also pretty awesome too … and dashingly handsome of course." He grins.

"Of course," I murmur, giving a nod of my head. I have to bite my lip to stop from laughing, it's creeping up my dry, aching throat. He really is quite funny in a sarcastic, confident, kind of way. Not that I'd tell him that. His ego's over inflated enough as it is. "I knew you were full of something," I murmur. "I just didn't realise it was wisdom."

"Oh yeah," he says in a brighter voice. "I've got tons of it. I'm full to the brim with wisdom." His lips tip upward again. A smile starts to edge the corners of my own. "Mostly it's utter crap," he adds. "But every now and then something good does show up."

"You're an idiot," I laugh.

And then suddenly I feel like I can't stop laughing; don't want to stop laughing. I'm laughing so hard tears have formed in my eyes. I clutch a hand to my stomach. I can't remember the last time I laughed properly, or wanted to. It feels pretty good.

"Hey, you're laughing!" Zeff grins, chuckling. "I knew I could get it out of you, and look, it didn't even take me long either. Told you I was awesome."

"I don't know about awesome, but you are a little crazy," I say, still laughing, wiping my eyes dry.

"Oh, that I am." He winks. "And you Bunny, well you're a rubbish fighter. You fight like a girl. A five year old girl to precise, and that's me being generous. It was embarrassing to watch the other night. That's why I had to intervene and save you – just to put him and me out of our misery. It was painful to watch your arms and legs flailing about like a toddler having a tantrum."

He grins but bites down on his full lower lip, trying to hide it.

I push my tongue between my teeth and up into my top lip, "Embarrassing, huh?"

"Oh yeah, completely." He gives a serious nod, as he puts his seatbelt on.

I reach back and retrieve my own seatbelt, pulling it across me I pop it into the holder with a loud click. "And what? You're going to teach me how to fight like a man instead?"

"Oh no, Bunny." He winks, rolling the car forward. "Tomorrow, I'm going to teach you how to fight like a Vârcolac."

Chapter 8: Training Day

I pop back to my apartment after I finish work to change out of my work clothes and into something a little more appropriate for today.

Because today is the first day of 'teaching Bunny how to fight', as Zeff puts it.

Shit. He's even got me calling myself Bunny now. I give myself a mental slap

Taking my work clothes off, I put on my black sweatpants and black ribbed vest, tie my hair in a ponytail, slip my feet into trainers, lace them up, put mthey rucksack on my back, and set off for Zeff's lodge.

Zeff did offer to come and pick me up, but I said no. Mainly, because I don't want him to keep putting himself out for me, he's doing enough already and I still feel guilty for last night's little outburst, and also because today I feel like having a run.

I know, not like me at all. But I just feel all pumped up and wired for some reason, and I thought it would be a good way to burn it off and loosen up for whatever Zeff has in store for me.

Surprising myself I've discovered I am actually looking forward to doing this training with Zeff. I'm looking forward to learning how to protect and defend myself properly, you know, instead of kiddy fighting.

I'm really quite intrigued to know what we'll be doing today. The only thing I am a little worried about is the shock treatment.

Obviously I'm going to have to touch Zeff. I can't learn how to fight without making some form of physical contact with him. And I'm guessing there will be quite a lot of physical contact. I'm hoping after the initial, I'll get used to it, and it won't be an issue for me.

My feet hit the pavement outside my apartment building and I set off running at a normal pace. I can't run at the speed I'm capable of in public, I have to wait until I'm under cover. Here I have to blend in and be just like any other normal person out for an early evening run.

Taking the left at the end of my street, heading out of town, I set a steady pace. The good thing about being Vârcolac Alex, is the uphill and five miles to Zeff's lodge will bear little to no effect on me.

It's so funny, pre-Vârcolac me would never in a million years consider running five miles. I couldn't even run five feet. But now I have all this superhuman strength and energy, I'm finding I really like it. It's blowing the cobwebs off and clearing out my mind.

I wish I'd gone running for pleasure long before today. It's just not something I've ever thought of doing. Of course I've run before, but mostly it's been when I've being running for my life, and when you're running for your life it doesn't really have the same effect.

I come upon the trees where I was attacked by that vampire a few nights ago. A shudder runs through me. Shaking it off because I want to use the shelter of the trees so I can run faster, I ignore my own fears and slip just inside the woods.

Keeping near to the edge, but not close enough so I can be seen,, I pick up pace, and soon I'm flying through the woods, my feet skimming the soft earth. The trees and bushes whizzing by, my ponytail whipping in the wind. It's absolutely exhilarating and kind of mind blowing being able to run at this speed.

The exhilaration doesn't last long though, and I'm very quickly at the point where I have to exit the woods, so I can take the turning off the main road which will take me up to Zeff's lodge.

Slowing to a jog, I exit the woods, cross the road, and set off up the narrow steep road that leads to the lodge.

It's an open road. If I look back I can see the town in all its glory. The woods I hunted in yesterday sit further out, at the back of the lodge, spreading down the right side. The woods here are probably as big as the one Jack owns, if not bigger.

Actually, thinking about it, it is kind of odd that Zeff chose to live here, in complete seclusion with a forest on his backdoor step. Being a hunter, isn't he just attracting the chance of the wrong type of creature showing up to visit him? My kind, and surely werewolves, and whatever else hides in the shadows, will use the cover of woodland to change, or do whatever it is they do. If I were him I would choose to live in a heavily populated area.

Isn't living secluded a clear danger for him if it's known he's a hunter? Or maybe that's the point; it lures them here so he can kill them with minimal fuss. I wonder if that's what that vampire was in town for – Zeff.

It does kind of seem funny, now I think about it, all these months of nothing, then I happen upon a vampire the very day I met him – a hunter, in the very town where he lives.

When I reach the end of the road, I turn into the driveway, slowing my pace to a walk.

Climbing the porch steps I knock on the front door.

No answer.

I can't *feel* him here, but he can't have gone out because his car's still here, and he was expecting me.

Cupping my hands around my eyes I peer through the window. He's not in the living room.

Feeling a little concerned after what I've just been thinking about, I step back from the window and reach my hearing out to see if I can pick up the sound of him or anyone else here.

I'm praying for a no, on the latter.

Hearing movement coming from around the back of the lodge, I inhale deeply.

It's Zeff.

He's alone, which eases my worry. But really, why can't I get a read on his whereabouts? It's starting to bug the crap out of me.

Jogging down the porch steps I make my way around to the back of the lodge.

And there he is, with his back to me. Top-half naked, wearing loose fitting grey sweatpants on his bottom half, and he's doing some sort of martial arts exercise.

I watch as the muscles in his back and arms tense and flex with each movement he makes. Movements which are so graceful it's like he's moving suspended, gravity defying.

There's a gleam of sweat covering his caramel skin.

He looks almost iridescent with the sun licking down on him. Even covered in sweat he still looks like he's just stepped off the pages of a magazine. My heart thrums a little harder in my chest.

Turning, he catches my staring and immediately stops what he's doing. A smile lilts his face. And I'm pretty sure mine has just gone bright read. Holding my hand up in a half wave, I start to walk toward to him.

"Hey," he says. Bending down he picks a towel off the floor and pats his face dry.

"Hey yourself," I smile. "What was that you were just doing?"

"Tai Chi," he says. "Well, a form of it, anyway."

"Ah, cool. It looks good – the exercise I mean – not you."

Zeff raises his eyebrow.

Oh God, here I go.

"Not that you don't look good, because of course you do – I meant that the Tai Chi looked good when you were doing it..." Stop talking Alex, now. Please.

Well, I suppose it's good to know something's never change; my mouth still has the capability to run away with itself. I just wish there was some way I could teach myself to censor the thoughts spewing from my mouth.

Zeff lets outs a laugh. "Thanks. I think. And I'm glad you think it looks good because you're going to be doing it in a few minutes."

"Oh, no. No. Seriously, I can't do that. I have no coordination. Zero. Not an iota." My voice comes out shrill.

Bloody hell, what on earth is wrong with me today?

He gives me an amused look. "You'll be fine. It'll help you loosen up for the fighting, and a lot of fighting and self-defence moves I'm going to teach you come from Tai."

His tone is beginning to sound like he's not going to take no for an answer.

I bind my hands in front of me. "Seriously Zeff, I really have no coordination. I'm not kidding. I can't dance or anything. Before the change, it took a lot just to keep one foot in front of the other. I'll make a complete arse out of myself."

"You can't dance?" he asks, brow furrowed.

"Nope," I shake my head.

"We'll have to change that too." The look in his eyes is as intense as his voice. It quickly clears, and his tone is back to that easy way of his. "There's only us here, so if you make an ass of yourself it won't matter." He beckons me to go to him. His eyes on me are all soft and inviting. And they strip away of all my insecurities.

Lifting a foot, I find myself moving toward him, without another consideration. Almost like there's a magnet pulling me in his direction. He seems to have the ability to be able to calm me with a click of his finger, a softly spoken word, or a look. At times when no one else would be able to.

"Take your sneakers and socks off," he says.

"Sneakers?" I wrinkle my nose, looking up at him. "Don't you main trainers?"

"Same thing."

"Sneakers is a very American thing to say," I muse, sliding the rucksack off my back, I put it to the grassy floor. I sit down beside it and start to unlace my trainers. Come to think of it, he calls coffee – Joe. And his mobile phone – a cell phone.

"Is that where you're from originally, America?" I pause untying, to look up at him. His accent is so indistinct it's hard to tell just where it is he's from.

He shakes his head. "I was born in Spain. I just lived in the US for a while; I picked up some bad habits." He grins.

So he's Spanish. I guess that explains the skin tone and black hair. And it's also quite sexy.

Crap.

I pull my trainers and socks off, and get to my feet.

Positioning himself in front of me, he says, "Just watch me first, then we'll go together. And don't worry," he adds at my worried expression. "I'll just show you the basics for now. You'll be fine."

"Okay," I murmur.

And then I watch him as he begins to demonstrate the basics of Tai Chi.

His movements are so ridiculously graceful for his size. I'm in absolute awe. And there is absolutely no way I'm going to be able to do this as well as he does.

"Did you get that?" he asks, when he's finished.

"Kinda." I grimace.

"Just follow my lead."

He starts up again and I try to follow his lead, really I do, but my movements just aren't good. I'm not graceful. I'm clumsy and awkward. And thank God there are just the two of us here and no one else can see, because they would be laughing their ass off at me right now.

Zeff lets out a little laugh, and shaking his head stops what he's doing and moves to stand behind me. My head follows him round.

"Just look straight ahead and close your eyes," he says with a gentle nod of his head.

Uneasy, I do as he asks.

He moves closer, leaving all but a sliver of air between us. He reaches down and takes hold of my hands, his palms flat against the tops of mine, resting his huge arms along mine. My skin vibrates and thrums from the electricity streaming out of him and straight into me. I don't like the sensation.

Okay, actually I do, it's not as shocking as those first few times, it's almost soothing, but I don't want to like it, so my whole body stiffens in line with my mind. I flick my eyes open.

"It's okay, Bunny," he hushes, feeling my tension. "Just relax and I'll lead you."

His voice carries like a whisper in the wind blowing down my neck. It's hard to relax when he's touching me like this. It feels all types of wrong, and plenty kinds of right.

"Relax," he whispers.

And then instead of fighting it, I just simply decide to let go.

I feel like I'm dancing. Like I've floated up into the clouds and I'm dancing on air. Zeff is barely touching me, but keeping me directed. Almost like he's in my head, whispering the words, guiding the way.

Right now I feel invincible. Like I could do anything. Fight off every single Vârcolac and vampire in the world out to do me harm, and obliterate them into extinction. Well, okay, maybe not obliterate, but maybe somewhere close.

Zeff slowly moves around so he's standing in front of me, his hand gently brushing across my lower back, coming round to my waist.

I open my eyes. He's staring down at me, his eyes opaque, impenetrable, his hand still resting on my waist.

I smile, looking up at him, heat rising in my body. A wrong kind of heat.

My thoughts suddenly jump to Nathan and my smile falters. I step back. His hand slips from my waist to drop to his side.

"We should start with the fighting now," Zeff says.

His voice sounds deeper than normal.

"Fighting. Yeah that'll be good," I say, awkward.

I turn away, trying to gain some balance, clear my head and bring my body temperature back to normal.

I do not fancy Zeff. I don't. It's just because I haven't been near a man in so long that I feel this way.

That is all it is. And nothing more.

Chapter 9: Awakenings

"Okay," says Zeff, standing before me. "Let's try out some of those moves collectively."

"Okay."

I flex my arms and legs out readying myself.

"Right, I'm going to try and take you out from the front. Vamp's and Vârcolac's are not afraid of frontal confrontation, Bunny. They're not interested in sneaking up from behind, they like to see the fear in their victims faces."

"Ack!" I grimace, containing a shudder. He gives me a firm, serious look. "Okay, I got it. Front attack, see fear."

Zeff gives me the nod and then without hesitation he grabs for my throat with his right hand.

As he said they would earlier in training, my hands instinctively go up when he grabs my throat. My arms either side of his, I overlap them, pulling them straight in, I yank his arm downwards and off my throat.

He moves in quick, trying to grab me again and without thinking, instincts takes over, I knee him in the groin, grab him, flip him over and drop him down onto the mat, landing him hard on his back.

He grunts a pained kind of sound, holding his groin, rolling away from me.

"Oh my God! I'm so sorry!" I say, instantly coming to my senses. I'm down and by his side in a second.

Shit, I've broken him!

"Are you okay, Zeff? Please tell me you're okay?!"

He doesn't answer, well if he does he's making no sense, all I'm getting is sharp intakes of breath between groans of pain.

Concern takes over and I put my hand on his arm and gently roll him onto his back. His eyes are squeezed tightly shut, his face red, knees bent up at his holds on to his manhood.

He actually looks kind of funny, but now's probably not the right time to laugh.

"Are you okay?" I ask softly, in a less panicked voice.

He lets out the breath he was holding in. "Yeah."

His voice is strained and a bit croaky.

"I'm so sorry," I emphasise. "I guess I just got a bit carried away."

He opens his eyes and looks at up me.

I smile, apologetically. "Have I broken you permanently?" I nod downwards.

"No. More like temporarily disabled." He gives a strangled grin.

I snort out a laugh, covering my mouth with my hand, I mutter, "Sorry."

He lets out a laugh. "Don't be. I'm actually kind of impressed. I mean, hellfire Bunny, you've got some strength in that tiny body of yours. Once I've got you trained up there'll be no stopping you."

I sit up on my haunches, feeling more than a little proud of myself. "You really think so?"

"Sure I do. I know I'm just a *regular guy,* but you took me down in seconds without even blinking. You've got a real fighter's instinct."

I don't know how to feel about having a *fighter's instinct;* something I never imagined anyone would ever say about me, but then I guess whether I like it or not, I need to have it.

"That's what I did to the vampire," I say, chewing on my thumb nail. "You know, when he had me pinned to the floor. I punched him in the nuts. It didn't last long though, and I managed to get away for a short while, but then he was back on me and then I couldn't get away. It obviously wasn't as effective on him as it is on you."

I scrunch my face up, realising my words.

He glances down at his hands, still on his groin, and moves them away. "No. But it was a smart thing to do, it gave you the chance to make that break to run. You hit a guy where it hurts, whether he's supernatural or not, and it will take him down, no doubt. Anything is worth a try to save your life. A swift punch to the throat, eye gouging, whatever it takes to save your life and keep you safe, Bunny." Giving me a small smile, he puts his hands to the floor and starts to sit himself up, but pauses, obviously still in a little pain, he puts a hand to his groin again, adjusting himself. I look away.

Biting my lip, I say again, "I am really sorry for hurting you, in quite possibly the worst way to hurt a guy."

He puts his hand on my arm. "Don't worry, *really*," he stresses, eyes dark yet soft on me, like warm melted chocolate. "I'll be fine."

Then leaning back away, he reaches over and grabs his bottle of water off the floor beside the mat. And I'm left with a tiny shock tremoring through my arm, making its way through the rest of my body.

The shocks I get from Zeff have lessened over the last few hours while we've been training, which we've been at for hours; actually, looking around, I notice for the first time just how dark it's gotten, and also that the flood lights at the back of the house have come on, illuminating the space.

I guess I was enjoying myself so much I didn't notice, and because I can see as well in the dark as I can in daylight my eyesight automatically adjusted.

The fighting has been way more enjoyable than the Tai Chi. Well up until the point I nearly broke his manhood that is. And don't get me wrong the Tai Chi was good, but it got me a bit too close to him. Way closer than I need to be.

I've been lonely for a long time now and being close to someone; a man, raises certain feelings in me.

I'm still a woman after all. And Zeff is ridiculously good-looking. I'm not made of wood.

"You want some?" he offers his water to me.

I shake my head. He screws the cap back on and sets the bottle down on the mat beside him.

"So, I think we should call it a day before you kill me, and my sense of masculinity, totally," he jokes, winking.

I nod, feeling a little disappointed the training is over with, I was really just getting into the swing of it, but I guess it is understandable since I just practically garrotted his nuts.

"We can carry on with the training tomorrow night if you want?" Zeff adds, slowly getting to his feet, almost as though reading my thoughts, and I wonder for a moment if they were clear to read on my face.

"I'd like that," I say, nodding. I shuffle back off the mat and start to roll it up. "And I promise not to knee you in the nuts the next time."

"That'd be good." Pause. "So I was just going to make some dinner if you want to stay and have some?" I glance up at him through my lashes. "I'm a pretty decent cook, or so I've been told. You can judge for yourself though."

Looking back down, I finish off rolling up the mat. I can feel my heart has started to beat just that little bit harder in my chest.

"Erm, no, but thanks."

Training with Zeff is one thing, but we've already had dinner together once when we went for pizza, twice would just be like a date. Especially if he cooks for me. Zeff might think an acceptance of dinner as I'm okaying it as a date, or something. I can't confuse things; I need to keep this neutral.

"I need to get back to my flat. I've got stuff I need to do."

Okay, I know it's weak, but it's the best I could come up with.

"Stuff," he echoes. "So you need to get back to your apartment to do *stuff*." He raises his dark brows. "What stuff?"

I get to my feet tucking the mat under my arm. "Stuff. You know. Woman's stuff." That'll shut him up. Men never like to talk about woman's things.

"Hmm," he murmurs. "So you need to rush back to your empty apartment so you can get on with woman's stuff." He air quotes. "And what are you going to do when you've finished doing your woman's stuff?" Again with the air quotes.

What's up with that?

I look from his hands to his lightened face. "Watch TV, go to bed." I shrug.

"Why don't you want to stay for dinner, Bunny?" he queries, his voice suddenly sounding deeper, more intense.

I look at him, then down at my feet, scuffing the grass with my toe. "It just feels odd … having dinner with you – twice now, and you cooking for me … well it kind of feels like it'd be a … "

"A… ?" he pushes.

"Date." I look up at him to catch his reaction. But I didn't need to look, hearing his laugh was loud and clear enough as to his thoughts on my response.

It does nothing for my self-confidence.

I'm kind of pissed off and severely insulted he thinks the thought of dating me is that funny. My whole face is burning with embarrassment. It's a good job I already crippled him before, or I might have been tempted to kick him there again.

"Yeah 'cause I let all my dates kick my ass – well nuts," he corrects, "before we have dinner!"

He's still shaking with laughter. I wrap my free arm over my other, getting the urge to walk off.

"Look, I'm not trying to get into your pants, Bunny. I just thought it'd be nice, two friends having dinner together. I know you don't like having them so much, but for now you're stuck with me as one." He winks. "And trust me, even if I wanted to get into your pants, tonight really wouldn't be working so well for me. Your swift knee saw to that one." He nods down at his groin.

I feel my cheeks heat.

"And you're not telling me you haven't ever had dinner with a friend before?" he continues.

"Of course I have." I flicker a look his way.

"Well there you go then. And I'll even let you load the dishwasher with all the dirty pots if it makes you feel better, you know, make it even less date-like," he adds, a smile ghosting across his face.

I suppress a rising smile. Sometimes I can't not smile at him. And I guess what he's saying does kind of make sense. I'm just over-thinking things.

"Okay, I'll stay for dinner," I say slowly, "but on one condition."

He folds his arms across his chest, intrigue capturing his expression. "Shoot."

"You stop calling me Bunny."

Releasing a hand, he steeples his fingers over his mouth. "Ahh, now come on that's not playing fair."

I put my hands on my hips, stifling a laugh. "Take it or leave it."

"Why do you hate it so much? Because personally I think it's cute."

I give him a look. "Um, where do I start … because you are totally taking the piss every time you call me it and because it makes me sound like a pet, or worse, like one of Hugh Hefner's Playboy bunnies or something equally as tacky." He raises his eyebrows at that one. "And before you say it, don't." I point a warning finger at him.

"What?!" He raises his palms, feigning that innocence he's so good at. "Okay, okay," he concedes. "How about I don't call you Bunny for the rest of the evening."

"Two days."

"One."

"Two. Or nothing. Take it or leave it." I give him a firm look, letting him know I mean business and that there'll be no flexibility.

"Jeez, you drive a hard bargain. Fine, two days," he huffs.

I hold my hand out to shake. He begrudgingly takes it and gives my hand a quick shake, then taking the mat off me, he strides toward the lodge.

Smiling, picking his water bottle up off the floor, I follow behind.

He waits at the back door, holding it open for me as I ascend the porch steps. "Bunny," he drawls, "you know when I said I'd let you load the dishwasher ... well actually, the clean ones need taking out first."

He makes a cheeky face at me as I continue on up the steps.

"Bunny is off the menu for two whole days remember." I give him my best stern look.

"Ah, right yeah, sorry." He nods solemnly, but I can see the glint in his lovely dark eyes. He knows exactly what he's doing. But I kind of have to like him for it too. He's just a bucket load of mischief and more.

"And of course I'll empty the dishwasher, it's the least I can do if you're making dinner."

"Atta girl!"

He playfully cuffs my arm with his fist as I pass by into the kitchen.

And it definitely doesn't feel like a date now. That couldn't be more of a 'one of the guys' thing to do if he tried.

Pausing, I stop to look at him as he overtakes me, heading straight for the refrigerator, it finally dawning on me.

I've finally figured out what it is I like about Zeff.

Reaching the fridge he stops and looks over his shoulder at me, catching me staring. But I don't look away.

"What?" he says, smiling his off centre smile.

"Nothing." I shake my head. "You just really remind me of someone I used to know."

"Oh, yeah," he says, mildly interested. "Well, I hope he was startlingly good-looking and charismatic." He winks at me before turning away and pulling open the fridge door, revealing its contents.

"He was," I say quietly. "He was the best."

There was never anyone one quite like Sol in my life, before or since. Well, not until now that is.

Chapter 10: Drunk Lips, Cause Slips

After dinner we go sit in the living room. I curl up on one of the leather chairs, sipping on my third glass of wine. Zeff sits across from me on the sofa I woke up on a few days ago looking relaxed with a glass of wine in his hand.

He's dressed in a black long sleeved sweater and jeans, which look like they cost more money than I could earn in two months at the café. He changed out of his sweats just before he made dinner, and I changed into the spare pair of jeans and T-shirt I always carry in my rucksack, I didn't fancy wearing my sweats all night either.

The fire is roaring to my left, the heat soothing on my skin, and I couldn't be more relaxed if I tried. It's crazy how comfortable I feel here with him, after such a short time knowing him.

Zeff is one of the easiest people I have ever met. He's so uncomplicated, so open and inviting, and yet, I barely know a thing about him.

"Do you want some music on?" asks Zeff.

"Sure." I smile.

"Any preference?"

"Nope."

Leaning over he picks a remote control up from the side table. His sweater rides up and I catch a glimpse of his tight toned abs. Heat courses through me.

I take a glug of wine.

He points the remote in no particular direction and then I hear the music melt into the room. The Doors, Love Her Madly.

I'm impressed. My dad used to listen to them like they were his religion. Hearing this song reminds me of being in the car with him and my mum, driving to my Nan's house on a Sunday afternoon.

Emotion starts to gather in my chest. Grief. Longing.

Then without warning a memory of Nathan in his Jim Morrison T-shirt flashes through my mind.

He's leant up against his car, waiting for me. He's taking it off in the woods …

I blink myself free from the memory and take another drink of wine.

Clearing my throat, I say, "Not that I'm not impressed, or dissing your taste in music in any way, because I'm not, all hail Jim Morrison. I actually grew up listening to The Doors. But I really didn't figure you for this kind of music."

His brows pull in together and he licks his lips. It's distracting.

"You've got a lot to learn about me." He winks. "Hands down the sixties and early seventies music was the best." He clicks his tongue in mock-reproof. "The Doors, Rolling Stones, Beatles, Fleetwood Mac, all the good music came from then."

"You see, and I had you figured as a Kenny G kind of guy."

He lets out a deep throaty laugh. "Hey, don't knock Kenny. Hot bubble bath and a glass of wine, Kenny playing in the background, I can really connect with my inner woman."

I'm sipping my wine as he says the last part and I laugh, snorting, wine goes up my nose. I start choking.

"Attractive," he chides, laughing. "You okay? You need me to get you anything, a glass of water …"

"No, I'm fine," I wheeze, wiping my hand over my mouth, the coughs beginning to subside.

"Pig trough … "

I snort again. This third glass of wine really is having the desired effect. "Stop it!" I chide.

"Bunnies and pigs, huh?"

"Hey," I warn, holding a finger up in his direction.

"Merely an observation," he says innocently, grinning at me over his wine glass.

I really like Zeff's smile. I like that it's crooked. That it diminishes his perfection. Makes him look more human, and not like something carved out of marble by God.

Okay, so now I know I've had too much wine when I'm thinking crazy shit like that. Well, seen as though I'm on crazy shit for brain and have had too much wine to care, I might as well ask what's been bugging me for a while now.

"Zeff, can I ask you something?"

"Is it clean?" he asks with a salacious smile. "Because I'm not talking dirty with you."

"Shut up!" I roll my eyes at him, but I can feel a flush rising in my cheeks. "I'm being serious."

His gaze holds mine, "Oh you're being serious. Well, okay, sure, I can do serious for a minute."

I drag my hand over my ponytail, pulling it around the nape of my neck. "I know you're human, of course you're human … but well, it's just … is there anything *special* about you?"

He lifts his eyebrow, part curious, part jokey. "There's a lot that's special about me – fancy narrowing it down a bit?"

"Well–" I fiddle with the stem of my wine glass. "Do you have any … powers of any sort?"

"Powers?" he echoes. "What do you mean, powers?"

"Just – can you do stuff that regular people can't do?"

"Um … not that I know of." A half-smile. "Why do you ask?"

"Well, it's just – every time I touch you, I get a shock – like an electric shock. It's not so bad now; I'm kind of used to it after having so much contact with you while training. But it was a little weird at first. And the other day when we were talking about my attack I could literally feel your anger emanating out of you and coating onto me."

And now saying it out loud I can hear how strange it sounds, but it's also really true.

He scratches the back of his neck. "Sorry, but that's not coming from me. I'm just a regular guy. Nothing extraordinary about me, except for my damning good-looks that is." A grin. "Are you sure it's not just something about you – a Vârcolac thing?"

I'm looking at him intently, spying for anything. A flicker in his eyes or slight change in expression. An increase in his heartbeat. But nothing. He either has no clue, like he's saying, or he's really *really* good at hiding it. I can't decide on which one it is yet.

I shake my head. "I don't know for sure, but it's only from you that I've ever experienced it."

My voice is a little quieter now, the alcohol confidence waning.

He shrugs. "I'm sorry, I don't know what to tell you. It's not something I've heard of before."

Zeff is a pretty open book, and if there was something special about him I think he would tell me. So it must be something to do with me. Around him. And now I feel kind of stupid bringing it up. I chug back on my wine until I drain the glass.

"More?" There's a smile in his eyes.

God, I must look like a real alchy. But then again I don't really care. The booze is numbing the part of my brain which makes life hurt just that little bit more.

"Sure," I say.

Zeff drains his own glass and reaches over, retrieving the half-full bottle from the coffee table. I clamber forward in my seat, holding my glass out, allowing him to fill it.

He sits back and picks his own glass up to fill, then pauses. "Actually, I better not have anymore. I have to drive you home."

"No." I pause glass on lips "Don't worry about me. I can walk – well run home." *Okay stagger*. "It'll take me five, ten minutes, tops."

"Now, I know you can take care of yourself, Bun-" I give him a hard stare, cutting off his slip up. "Sarah," he corrects. "But I'd feel a whole lot better if I drove you home."

It's kind of funny to hear him calling me Sarah; I'm so used to him calling me Bunny.

Then I realise I actually like him calling me Bunny. Or the wine does. Well either way, I'm never telling him that.

"I know. I just don't want to spoil your evening because you have to drive me home."

"I don't need alcohol to have a good time." He smirks that devilish grin of his.

My skin shivers, pleasantly. "Me either."

I give an ironic snort holding my fourth glass of wine up. Oh God. Why do I keep snorting tonight? I rub my nose, embarrassed, realising how that could actually sound.

"I mean, I'm kidding of course – of course I'm having a good time."

"You're having a good time – with me?" His voice is warm, amused.

He's trapped me there. I have this urge to say no, because he can be so confident, so cocky at times, and I hate for him to be right, because it is the truth. I am having a good time here with him.

I swallow nervously and tuck a stray hair behind my ear. Pressing my lips together trying to cover a rising smile, I say, "I'm having a good time."

His smile deepens, filling out his eyes to a shade of breathtaking. It casts an unwelcome but warm shadow deep inside of me. "And you've managed to hold up a full conversation with me, lasting what – nearly two hours now, without having a go or yelling at me. That must be some kind of record."

"Funny!" Relaxing, I pull a face at him. "You need keeping in check."

"If anyone can do that it's you," he says dryly. I think I see the hint of a smile.

And once again, his words have an unnerving effect on me.

"Are you going to have that drink or not?" I say, slightly rattled,

"Well I'm not drinking and driving, and you're certainly not walking home alone, so the only other option is if you stay here the night."

His words thud into the room like a pair of heavy boots and stomp all over my good mood.

Dropping my feet to the floor, I sit up bolt straight. "Erm, I don't think–"

"It's a good idea," he smiles, but it doesn't quite touch his eyes. "I thought we were past all that. I have a guest room at the bottom of the hall, far away from my bedroom, and it has a lock on the door just in case you're worried I might try and seduce you in the middle of the night."

There's a level of forced humour in his voice. I guess I must be kind of irritating him by now. And also it makes me sound conceited and incredibly vain, insinuating he's trying to get into my pants every five minutes.

A flush rises up my neck, hitting my face at record speed.

"I didn't mean it like that." I'm stuttering. "I don't think you like me – in that way – I know it sounds like I do but –"

"And if I do?" He cocks his head to one side and regards me intently.

I'm confounded and heated by his gaze. The blood quickly drains from my head.

"Eh?" I squeak.

He holds my gaze for a long moment. I can feel my body heating from the inside out. Then laughter starts to shake in his chest, spreading throughout his whole body.

"I'm kidding! The look on your face! I get that you're immune to my good looks and charm, but really I could never date a girl like you."

"Too witty for you?" I smart.

His eyes alight with wicked thoughts. "Nah, way too high maintenance." A grin. "Look, I know you feel like you'd be disloyal to your guy by staying over, but really it's no big deal. Men and women sleep, platonically, in the same house together, all over the world. It's nothing new. "

My back has stiffened ramrod straight, thoughts tossing out all over my befuddled brain. "I never said I had a guy."

"You didn't have to."

There's a long, distinctly noticeable pause, where we're both staring at one another.

"It's the guy who saved you from the Vârcolac?"

It's not a question, not really, because he already knows the answer. He knew from my reaction the other day when I dressed myself in coffee.

Deep breath. "Yes." I wrap both my hands around my wine glass, interlocking my fingers.

Then just being here with Zeff, and him reminding me so much of Sol, it just forces to the forefront everything I have lost since the day I became this version of myself. The one that brought me to the point of being sat here with him.

Tears spring to my eyes. Closing them briefly, I will them back.

"Are you okay over there?" Zeff asks, concerned lacing his voice.

I open my eyes. His are still fixed on my face.

"Hmm." I nod. "I'm fine."

Zeff reaches over and places the bottle of wine back on the table, along with his empty glass.

"You don't look it," he counters.

"No, I am. I guess, I just find it hard sometimes …" I murmur, confounded by the direction of this conversation.

"You miss him?" he queries. I note the weariness in his voice.

I nod.

"Why did you break up?"

I smile. It's not a happy smile. More of an ironic one. "We didn't actually break up. To do that you'd have to have an actual relationship."

"Ahh, he a 'love 'em and leave 'em' kind of guy?"

Now that makes me laugh. That's not the way I would ever choose to describe Nathan.

"No." I shake my still laughing head. "We never actually got to the relationship stage. Things were *difficult*."

That's putting it mildly.

I don't even know why I'm talking to him about this. It's the wine. Note to self. Never drink wine again. Drunken lips cause slips.

"Difficult – because you're a Vârcolac?"

"That … amongst other things."

Then from out of nowhere a tear leaks from out the corner of my eye, unexpectedly. I catch it before it falls too far. I don't think Zeff notices. If he does, he has the courtesy to pretend he doesn't.

"You loved him?"

"Mmm."

"So why leave?"

"Because too many people had died already." I pull in a deep breath. "His brother was killed trying to save me from Vârcolac's. And I didn't want him to die too. Being with me is …" I look straight into his eyes. "Dangerous."

If I meant to scare him, I don't. Seemingly, it just simply rolls off him.

"And he just let you go? Just like that."

"No. I didn't … erm … exactly tell him I was leaving."

"Ahh." He nods. His gaze is unwavering. "Do you think he's looking for you?"

"At first, maybe. But not now, no."

I might like to believe in an ideal world he is, but my world has never been ideal and I know he isn't. Nathan stopped looking for me a long time ago.

"If I were him, I'd never stop looking," Zeff say low, deep.

I halt at his expression, his eyes darkening. I really don't know what to say to that. I don't think I've ever been as confused by someone as I am by him, right now.

Moving his heavy stare from me, he picks the wine up and fills his glass, emptying the bottle into it. Then picks his glass up and downs it in one.

Watching in confusion and wanting to clear the air of the tension I can feel coming from out him, I say, "You're letting me walk home?"

I raise my eyebrow.

He pulls one side of his mouth up in a half-smile. "Nope. I'm just taking the choice away from you."

"Ha!" I laugh in spite of myself. "You're a confident son of a bitch."

"Yeah and you're a pain in the ass." He stands up. "So you're staying?"

I nod, yes.

"Good." A smile. "You want any snacks from the kitchen? I'm gonna need some more food in me to soak up the amount of alcohol I'm intending to drink tonight."

I raise a half-smile. It's impossible to not smile at him, even in the weirdest of moments. I shake my head. "No. I'm good, thanks."

Curling my legs up onto the chair I watch Zeff as he walks over to the kitchen. I drag my stare from him, and down into the honey liquid in my glass, feeling an intense mixture of emotions, praying the wine has the answers to ending the eternal ache for Nathan I feel, and the sudden and very confusing attachment I seem to have developed for Zeff.

Chapter 11: Losing Battle

I wake with a start. Not because I'm not used to waking up in strange places, because I am, believe me, but because I'm waking up at Zeff's place.

The night quickly regales to me.

Wine. Lots of wine. Bottles and bottles of the stuff. Then vodka and whiskey … possibly gin.

Blurgh!

It takes a lot of drink to affect me nowadays, but holy crap we drank a lot; I think we may have drunk Italy dry.

And boy I was wasted.

From what I recall, Zeff is a good drunk. A fun drunk. Me on the other hand, not such a great drunk. Emotional. I actually think I cried at one point. Oh God, and Zeff had to carry me to bed.

Double God.

I reach a hand down feeling for my clothes. Still dressed. Thank you Lord.

Thirst suddenly overcoming me, I drag my parched body out of bed and straight to the en-suite bathroom. Running the cold water tap I drink straight from the faucet.

After using the bathroom I stumble back into the bedroom and sit down on the edge of the bed. I listen out for movement and can hear Zeff's deep breaths. He's still sleeping.

Good. It makes my exit from here all the easier.

I make the bed. My good manners stopping me from not being able to. I can't leave a mess when he was so kind as to let me spend the night.

Then moving quickly and quietly, I go out into the living room to retrieve my shoes and rucksack. Slipping them on, I leave the three hundred euros and the passport photo on the counter, and let myself out the front door with a quiet click of the handle.

I quickly pick up pace running, heading back toward town, back to my place to get showered and ready for work.

The day passes by in a blur. A haze of customers, coffee and sticky pastries. When my shift is finished, instead of going to Zeff's for training as planned, I go back to my flat.

To hide.

From him.

I feel weird about staying at his place last night. I can't explain why, I just do. I mean it's not like we slept together or anything. But the fact it feels weird is ringing serious alarm bells for me.

And when the time comes, and long passes, that I should have been at his place, and I don't hear from him and he doesn't come looking, I take it that maybe he feels weird about last night too.

I make myself dinner; well beans on toast, and it's more out of routine and for something to do than actual hunger. I push the food around my plate, then bin it. I don't even feed because my stomach just feels all hollow and empty, the thought of anything going into my body makes me feel like I want to throw up.

I know why. Because I'm feeling guilty.

I haven't thought of Nathan much in these last few days. Not like I used to. I know I want to get over him, but suddenly, since the appearance of Zeff in my life, it's been happening all too quick and all too easily.

Look at me. A few days around a new guy and I'm forgetting about Nathan. I know I said it was what I wanted, but I didn't mean right now, and not so quick. I wanted a gradual slip.

But now it's started to happen way too fast. And I'm not ready. I can't lose Nathan from the only place I have him. In my memories.

Pulling exaggerated breaths, I try to calm myself and gain some perspective. My head is buzzing.

Going into the bedroom I change into my pyjamas.

I'm probably being stupid stressing over Nathan like this. I mean, I don't have to forget about him if I don't want to.

And Zeff … well I know I don't have feelings for him and he doesn't have them for me. I got that from the way he laughed when I mentioned about last night's dinner feeling like a date. So his interference in my feelings for Nathan is a moot point.

But, well … I guess what worries me is in the short time I've known Zeff he hasn't mentioned any other friends or family, except for his dead parents. I've never seen him take a phone call or make one, except for the call to the passport guy. He's never mentioned any plans he has with people, and always seems available to train with me.

I get the distinct impression Zeff spends a lot of time alone. Like me. And when you put two loners together, well, then that loneliness can sometimes surface.

And not in the right way. Usually in a sex way.

A way of staving off the loneliness, for even just a short time. And that can't happen.

But I'm just worried that the more time I spend with Zeff, that I'll stop thinking with my head and start thinking with my hormones. They're already rearing their crazy ass head, and when they take over – well if Zeff's a willing participant then it'll just be a forgone conclusion.

I need to stay away from him. While I wait for my passport to arrive I need to put a big thick dividing wall between us, you know the kind with solid concrete blocks, before things go to a place they were never meant to.

No training. No dinners. Nothing.

My mind is made up.

Only, for the rest of the evening, no matter what I do or how hard I try, I can't seem to stave off thoughts of Zeff from my mind. Ones threatening to override Nathan.

Maybe my fears were founded after all. Maybe I am just fighting a losing battle when it comes to Zeff.

Chapter 12: Out of the Blue

I'm leaving work the next day when I see Zeff's car parked just down the street from the café, him casually leaning against it, assumedly waiting for me.

I have an involuntary lurch in my stomach.

He's wearing a fitted cotton black shirt and black trousers. He's leant up against the side of the car bonnet, elbows resting back on it. He lifts his head in my direction as if sensing my appearance, and his face alights with his crooked smile.

He looks exactly like a ray of sunshine in my world filled with bleakness. And any resolve I had about staying away from him quickly filters out of my mind.

Straightening up, he says, "So yesterday, I woke up and you were gone, Bunny. No note, no breakfast, not even a measly cup of coffee waiting for me … and I'd thought we'd had such a good night together. I thought we had something special. I'm completely heartbroken." He casts his large hand over his chest, feigning drama. "I don't think I can ever forgive you for this."

My lips crack into a smile as I walk over to him. I slap his firm bicep lightly with my hand.

The shock I feel at the connection momentarily stuns me. I thought I was used to it but it seems to have doubled, tripled in strength. Maybe it's because I've not been around him for the last few days.

Finding my voice, although a touch croaky, I say, "Hey, remember we had a deal. No calling me Bunny." And discreetly, I clench my fist, flexing my fingers in and out by my side, trying to dispel the feeling he's left me with.

"Our deal was for two days. It's been two days." He lifts his arm, shifting back his shirt cuff, he casts a glance at his watch.

"Not for another three hours," I say, leaning forward, tapping the face of his watch with my fingernail.

He lets out a small laugh. "Now if I'd have known, I'd have waited the extra three hours. That's why I've stayed away. It's been absolute torture not being able to call you Bunny."

I grin up at him. Then I realise just how close I am to him. So close I can feel the heat licking off his skin, diving straight into me. I take a large step back.

"So what have you been up to?" I ask, moving into neutral territory.

"I've just had some business to attend to." He sounds suddenly different. Businesslike.

I get the distinct impression it's not business he wants to talk about with me. And it's quite possibly not business I would want to know about.

"So anyway," he says, lifting his voice. "I just stopped by to see if you wanted do some more training tonight. We missed out last night and I've still got plenty to teach you, and I might even let you cook me dinner if you behave yourself."

I like that he doesn't question my noticeable absence from our arranged training session. Or the fact that I didn't even call to let him know I wasn't going.

I don't even hesitate in my answer. "Sure it's been a few days since I kicked your arse – sorry nuts." I raise my brows. "Don't want you getting complacent now, do we?"

"Is that a challenge, Bunny?" Brows furrowed, he gives me a serious look, with a soft edge.

"What do you think?" I'm feeling mischievous.

He has the ability to bring that side of me out. Actually, he has the ability to bring a lot of sides of me out. He opens the passenger door for me, and I hop in.

"I'd say … yes, and challenge accepted. Prepare to get your ass kicked little lady." He shuts my door with an expensive clunk, and I watch as he walks around to the driver's side and climbs in.

The minute he's in the car, I say, "In your dreams, pretty boy." I give an evil villain laugh.

"You already are, Bunny. You already are." His voice is low, he's staring straight ahead, face unreadable, hands resting on the steering wheel.

I tilt my head and stare at him. I wait for him to laugh. To say he was joking. But he doesn't. And a sensation grabs a tight hold of my heart, twisting and turning, sending a shiver right through me. I swallow against the sudden thickness in my throat, unsure of what to say next.

Then he breaks his gaze and offers a grin my way. He cranks the car to life, "Let's get going, so I can give you that ass whooping."

He laughs, but it feels forced somehow.

I laugh too. "You're a jerk."

I grin, but nothing about this moment feels right. I feel like I've intruded on thoughts I was never meant to hear. And I have no clue how to feel.

So I do what I do best, I scratch over the moment as if it never existed. I erase it from my memory.

Because if I don't, then I won't get though the rest of the evening without doing or saying something stupid. Something that could potentially put me in a place I really do not want to ever find myself in with him.

Chapter 13: Weapons

I'm back at Zeff's place again today.

The training we did last night was excellent. He taught me some great self-defence tactics, and we worked on boxing, and a little kickboxing. I didn't even know I could kick that high.

It was awesome and really energising, and I also managed not to break him once. I feel like really soon I'll be in a position to be able to defend myself if I need to.

Afterwards we had dinner together. I offered to cook. It's been a while. The last time I cooked a meal was when I was still living with Eddie. Zeff has plenty of food in so I rustled up a Spanish omelette with salad.

I thought he might like it, being Spanish and all. He seemed to enjoy it, it went down pretty quick. Then we talked until late, drinking beer, regaling stories from when we were kids, things we'd done, mischief we'd gotten into.

And even though I felt I was getting to know him better, he still eluded details. He didn't once mention his parents in any of his stories. Only a few names dropped in, cousins and friends he said. But that was it.

And I realised. He talks like I do. He holds back any real detail, like there is something in his past he has to hide.

It makes me curious, but I also respect it. Because there are a lot of things I can't disclose. Things I have to keep locked up inside.

I suppose I could tell him my real name; who I am. Where I came from. I trust him now.

Well, I think do.

But then, Alex Jones, died a long time ago. So maybe she should just stay dead.

I'm sat at the breakfast bar, sipping on lemonade. Zeff's out back, setting up. I have no clue what he's setting up for. We're trying something new today, and apparently it's a surprise.

I'm not so keen on surprises. But I'm just going along with it.

As long as I get to punch some anger out on the punch bag today, I'll be a happy lady.

Lately, I've been feeling an anger growing inside me. Simmering, bubbling away, but just recently it's been growing with intensity, and quickly. It's starting to worry me a little. Okay, a lot.

And I don't know if it's because I tasted blood. My – sort of – preferred kind of blood. I know it wasn't exactly *human*, but I would think vampire blood nears close to humans, and I know it was only a drop from his finger when I bit him but since then my urges have increased somewhat.

The other thing it could be is the wolf in me. She's there in my head constantly fighting to get out. I keep caging her up, but for how long can I continue to do so, I don't know.

It just frightens me what could happen if I do release her.

"Come on Bunny," Zeff says, head poked around the half-open door. "It's ready."

I turn in my seat. "What's ready?"

He raises an insolent brow. "Well if you get your ass out of the chair and come out here, you'll see."

Putting my drink down, I meander over to him. He pushes the door wide open for me and I follow him out onto the porch.

Immediately I see beer bottles lined up ahead on a makeshift wooden ledge, situated between two high stools. A table with an impressive array of guns and knives. A dummy hanging up off a makeshift stand, and a target board, with a crossbow resting at its side.

I look sideways at him, mouth agape. He meets my eyes, clearly impressed with himself.

"Today is weapons training, Bunny."

"Eh?"

"Well," he says descending the steps. "You carry a blade around in your bag, so you might as well learn how to use it."

"And the guns and crossbow?" I gesture around, following him down the steps.

"Ah, they're just here for my pleasure." He casts a grin back over his shoulder, winking. "You might not carry them around Bunny, but you never know what lies ahead and it'll be good for you to know how to handle them. I'm taking it you've never handled a gun before?"

He stops at the table and picks up a fierce looking gun. Silver, shiny and deadly.

"No." I shake my head. "I've seen one before." *Nathan's*. "But never touched one."

He gestures it forward.

I look from it to him. "What? You want me to hold it?"

"I do."

"Can't we just do training with the knives?" I gesture to his impressive collection.

I just don't trust myself with a gun. I might shoot him by accident or something, and I certainly don't fancy explaining that to the police. But mostly, I just don't like them. Guns give off a bad vibe.

"We'll get to the knife training later. First guns, I want you doing this while you're fresh and alert." He pushes it forward and I can tell he's getting impatient with me.

"Look, I just don't like them, okay. They freak me out. They're dangerous."

Ever since I saw that gun in the back of Nathan's jeans, intended for me, I just can't bear the thought of them, let alone holding one.

"Bunny, you need to get past whatever issue you have with guns, and fast." He lowers his tone to a range I don't like. The hairs on my skin prickle. "Because one of these." He holds it up between us. "Might just be the difference for you staying free, and alive."

I close my eyes in brief contemplation, and I see behind my lids the look on that vampire's face right before he bit me. Then I see Albino. His hands on me. Then I see Jin, biting Sol.

I open my eyes and take the gun from his hand.

It feels cold and smooth on my skin.

"The safety's on so you've nothing to worry about," he adds. "We'll go as fast or as slow as you want. We've got all day."

I look up, seeing the tenderness in his eyes, his face. Seeing all he's doing for me. Knowing how much he cares about me.

"Thank you," I say. "For doing this for me. For helping me as much as you have done. I'd have been up shit creek without a paddle if it wasn't for you. Well, actually, I'd probably be just – dead." I add a weak little laugh onto the end. "And if there is anything I can ever do for you, just tell me, okay?"

His face stays impassive, smooth, but he smiles a little. "Just stay safe and alive. That's payment enough."

My heart does something funny; bumping its way clumsily around my chest.

"Come on," he says, pulling his eyes from mine, he picks up a gun, a black one. It looks similar to the one I'm holding. "I'll show you how to do target practise."

Anchoring my heart down in my chest, I follow him over to the makeshift target of beer bottles.

"This why we were drinking beer last night?" I offer a grin.

He chuckles. "Well that and simply for the carnal pleasure of it

"You know, I drink way too much when I'm around you." I giggle.

"Well you can get back on the wagon next week, when you're free of me." His words thump into the warm air, instantly cooling it.

"Yeah. I guess I can." I swallow against my dry throat. It doesn't run smooth, just like his words didn't.

"Okay … oh, put these in your ears." He delves into his jeans pocket and pulls out a pair of ear plugs. "You're not used to the sound yet, and with your hearing it might shock you a bit. Wear for the first few rounds and then we'll try without, okay?"

"Sure."

I take the ear plugs from him, gaining a little shock from the contact, like normal, and push the plugs into my ears.

"Right, just watch me." He takes the safety off and raises the gun in his hands, finger on the trigger. "I lift to aim, eyes following down the barrel. With what you are going to be shooting at, there's no blind aim here hoping for a hit like you could with a normal person. You've got one – two shoots, if you're lucky, before he'll be on you. You're going for the heart, so that shot has to be a good one. Make it count, because you're aiming for a very small part on the body." His voice is so smooth, I feel kind of mesmerised watching him. "Think of it as throwing a dart into the bulls-eye on a board."

"You're not selling this you know. And I'm really shit at darts."

He slides his smiling eyes to mine. I can't stop the grin on my face.

Aiming his gaze back in place, he says, "Okay, so I focus on the target, then gently squeeze the trigger."

I hear the loud pop of the gun when it goes off. Even though I have plugs in it's still crazy noisy. The smell of sulphur hits my nose straight away. I watch as a bottle shatters to pieces. Then he shifts the gun to his right, marginally. Pop. Another bottle shatters. He takes three bottles down in a few seconds.

"Impressive," I nod.

"I had a great teacher and it took a lot of years of practise," he replies modestly. "I don't have years to teach you, so it's a crash course in weapons training. You just need to hit one target at a time. The only problem we've got," he says walking over to put some bottles he just picked up out of the bag beside the table and replacing the ones he just smashed, "Is you're going to be aiming for a moving target."

He starts walking back to me. "And I don't have a moving target. Not unless you use me of course." He smirks.

"I'll pass. Thanks."

Coming up to stand behind me, he says, "Your turn."

Nerves start to tremor under my skin. He reaches over and takes the safety off.

"You'll be fine. Trust me."

"I do trust you. I don't trust myself. You joke about letting me shoot you, knowing me, it might just be a possibility."

"Have a little more faith in yourself." He chuckles deep and low. "But I'll stay back here just to be on the safe side."

I glance at him over my shoulder. "You think you're safe back there? You really don't know me at all."

He smiles and it lights up his whole face. My stomach does a little flip.

"Eyes forward Bunny, sooner we get started the more confident you'll feel with that gun in your hands."

"Okay, well don't say I didn't warn you." Eyes facing ahead, I take a deep breath, holding the gun with both hands, I lift it up to chest level.

"Okay." His breath blows over the skin on my neck. It's distracting. He's not touching me, but he's close enough for me to feel his heat. "Cup your left hand under the gun; it'll give you something to rest against, help keep it steady and level. Yeah that's right," he adds as I move my left hand to position.

"Next rest your index finger ever so lightly against the trigger … good… now slide your eyes down the barrel of the gun to your target, does it meet with it?"

I shake my head.

"Adjust it until it does."

Keeping my eyes in line, I shift the gun ever so slightly higher.

"You there?" he asks in a murmur.

"Yes"

"Okay, so when you're ready, squeeze the trigger."

I focus my attention in on the bottle I picked. Taking a couple of deep breaths, I ready myself and squeeze the trigger in.

The jolt of the gun in my hand is more forceful than I was expecting, it pushes me back a bit and I bump into Zeff. His hands go to my waist steadying me.

The bullet whizzes straight past the bottle and smashes into the trunk of a tree.

I turn, giving Zeff a 'that was crap' look.

"Hey, you hit something. That's good for your first time. Let's just keep at it 'til you're hitting the bottles."

Then I'm acutely aware that his hands are still on my waist. I glance down, then back up at his face. Seemingly, coming to, he moves his hands away.

My skin feels instantly cold where his touch was. I hate that I like the way his hands feel.

Taking a deep breath, slamming my focus on another bottle, I line the gun up. "I'm really sorry to all of you trees if I shoot you again."

Zeff chuckles. "You're apologising to the trees?"

"They're living things."

"You're odd."

I bump his leg with my hip. "Yeah, well, it takes one to know one."

Then I lift the gun a little higher, aim and … fire.

Hit another tree.

"Sorry!" I shout.

Another chuckle from Zeff.

"Concentrate," he whispers in my ear.

"I'm trying."

"Try harder." He's too close to me, it's distracting.

Okay, focus. Eyes on the target. Squeeze the trigger …

Miss.

"Arrgggh!" I cry.

I can't hit one measly bottle. Plenty of trees, not bottles. He made it look so easy. I start to fire the gun in anger, trying to hit one bottle.

I miss every one.

Zeff says nothing from behind me. Frustrated, I walk away and slam the gun down on the table.

"I can't do this! I don't even know why I'm bothering." I feel really angry, and I'm not exactly sure why.

"To keep your ass safe." Zeff is at my side. "You've only just started, you need to give yourself more time to get it right."

I round on him. "Yeah, and like I'd be able to stop one of the Originals anyway if he got within spitting distance of me! They're stronger than me, and they're immortal for fuck's safe!"

He grabs hold of my shoulders, firm fingers digging into my skin. "And so are vampires, but I've killed plenty of them." Zeff stares at me seriously. "If it bleeds you can kill it, Bunny, remember that."

I stare back into his dark pooling eyes, watching the adrenaline in them settle and turn into something else entirely. Every part of my body starts to prickle with the sensation. And my anger switches into something else too. The same as his.

Lust.

Nathan.

I step back freeing myself from him. His hands drop to his sides. He folds them over his chest, almost as if he's looking for something to do with them.

"Okay. Sorry. You're right. Let's carry on." I turn away from him, picking the gun back up with trembling fingers.

"Don't be sorry, Bunny." His deep soft voice runs over my skin in delicious waves. "If you just let go of your fear and anger, the rest will all just fall into place."

Yeah. And that's what I'm worried about. Fear and anger are the only things keeping my hands on this gun right now, and not on you.

Chapter 14: She Wolf

The afternoon is rolling to early evening. I'm sat beside Zeff, resting back on my hands. Zeff is laid flat on his back basking in the sun that's just making its final appearance for the day.

We have been at weapons training all day, stopping for a short lunch. Zeff made us sandwiches and had kindly thought to have some blood ready for me.

Sweet. In a weird kind of way.

We sat out on the porch while we ate, and then we were straight back on it. I think he's trying to fit everything in before I leave. The days are quickly creeping up on me.

Zeff focussed mainly on teaching me how to shoot a gun. By the end of the session I was hitting three out four bottles on target. It took me quite a while, and a shed load of bullets and curse words, but I'm really proud of that achievement.

It was after lunch when Zeff showed me how to handle a knife properly. Using the hanging dummy as a target, he showed me the best tactics and moves to get myself in a position to stab my intended through the heart. After I got a hang of that we moved onto shooting a crossbow. That was fun, but really hard. I hit the target once, on the outer edge.

Zeff said not to worry, so long as I can shoot a gun and stab using my blade, I'll be fine.

Personally, I'd rather not have to do either.

"Thanks for today," I murmur, tilting my face to the sun, enjoying its warmth. "I had fun ... which is a weird thing to say considering I've been shooting beer bottles, stabbing dummies, and firing off arrows at a huge dart board."

I hear a little rumble of laughter in his chest. "Welcome to my world." His voice sounds deeper than normally, a little sleepy.

"I mean, I'm no Nikita, but I think I did all right."

"You did good, Bunny. You could kick Nikita's ass, hands tied behind your back, blindfolded."

I laugh, feeling a warm glowing coating my insides. "I highly doubt it, but thanks for the confidence."

I always get this feeling when he praises me. There's a real teacher-pupil thing going on here.

"Are you tired?" I add. Looking down at him, I rest my chin on my shoulder. "Because I can get off if you need to crash? I do need to get back to my apartment for my next feed soon anyway."

I've been a little lax with my feeds lately and I want to make sure I get back on track with my timings.

He opens his eyes, looking a little more alert than I was expecting. Then sits up, resting on his elbows.

"I'm fine," he says. "I would have hunted more blood for you than I did if I'd considered it."

"Don't be silly," I chide good-naturedly. "I appreciated you doing just that. It was really thoughtful."

"I aim to please." He winks. He can be such a flirt at times. "Actually thinking on it, why don't you just feed here, use the woods to hunt?" He nods his head in the direction.

"Hmm, I suppose I could." I shrug.

Actually, thinking about it, I can just hunt, then I get to hang out here a bit longer. It's better than going back to my empty apartment. And he seems to want me here, with him offering. Yeah, I think I'll do just that.

"Bunny, can I ask something?" he breaks into my reverie.

There's that nosey tone to his voice, the one I've heard before when he's questioned me about my change into a Vârcolac.

"Depends on what it is." My voice is light, but I give him a curious stare.

He sits up the rest of the way, shifting to the side, so he's facing me. "Why don't you shift into your wolf form for hunting? I'd think it would be easier for you, you know, considering the type of things you're hunting."

I sit up straight. "How do you know I don't?"

A smile. "Call it an educated guess." There's something behind his eyes that I can't quite grasp a hold of.

Pulling my eyes from his I look down at my T-shirt and start fiddling with the hem. "Okay so you're right, I haven't turned."

"Why?" His voice is soft, tainted with interest.

I blow a breath out. Then taking hold of my ponytail I yank the band out, freeing my hair. I fan it out around my face with my fingers. I need it as a shield. "Because I'm scared," I breathe the words out.

"Of?"

I bite my lip. I still haven't had the nerve to look at him yet.

"I'm afraid I'll get stuck and won't be able to change back."

I expect him to laugh, but he doesn't. So I glance up at him, through the veil of hair. His eyes are intent on my face. No humour there, just intrigue and kindness. It eases me somewhat.

"I get that, but Bunny it's a natural thing for you do now. You shouldn't repress it."

"I'm not repressing it." My voice hitches up an octave.

He raises an eyebrow. I look away.

Okay, so he's right. I am suppressing it. I can feel it deep down inside fighting to get out. A wild animal in me caged up, desperate for freedom, and she's getting more and more frustrated and antsy as the days roll on and on.

"It's not good for you," he adds. "You have to let that side out of you. If you keep caging it up then it could turn on you one day."

Sitting up, back ramrod straight, I flick my edgy eyes to him. "Turn on me?"

"Look I'm no expert, but I think it's a possibility that if you suppress that side of yourself for too long, then …"

"It'll turn me into the killer I'm meant to be?"

He shrugs. "Maybe. I guess that could happen. You do seem highly strung. Is that just you naturally?"

"No!" I say offended. "Okay, well … I can be a bit demanding and argumentative at times," I concede. "But not as bad as I have been lately, no." I release a sigh. "I'm going to have to do it aren't I?"

He nods. "Just look at this way, you're taking control of it, just like you have with the vampire need in you – feeding on animals not humans, so in my opinion taking control and turning into who you really are can only be a good thing."

I brush my fingers through my hair, contemplating.

I guess he's got a valid point. I'd never thought of it that way before.

"I can't do it alone though, and I have no one, like me, to help me." Nathan would have been able to help me.

Zeff limbers to his feet and holds a hand out to me. "I might not be able to change like you can, but I can be there for you, and with you, while you do."

I glance at his hand, then his face. He means it. Something funny churns in me. Nerves. I am honestly considering this. How does he do that? Having a way of making me feel like I can tackle anything.

"Remind me again, why you – a hunter, are helping me – a Vârcolac?" I put my hands in his and allow him to pull me to my feet. "You're supposed to kill things like me."

"I know, but I kind of made myself a promise long ago that I'd try and not kill my friends." He grins, but it doesn't last long. "And because Bunny, in a few days you'll be back out in the big bad world all alone, and the only way I can feel better about that is if I know I sent you back out there fully equipped."

My own smile drops from my face. And if I'm being honest I feel kind of winded.

Keeping hold of one of my hands, Zeff turns and starts to walk toward the woods, but I don't move and it tugs him back to a stop. He turns and looks at me curiously.

"You said if I cage this part of me up it could turn on me one day, but … what if I let it out and then there's no going back for me. What if what I have caged up in here is a monster and I release it, and then I'm done for? I lose the scrap of humanity I have left and I become a monster."

He moves close to me, and the hand he's holding he takes hold of with his other too, bringing them to rest against his chest, cradling it in his huge palms. He stares down into my eyes. Heat starts to burn through me.

"There is more humanity in you than I see in the average person on a daily basis." His voice is rough. "Being what you are, won't change *who* you are."

He words coat around me like silk armour. "How do you know?"

"Because I know you."

I hate that he does, and how much I like the fact.

It's like a huge band-aid on my long open unhealing wound.

Pulling in a deep breath, I say, "Okay. I'll give it a try."

We stand for a moment, my hand burning in Zeff's hold.

Finally loosening his grip, he says, "Come on. Let's get this show on the road."

He holds my hand for the whole walk there. And I don't once try to move it away.

"So now what?" I ask once we're safely in the trees.

"Well, you do your thing." Leaning his back against a giant oak tree, he gestures to me with his hand.

"You do remember our conversation out there, don't you?" I thumb toward the clearing. "You know the one we had a few minutes ago, the one when I said I'd never done this before."

A pirate smile. "I guess you'll just have to concentrate on what you want to do and then allow your body to change naturally. I'm sure your natural instincts will just take over."

"Seriously," I say, quirking an eyebrow. "Where are you getting this crap from? And please don't say, the 'Vârcolac How To' manual."

He laughs. "I don't know. It just sounded like a good thing to say. It seemed appropriate."

"Okay, so I just concentrate and allow my body to change naturally?" I feel like an idiot. I have no clue what I'm doing. I'm stood in the middle of the woods trying to turn into a wolf.

Sometimes I really can't believe my life.

I cast my mind back, trying to think of the time I was with Nathan in the woods when he shifted, what exactly it was he did.

But then I wasn't so much focussed on what he was changing into and more what he was changing out of. I get a flicker of the moment in my mind. A shiver runs over my skin, prickling my hairs.

That was one thing he did though. He undressed so he wouldn't shred his clothes. And I'm going to need to do the same. I don't have many clothes and can't afford to tear the ones I do have.

"I think … well, I'm erm … going to need to undress," I utter. I can feel my cheeks starting to burn already. I see his brows go up, so I add, "It's so I don't tear my clothes when I shift. Would you mind turning around while I undress."

"Sure." He turns away, leaning his shoulder up against the tree.

I kick my trainers off, removing my socks and stuffing them in my shoes. I peel my T-shirt off, fold it up and lay it on my trainers, then unbutton and shimmy out of my jeans, fold and put them with the rest. My eyes keep flicking ahead, to Zeff. I feel really uncomfortable undressing in his presence, whether he can see me or not.

Okay, so I'm just in my bra and knickers. In the middle of the forest. With Zeff.

I've decided I'm not taking them off. I don't care if they do get wrecked. I'm not standing completely stark naked with him, whether he can see me or not. Standing here in my bra and knickers is bad enough.

I let out a sigh.

"You okay?" he asks.

"I feel like an idiot."

"Why?" he starts to turn around.

"Hey!" I yell, wrapping my arms over my body, trying to cover myself. "I never said you could turn around!"

But it's too late he's already seen me.

"Turn back around!" I yell.

"Bunny, I've seen you now, so what does it matter. And if you want my help, I'm kind of going to need to be able to see you to do that. You're not the first woman I've seen half-naked, and I'm pretty sure you won't be the last. Why don't you just think of it like we're on a beach and you're wearing your bikini." One thing he does do is give me the courtesy of looking at my face and no place lower.

I glance around at the trees and the earth beneath my feet.

"But it's not a beach and my underwear most definitely is not my bikini." And honestly I'm really embarrassed of the underwear I'm wearing. I don't exactly go for sexy and expensive nowadays. Just my basic white T-shirt bra and plain white knickers. Not that I want to impress him in any way, but, you know what I mean.

"Just use your imagination," he coaxes, resting up against the tree, a grin spreading across his beautiful face like a wildfire.

Using my imagination too much is what I'm currently worried about. It's vivid and runaway. A little irrational at times. And he is seriously handsome.

I cross my arms over my chest, covering my boobs up, "Fine."

There's a huge silence between us. I'm staring at him. He's staring at me. My skin starts to tingle and something starts to flicker and flare in my stomach.

His eyes move down to my scar. I instantly feel self-conscious. Even more than I already was. But this time for a different reason.

"Erm..." I put my hand over it. It doesn't cover it fully, but I just need to do something. I can feel my face reddening. I cast my eyes to the floor and start to shift uncomfortably on my feet.

"Is that– "

"Yes."

I hear him start to move toward me. My whole body tenses up.

"I'm so sorry that happened to you." His voice is soft, soothing. "I just wish – " A sigh. "I just wish I could have done something to stop it."

I lift my eyes to his. The intensity there surprises me.

"You couldn't have done anything. You didn't even know me then."

His lips turn down at the corners. He lifts his shoulders slightly, shrugging. "You just deserve better than this, Bunny."

He lifts his hand, and for a moment I think he's going to touch me, but he corrects himself and shoves his hands in his pockets.

The level of disappointment I feel surprises me.

"So … " He purses his lips and I see the Zeff glint back in his eyes. "Not that I don't enjoy being in the woods with you in your underwear, but shall we get this show on the road?"

"Sure." I shrug. "I'm just not really sure how to – start the show." I give him a helpless look.

Releasing his hands from his pockets he holds them out for me to take. I stare down at them for a moment, then place my hands in his.

He holds them out loosely between us. "Okay, so just close your eyes and relax, just like you did when we were doing Tai Chi."

Oh God. I don't want to feel like I did when I was doing Tai Chi with him. Especially not while I'm stood here in my undies.

Seeing my hesitation and reading it wrong, he gives me a 'humour me' look.

I close my eyes, squeezing them tightly shut. I think of anything but this situation I now find myself in.

"Okay, so try and let your body go. Drift into your mind. Find your *wolf* in there. Your other self that you've locked tightly away into that cage in your mind."

A thought occurs to me. I flick open my eyes.

"I won't attack you or anything when I change – will I?"

He gives me a sly grin. "I hope not."

"Okay, I'm not doing this." I step back.

He pulls on my hands, keeping me there. "I'm winding you up. You'll be fine. I'll be fine. Now close your eyes."

"Not funny," I mumble. I close my eyes again.

"Find her again. Go to that cage." His voice is soft, deep, flowing through me, as I move through my mind, trying to find her. And then I see her.

"Let her out, Bunny. Just reach out and unlock the cage. That's all you need to do …"

I can see her, titling her head at me in silent contemplation. She looks so beautiful, yet so terrifyingly dangerous. I reach out a tentative hand to the lock on the cage.

With shaking fingers, I slowly slide the bolt across, unlocking it.I take hold of the handle and start to open the door. I'm expecting her to barge her way out. I can see her frustration. Smell it. Taste it.

The door is wide open. She hasn't moved yet.

I step back, giving her space.

Then very slowly, she starts to walk toward me…

I feel a tingling through my body; it quickly turns to an ache.

Then discomfort.

Nathan said it would feel uncomfortable, odd, the first time I shifted.

My heart starts to pump faster.

Faster.

Almost beating out of my chest.

I can feel my body moving in the worst kind of way.

Where's Zeff? I can't feel him anymore. I don't even know if he's holding my hands any longer.

I start to panic. It's hurting. I want it stopped. But I can't make it stop. She's free now and she's not going back in that cage for anyone.

I try to open my eyes but I can't. They're stuck. Glued tightly shut. My mind blurring. Changing in contest somehow. I try to conjure up an image in my mind. Something safe.

Nathan.

But I can't find him. If I just find him, my anchor, I'll feel safe.

But he's nowhere in my mind.

Zeff. Where is he?

I try to find my voice. I try to speak.

I hear a sound. I growl. A snuffle.

And that's when I realise the sound is me. It's coming from me.

I force open heavy eyes, blinking hazily, and everything looks different. I'm seeing the world through different eyes. New eyes. Her eyes.

Then I feel a hand on me, touching face, stroking me. I turn my head. The sensation odd, off.

I see Zeff crouch down beside me, smiling at me, awe and wonder on his face. "You look beautiful," he murmurs.

I try to speak, but it comes out a snuffle.

"Go," he whispers. "Hunt. I'll be waiting right here for you when you're done."

I press my face into his hand, nuzzling him, inhaling his scent.

Then I feel the lure, taking me away, and then I take off, in my new body, running at a speed that even my human legs wouldn't take me to.

Chapter 15: Passport Control

I stretch my well rested limbs out. Oh my God, I'm so comfy and cosy. I don't want to move ever. I can't remember the last time I slept so well.

Easing my eyes open I rub them free of sleep with my palms, stretch my arms out over my head linking my hands, and let them fall back onto the fluffy pillow. Its early morning. I can tell from the scent of the rising sun in the air.

I'm in the guest bed in Zeff's lodge. I slept the night at his again. I spend more time in this bed than I do in mine at the apartment.

But seriously, how did I not appreciate how comfy this bed was when I slept in it the other night? It must have been the block out from the amount of alcohol I'd consumed.

How am I even here? The last thing I remember was shifting, running, hunting, feeding. I can't believe I finally did it. I turned into my other self. And it was amazing. Exhilarating. And it felt so natural being that way. The most natural thing in the world,

Then I remember after what seemed like hours and the dark was rolling in, I started feeling tired so I stopped to rest for a while. I must have fallen asleep in the woods.

I'm guessing Zeff found me and brought me back.

Hang on. Had I shifted back to *me*, when he found me? If I had then that means…

Oh God.

I reach my hand down under the duvet. Yep, I'm naked. Zeff saw me naked. And presumably carried me back here to the lodge – naked. And put me in this bed – naked.

I pull the duvet over my face, trying to conceal my own embarrassment. I really *really* hope he had the good grace to at least have covered me with something. Knowing him as I think I do, I'm sure he will have.

God, I hope so.

Relieving my face of the duvet, I sit up, tucking it around my chest and under my arms and spy my clothes set out on the chair at the dressing table.

Climbing out of bed, I retrieve them and take them into the en-suite bathroom with me. Tying my hair up into a bun, I have a shower. When I'm done, I brush my teeth using the new toothbrush I found in the cabinet. I'll replace it for him; I just really need to brush my teeth.

I get dressed into yesterday's clothes and head out to the living room. Zeff is at the breakfast bar eating breakfast, reading the newspaper.

Lifting his eyes, he smiles and indicates the pot of coffee in front of him.

Trying to repress the blush I can feel rising in my cheeks, I say, "Yes, please."

I walk over and sit on the stool opposite him.

He hands me the cup. I take it, then rest it down on the counter and start to add cream.

"You sleep okay?" he asks.

"Really well, thanks." I curl my fingers around the cup and lift it to my lips.

"So that was kind of crazy yesterday," Zeff says, picking his own coffee up and taking a drink.

"Yeah it was," I murmur.

Putting the cup down I pick a croissant from the plate laden with them, and start nibbling the edge.

"It was impressive stuff though. You changing like that – it was amazing."

Meeting his eyes, I feel a glow in my cheeks. "Really?"

He smiles, warm. "Really."

I pull a piece of the pastry off and pop it in my mouth.

"Zeff …" I start, readying myself to ask him the one question that's burning my brain. The main one. "What did I look like?"

He stares at me for a long moment, his dark eyes softening around the edges, liking melting chocolate over the stove.

"Stunning. You looked stunning."

I grin, like an idiot. I can't help it. "Stunning's pretty cool."

"I'd say so."

"What colour is my fur?"

"Grey."

"Grey. Hmm…" I ponder. I wonder why grey? Cool though.

I take another bite of croissant.

"So how did I end up back here?"

He takes a bite of his toast and turns the page of his paper. "I brought you."

It drives me crazy when he does that. Answers a simple question with a simple answer, making me sound dumb.

"I gathered that, dopey," I chide, good-naturedly. "I meant did I come back or …"

Without looking up from his paper, he says, "No. You'd been gone a long time. It was getting late. So I went looking for you."

"How in the world did you even find me in the dark, in the woods?"

He drags his eyes from the paper to give me a curious stare. "I'm a hunter, Bunny. I track things for a living."

"Oh." Pause. "So was I still a wolf or …"

"You were back to you." A grin.

"You saw me naked." I cringe as the words leave my mouth.

He closes his paper. I see the smile flicker over his features. "Do you really want me to answer that?"

I put my croissant down, instantly losing my appetite. "Actually, thinking about it, no I don't."

"Well, if it's any consolation, I was a complete gentleman. I didn't see anything … well, just that mole on your left bum cheek, but that was it."

"I don't have a mole on my left bum cheek!" I screech, wondering if I actually might have. I'm sorely tempted to check.

His face breaks and he starts to laugh.

"You're such an arsehole." I reach over and give him a playful punch on the arm.

"Hey, there's no need to get physical, Bunny. If you want to touch me, you only have to ask." A cheeky wink. When I shake my head at him, he says, "No seriously, when you hadn't come back I went looking for you and found you curled up asleep at the foot of a tree, exhausted from the whole shifting business, I guessed. And well, you looked so peaceful sleeping, I didn't want to wake you, so I covered you up best I could with your clothes and carried you back to the lodge, and I put you straight into bed."

I feel instantly touched. "That was really nice of you, thanks."

"Well, I couldn't just leave you sleeping out there, alone."

Alone. I used to feel so alone. Now here with him, not so much.

Then almost in a reflex reaction to that thought, the words are spilling out of my mouth before I even realise I'm speaking, "So have you heard anything from your friend about my passport?"

I see the flicker of surprise in his eyes, which he quickly conceals.

"Yes." He puts his toast back down. "I was just going to tell you. He called late last night while you were sleeping. Your passport will be ready tomorrow."

"Oh. Cool. Brilliant. That's really, really excellent news." I don't think I could have used anymore synonyms if I'd tried. But even though I'm saying those brilliant words, for some reason, it doesn't feel quite so – brilliant.

He flickers a look my way, then says, "I said I'd pick it up from his place tomorrow morning. So I'll swing it by yours straight after if you want?"

"Oh cool. Sure. Thanks." I pick my coffee up just for something to do with my suddenly fidgety hands. "I guess I best let Joe know I'm leaving the café and apartment tomorrow. I don't think he'll be too gutted about the apartment as I paid up front for the lease and there's a while left on it. But he might be a bit pissed at having to find another Barista at such short notice."

"Or you could just stay a while longer." The air freezes into blocks of little tension all around us. "I mean you could just give Joe notice now and leave then when your lease has run out. You know, so you don't lose any money."

I don't think I've wanted to agree to something more than I do that statement right now. But I can't.

Shaking my head, but not meeting his eyes, I utter, "I've stayed too long already. It's time I moved on."

That's not strictly true. And apart from the vampire attack, there has been no danger since. I'm safe here as anywhere.

But, I have to leave for another reason.

Because I'm getting too attached to him. Way too attached. More than I ever should have allowed.

I care about him. A lot.

And because that very fact puts him in danger. The very danger I put Nathan and the rest of them in.

Sol.

I'm not losing anyone else. I made myself that promise when I left Nathan. I'm not breaking it now.

I allow myself a look at him, meeting his dark eyes. It's intense. There's something in his stare I'm not willing to see yet, or maybe ever.

I press my lips together and look away, shifting in my seat, I pick my half-eaten croissant up and tear a piece off, forcing myself to chew on it.

"So … seen as though it's your last day with me," he says in a brighter voice. I can tell it's forced. "I thought we should go out for dinner – you know a good-bye dinner."

"Dinner?" I echo, offering him a glance.

"Yes, Bunny, dinner. No sex though." He grins. And the atmosphere is instantly back to easy.

But it still doesn't stop my insides from flipping over like an acrobat performing in the circus, the instant the word 'sex' left his lips.

I tense my stomach tight, alleviating the fuelling sensation. "You mean to tell me they don't serve sex at restaurants nowadays? *Shocking*." I flash him a wide-eyed look.

"I know." He nods seriously. "I can't believe it either. I've been considering setting up my own restaurant. You know, two hookers for the price of one – free blow job with your slam, that type of thing."

"Slam?" I snort out a laugh.

"Sorry – *shag*." He sounds all British when he says it. And kind of sexy. Fuck. No, not fuck –shit, yeah shit is a much better word to use.

I raise an eyebrow. "Don't they just call those places brothels?"

"Yeah, but brothels don't serve up food, do try to keep up Bunny." His face is serious, but his eyes can't hide his grin.

I'm really going to miss his humour. Actually, I'm just going to miss him, end of.

I laugh again; no snort this time. "You really are strange, Zeff. And kind of gross come to think of it."

"Oh, I know." He runs his hand through his dark hair. "So is that a yes then?"

"To the sex or dinner?"

"I'm easy either way." He shrugs. "We could have dinner first, save the wild sex for later."

Even though we're jesting, I can feel my insides starting to heat up in the worst kind of way.

I stare straight into his lovely dark pooling eyes. Eyes that a girl could easily lose herself in. But not me. I can't. I won't.

"I'll say a yes to the dinner, and a rain check on the sex." I take a sip of my coffee maintaining my steady gaze.

It's his turn to choke on his drink. "Rain check?" he wipes his mouth clean with the back of hand.

"Yeah." I put my coffee down on the breakfast bar, pull a piece of toast onto my plate, and slide off the stool. "You know the kind of rain checks that are cashed in when hell freezes over."

Grinning at him, I head to the fridge to get the jam out.

"You see, now that's what I like about you, Bunny," he says from behind me.

I pause, opening the fridge door and looking over my shoulder. "What? The lack of sex I have to offer?"

"No." He shakes his head. "That you somehow always manage to keep things interesting, even when they shouldn't be."

He takes a bite of his toast and opens his paper back up.

I'm not really sure how to take that comment. But for some reason it's made my heart thud in my chest. Stilling it, I reach in and retrieve the jar of jam.

"So do you want me to run you back to your place after breakfast?" he asks, as I slide back onto my stool.

"Yes," I say nodding. "Now that is something you definitely can do for me."

*

Climbing out of his car, I thank Zeff for the ride to my place. He tells me he'll pick me up at half-seven to go to dinner.

I go in and change into work clothes. While I'm looking in my wardrobe, I realise I have absolutely nothing to wear for dinner tonight. The last time Zeff and me ate it was just pizza, and it was straight from work, but this is an actual night out.

It's been so long since I've been out. The last time I went out was … well, the night everything changed for me.

I have a feed, then leave the apartment, going straight to work.

Joe's already there when I arrive, so I take advantage of the quiet to let him know I'm handing my notice in and that tomorrow will be my last day. He's not pleased at the short notice, but overall he's pretty good about it.

Really I could do with staying as I have used nearly all of my money on the passport. Once I've paid the money for the passport I'll only have a hundred and fifty euros left to travel. I don't like it, but I can't stay here any longer. I need to move.

On my lunch break I decide to go for a walk around the little town centre where the café is situated. I haven't really ventured around here much. I've had no reason or care to.

Passing a charity shop I decide to go in and see if I can pick up an affordable dress to wear tonight. Luckily, I find a vintage wrap dress and some ballet pumps. For both of them it comes to five euros. I'm sure I can stretch to that. Funny the old Alex would never have dreamed of shopping in a charity shop.

As it's a nice day I stop to get an ice-cream from a vendor. Mint choc-chip. Sitting at the fountain with my ice-cream and new purchase I just enjoy watching people. Sitting here, licking on my ice-cream, I actually start to feel normal.

As I look around, I see there are couples everywhere. Shopping together. Eating lunch together. Holding hands. Kissing.

Loneliness and envy creeps into me.

And then I start to think about Nathan. I wonder what he's doing at this exact moment in time? He'll probably be on the farm working.

I wonder if he's happy? I hope he is. I really do.

Being away from him, and for it to hurt as much as it does … well, it has to be worth it for that reason alone.

Closing my eyes I conjure his image in my mind, opting for the last moment I have of him – Nathan asleep, peaceful and content in the bed we shared together in that hotel room.

I savour it for a moment. Then open my eyes. Pushing Nathan back in a deep recess of my mind, I get to my feet and make my way back to work, finishing off the ice-cream on the way. And for the first time ever, with a slight spring in my step as I think of tonight. My first actual proper night out in a very long time. Something I never thought I'd do again. And Zeff's made that happen.

He's made a lot of things happen.

Chapter 16: The Date

"Thank you again, for dinner," I say to Zeff as we're walking out of the restaurant and into the balmy night.

"Again, you're very welcome." He nudges me with his shoulder. "And Bunny, if I didn't say it already … you look really nice tonight."

Tucking my hair behind my ear, I slide a look his way, smiling. "You did. But thanks, *again*."

He smiles, locking out gazes, then looking away we continue to walk on side by side.

I know this is a last night together dinner, but everything about it screams, date.   And I'm actually okay with that. I know I shouldn't be, but I am.

He looks more handsome than normal tonight, smells ridiculously good, and I'm proud to be on his arm. I could see the envious flickering looks from other women in the restaurant, and I know I shouldn't have, but I felt kind victorious that he was there with me. They don't know we're just friends.

But then I don't even know that anymore. There's a really fine line that has slipped between Zeff and me over the course of the week we've spent together, and tonight I'm treading very close to the edge.

I feel disloyal to Nathan for even thinking these things. I know that sounds stupid because he will have moved on to better things. And I really shouldn't be considering any type of thing with Zeff. I leave tomorrow. I can't keep on having sex with guys, and then disappearing the very next day.

But I just can't help that little voice that keeps popping into my head, telling me to stop thinking, to stop overanalysing and to just let go. Let happen whatever will happen.

Tucking my purse under my arm and then wrapping them around my chest, I ask him, "So what's the plan for the rest of the evening?"

"Well, I had a thought…" A smile starts to play like a tune on his face.

I've fast learned that when Zeff looks like this, it usually involves me doing something I'd rather not. "Does it involve me making an arse out of myself?"

His smile turns to a grin. "Bunny, when have I ever made you do anything to make you look like an ass? Actually no, don't answer that," he interjects, as I open my mouth with my listed tirade. "Come on …" he urges. "Trust me, just this once."

How can I not when he's looking at me the way he is. All soft and sweet, with chocolate eyes, and his, oh so, very handsome face, while smelling like he's the devil's cake.

I reach out and take hold of his hand. He looks down at it surprised, then up at me. He gives me such a warm smile that I nearly melt into a puddle on the floor.

"Let's go." Then he's picking up pace, pulling me along with him.

"Hang on, what about your car?" I ask, realising we're heading off in the other direction, away from where he parked it.

"We're not going far, we'll come back for it later."

"Where are we going?" I ask, laughing, stumbling along, tripping over the cobblestones of the road as we cross it to round the corner.

"There."

I look up to where his finger is pointing and see we're across the road from a nightclub. "You want us to go clubbing?"

"No, Bunny. I want us to go *dancing*." He smiles that delicious devilish smile of his again. The 'I'm not taking no for an answer' one.

I pull my eyes away, mustering myself up to fight his charm. "I don't want to go dancing." I plant my feet firmly into the ground. "Let's go drinking, I'm good at that – great in fact. Look there's a pub over there." I point to a little pub I just spotted down the road.

"I don't want to drink, I'm driving anyway so I can't. I already had my one with the glass I had at dinner." He makes puppy dog eyes on me. "I want to dance. With you."

"But I don't dance. Seriously, I have three left feet."

He glances down at my feet. "Three?"

"Yeah. That's how bad I am."

He lifts his eyes and they practically burn into mine. He moves closer, just a fraction, but it's enough. And I don't stand a chance.

"Let me teach you," he murmurs. "Just one last thing before you go."

After those words, he might just be in for teaching me some other stuff too.

Did I actually just think that? I shake the crazy out of my head.

Zeff continues to stare at me, then a sympathetic tug of his mouth, and before I know it, I'm nodding agreement. Then he's leading me by the hand, toward the club, passing by the door staff, then we're through the door and he's paying the entrance fee.

I follow Zeff in through the main door which leads us straight into the heart of the club. I glance around taking in my surroundings. The beat of the bass is pumping up through my body, banging loudly in my ears.

At first it makes me want to switch my hearing off, until I adjust to it. Then I start to enjoy the thrum of the music and the people milling around me. And as I do a quick look around I start to notice a lot of people, not everyone, but most are dressed like they're something out of an eighties rock video.

Has he brought me to an eighties night? I feel the sudden urge to laugh. This is so *him*, to do something like this.

As if sensing my humour, he turns to look at me. His dark eyes shine under the flicker of the fluorescent lighting. I feel momentarily paralysed in his gaze. He tilts his head in the direction of the dance floor, a question on his face. And suddenly things don't seem quite so funny anymore.

I gulp down the instant nerves. My body simmering back to life. Then by way of answer, I offer a smile, and let him, once again, take me by the hand and lead me to the dance floor.

He works his way across the dance floor, weaving us through the hot gyrating bodies, until he stops, finding us our own small space in the centre of the floor.

For a moment, I stand here, close to him, looking up, but struggling to see past the flickering lights, to his face, wondering what now.

Does he expect me to just start dancing? Because the song sounds more rocky, less poppy, a little too heavy to dance to. And I am no way dancing to this.

Then the song ends. Almost abruptly. 'Is This Love' by Whitesnake starts to hum through the room.

If I didn't know better right now, I'd think he requested it.

The thrum of the beat kicks in. Moving closer to me, Zeff clasps my right hand, drawing me against him, he slides his arm around my back. I've never danced with anyone like this before in my life. Sure, Carrie would get me drunk enough to drag onto the dance floor and we'd end up with pervs grinding up against us. But dancing like this, with a guy, never before tonight.

My heart starts to tap an unsteady rhythm. Mostly thanks to the lick of electricity that's surging through me. But it's not uncomfortable and hasn't been for a long time. I'm used to it, just like I'm used to him. Used to being with him. It's going to be hard saying good-bye tomorrow.

And tonight, I'm starting to realise for the first time, just exactly how hard it will be.

Zeff's hand encases my small one. His other spans my back. His body is big, strong, warm, and ridiculously inviting.

He has this undeniable way of making me feel so comfortable, but yet so very uncomfortable at the same time.

How is that even possible?

I start to feel a stirring deep within. Like something long hidden is awakening. My knees suddenly rubbery, my breaths coming in faster. I know I'm treading down a slippery slope, and despite everything and everyone I just want to lean against him and let myself go.

I have to fight to hold my feelings in check.

As the lyrics begin, Zeff starts to sway his body, moving me in a slow dance with him.

It's good. Better than good. I feel like I've been transported somewhere else. Almost as if I'm a movie, one of my own creation and imagination. Something ideal, something perfect, but not real. Never real.

I shouldn't be doing this. Feeling this.

I can't bring myself to look him in the eye. I know he's staring down at me and I'm looking everywhere, but at him. I'm intoxicated by the music. The moment. Him.

"And she dances," he murmurs in my ear. His warm breath on my skin almost has me singing.

I gulp back my nerves and glance up at him. I meet with his eyes. They look opaque and impenetrable.

"Not really the case." My mouth is dry, tacky. I moisten my lips with my tongue. "You're doing all the work for me."

"Suits me," he murmurs, close.

Heat licks over my skin.

"So this was your plan? To bring me here to dance to Whitesnake." I smile, but it comes off nervous and awkward.

"Not specifically. Not your thing?"

"I thought, more like not your kind of thing."

A grin. "The perms, the tasselled leather pants, what's not to like?"

Leather pants. Nathan wears leather pants. Just without the tassels. I feel a sharp stab of guilt. Hard in the chest.

What am I doing? I'm supposed to be in love with Nathan, yet here I am dancing with Zeff.

Dry ice sprays out from nowhere, covering my legs, rising upwards, seeping into my lungs, intoxicating me further, extracting out the Nathan guilt with ease.

This is wrong. All different kinds of wrong, in the very blackest sense of the word.

My heart steps up its beat to a little past nervous. I need to stop dancing. I'm getting foggy brain. It's this dry ice. It's wreaking havoc on me. It's making me feel things I shouldn't – don't want to be feeling. It's making me want things, I don't really want. I should move away from Zeff. I know I should.

I should excuse myself to the bathroom, or go the bar or something, anything. But I just can't seem to connect the part of my brain telling me to extract myself from him, to the rest of me. My body is fighting my brain, putting up a good show, and I'm just caught in the crossfire.

I have a strong feeling which one is going to win. The way my body is moving closer and closer to his, telling me that.

Deep breath. One … two … three, in and out.

"Celine at my work has got the hots for you big time."

I don't know why I just said that. Yes, I do. Diversionary tactic. But really kind of obvious too. And by the way his eyes just widen and lips quirk to smile, tells me he figures that too.

He tilts his head to one side, his smile now playing on his whole face. His look shivers its way right through me.

"The blonde one?" he inquires.

I'm spiked by jealously that he cared to inquire. Jealous of something that I initiated. I've lost the plot, completely.

I nod my head.

"Not my type."

Relief. Stop it, Alex.

"Blonde hair, big boobs, and legs like a barstool aren't your thing?"

"No."

I'm nervous, very nervous, and sliding into dangerous territory, but knowing I'm no longer in control over what's coming out of my mouth, not that I generally am anyway.

"So what is your type?" My voice comes out husky and breathy.

He stares at me for a long moment.

"Someone a little less obvious and a lot more beautiful. Unassuming, smart, and full of wit. She survives everything life throws at her. She's not jaded. She has a unique take on the world, and her mouth doesn't often connect with her brain. But that's what makes her, her. And no matter what bad stuff has happened to her, deep down she still believes in the happy ending. The one with the white picket fence."

I make an attempt to swallow down my heart that's climbed up into my throat.

"That's quite a specific list." I try to keep my voice light, but it still sounds husky. There's no controlling it.

He nods, keeping hold of my eyes.

"Not so easy to find. One in a million kind of girl. The kind, once you have, you keep a tight hold of and never let go."

My heart whams into my ribcage like a speeding car hitting a safety barrier. I'm pretty sure I just broke a rib.

"Anything else?" I'm skirting close to the edge, but I just can't seem to help myself.

He nods again, his eyes still scribed to mine. "Brown hair … huge blue eyes … full pouty lips." His voice mirrors mine, husky.

It sets a run of hot fire down my spine, like someone's just poured a line of petrol down it and struck a match.

I know he's describing me. Of course I know. I got that after his third sentence. I'd have to be completely dumb not to have. And yes, I know I'm dumb generally, but not *that* dumb.

Pressing my lips together, I cough an awkward gargled kind of sound and start to fidget uncomfortably.

"I really can't believe you brought me to an eighties night."

A terrible attempt at a subject change but I need to take my own edge away.

A smile. "A bad thing?" He tightens his hold on me, stopping my fidget.

"No. You're just full of surprises."

"Right back at you." Unreadable passes over his face.

I raise an eyebrow. "And how have I surprised you?"

He reaches into my eyes with his, almost pulling me back out with him. I'm confounded and heated by his gaze.

"You're just not what I was expecting at all," he murmurs.

His words snap me to attention. I stop dancing. "Not what you were expecting? And just exactly when were you expecting me?"

"I wasn't," he replies smoothly resuming our dance, moving me with him again. "I just meant the day I met you in the café. I knew straight away what you were … and I just expect my Vârcolac's to be a little less female and a lot more vicious."

His hand on my back draws me closer. My defences break down.

I don't want to admit it but being with Zeff for this last week has made me feel alive again. I haven't felt alive in a really long time. Not since my last night with Nathan. And being with Zeff now, like this, is making me feel alive in the way Nathan did, then.

It's terrifying and exhilarating.

The smart and sensible part of me wants to dissect those emotions and crush them to nothing. But the physical part of me is just tired. Tired of fighting feelings and overcomplicating things. I just want what any other person wants. To feel a part of something. To feel needed by another. Even if for just a short time. And if that means tonight, I get the chance to feel human again, then I'm going to grab it with both hands.

I close my eyes briefly, drowning in the sensation. And then, just like that, I switch off my brain.

When I rest my head against his chest I feel his sharp intake of breath. Then he moves his hand over my back, upwards, and smoothes it over the bare skin on my arm. I notice it feels different; slow, deliberate.

He wants the same. He wants me.

"What are thinking?" Zeff's words blow down through my hair.

I close my eyes and revel in the sensation.

How alive I feel right now. How heedless of everything I feel right now. That I want to be with you in a way I should never want. But I can't find the will to stop anymore.

I lift my heavy head from his chest, looking up at him. He stares down at me. I let my eyes connect with his, knowing everything I shouldn't say … could never say, is readable within them.

Our faces are literally inches apart. I can feel his breath on my face. My own coming in faster, matching my heartbeat.

"Zeff, I …"

I halt at the instant change in his expression. His eyes darken. And my heart stops for a moment.

"We need to go. *Now.*"

Then he's pulling me through the club, elbowing his way through the crowd of dancing bodies as I struggle to get my brain working.

Then all my senses click in.

Vampires. Here. Now.

Fuck.

Chapter 17: True Colour

Zeff slams out of the exit door of the club, bringing us out into an alley. With a tight hold of my hand he keeps us moving forward quickly.

My mind can barely keep up in time to function my feet. How did he know before I did there were vampires in the club? I know I was a little off my game, but still he doesn't have my senses. Yet, he somehow seemed to know.

Maybe he spotted them. Yeah, that could be it. But his eyes were on me – nowhere else. I'm trying to pull a coherent thought out of the convolution currently going on.

He's a hunter. He's trained to spot vampires. That must be it.

Still, now is not the time to think about it. Now is the time for running.

I start to realise we're heading away from the main street where the thick of people are and, further and further into the alleyways of this town, where people are less. Well none existent.

We round a corner, and I see, we are yet again, faced with another alleyway. I just catch hold of my voice to speak when he stops abruptly. I crash into his back.

He turns, facing me.

"You remember everything I taught you in our training?" His tone, like his eyes are deadly serious.

Meeting his eyes, I nod, knowing why he's saying this. Knowing they are now soon upon us.

"Just stay calm, I got this," he whispers.

He's got this? I'm supposed to be the one to protect him. I'm the one with superhuman powers.

"Zeff, no. I'm–"

Then I see them - five of them. Three emerge from the alley branched off to my left. Two come up the alley we are on, just up ahead of Zeff.

We are fucked.

I know Zeff is a hunter and he's trained for this kind of thing, it's what he does, but he's also unarmed right now. And so am I.

I'm not going to be able to fight all five of them off.

"So the stories are true," the tallest of the vampires says. He speaks with a distinct European accent. "A female Vârcolac."

What the hell? Has my existence been broadcast on the supernatural news or something?

"And don't worry," the tall vampire adds, placating. "We're not here to kill you. We're just here to take you to see someone important."

"Yeah, still not feeling so great about that idea. I'd rather you off me – thanks all the same."

I'm pretty sure I hear Zeff snuffle a laugh beside me.

"No can do, sweetie. I have my orders. And they are to bring you to my boss in one piece. So if you'd be so kind." He gestures for me to go over to him.

Not bloody likely.

"Elijah's here in Italy?" I hear Zeff ask calmly.

He's not laughing now.

Elijah? The head vampire. Something in Zeff's hard tone is telling me there's a very important story here. Just one I can't get a handle on right now. But I'll get there soon enough. I hope.

Interest passes over the tall vampire's face and he steps forward with interest. "You know of Elijah? From where? Because the only interest he has in humans is for lunch. And by looking at you – you certainly do not look like his, *type*."

Zeff lets out a laugh. It's not a pleasant sound. It's surprising to hear coming from him. He rubs his hand over his face, almost like he's bored now, like he's fast losing patience.

"Okay so here's how it's going to go," he says conversationally, in a voice that he makes my head whip around to look up at him. "You tell me where Elijah is and who's with him, and I'll give you the courtesy of letting you live." He glances around at them. "Well most of you, anyway," he adds with a shrug.

Sorry, am I missing something here?

My mouth is wide and hanging open, eyes popping. Zeff knows I'm looking at him but he doesn't flicker a gaze my way. It's almost like he's forgotten I'm here. Or is choosing to pretend I'm not.

The vampire laughs, but I catch the hint of nerves in it. It gives me a sudden sense of confidence. Well in Zeff anyway, not so much myself. He may only be human, but his cool calmness is fighting the crap out of me, so it's for sure unnerving them.

"And what's a human and a tiny lady Vârcolac going to be able to do to the five of us?" The vampire gestures around at his comrades confidently.

"You'd be surprised," Zeff says.

There's an amused menace in his voice which frightens the skin off my bones. Then before I even get a chance to blink, Zeff is moving at inhuman speed, heading straight for the tall vampire and I see the flash of the silver blade as he raises it and in a matter of a second, I'm seeing the vampire dissipate to dust before my eyes.

Fear and adrenaline and utter bewilderment wrap themselves tight around my stomach.

Zeff lifts the silver blade in his hand, turning fast to his right and plunges it straight into the heart of the second vampire, all the while his hand has somehow found its way around the throat of the third vampire, and he is holding him out like an inconvenience.

I don't know whether to feel safe or absolute terror right now.

The vampires, who are behind me, quickly descend. Turning swiftly, I slide out the grasp of one. As he passes by me, I kick down hard into the back of his knee, he falls to the floor. The other one catches hold of me, from behind. His arm goes quickly around my throat, holding me firm against him.

But I know what to do, because Zeff taught me. Arm up, bend at the elbow, ram back into the rib cage. He doubles back, loosening his arm from around my neck, so I press the advantage.

Grabbing hold of his arm I twist it up, and I'm under and out. I yank it back, hard. I hear the distinct crack of bone and a grunt of pain.

As I turn, I see Zeff has the one who I kicked to the floor. He must have offed the other one. He picks him up by his clothes, one hand, lifting him off the floor like he's a doll. I can see the utter fear in the vampires face. Zeff drives him hard into the brick wall. Then with no hesitation he stabs him, swift, and he's gone.

Catching my eye, he sends me a silent message with his eyes, then tosses the blade to me. I catch it with my right hand, spin around and drive it hard, straight into the vampire's back, aiming for the heart, praying to God I hit just right. I watch as he dusts before my eyes, at my hand.

I just made my first kill. And know for certain it won't be my last. The blade is still in my trembling hand. I turn, lifting my fearful eyes from it, to Zeff.

I see he's stood here in the dim of the moonlight, a safe distance away, looking at me. I'm getting nothing from his even expression. All I can do is stare back confused and terrified.

I lift the shaking knife, pointing it at him. Adrenaline and fear are running through my veins, controlling my actions. Self-preservation has really kicked in. He might have just saved my ass, again, but he's certainly not who he claimed to be. He's not human for sure. No human I know can move as fast as he does. Or kill fours vampires without even breaking a sweat.

He raises his eyebrow in question. "You planning on using that on me?"

I look down at the blade again, it glints under the low light.

"Wh-what are you?" my voice stammers the words out. "You're not human. No human could do what you just did to those vampires and …" I lose my words.

I reach out trying to grab a read on him, anything. All I'm getting is human. But he's not fucking human! Why can't I tell what he is?

He sighs, a tired sound. "Bunny, we should get out of here before any more of them turn up looking for you."

"I'm not going anywhere with you until you answer my fucking question!"

My voice echoes down the alley, bouncing off the brick walls, caging me in. My whole body is shaking, my hands uncontrollably. I have no idea how I'm keeping a hold of this blade to be honest. If he came at me right now, I wouldn't be able to defend myself even though armed. And not just because I'm afraid, but because it's him.

"Are–are you here to kill me?" My voice drops to a tinny sound.

Something flickers over his face, if I'm not mistaken, hurt.

"No, of course I'm not."

"I don't believe you!"

He narrows those dark eyes of his into a frown. "If I wanted you dead, you would have been dead a long time ago, trust me. Believe it or not, I am trying to protect you." I note the sarcasm.

"Protect me! From what?!" I scream at him. "Just tell me what the hell is going on and just exactly who the fuck you are?!"

He says nothing. He just stays absolutely still. And then the moment suddenly freezes. It's just complete and utter silence. Like everything has stopped moving. The world has stopped turning.

Zeff closes his eyes and starts muttering under his breath. I can't catch the words, properly, they sound foreign.

Then I feel it. The electric force that I always feel when I touch him. But now it's in the air, all around me. And it's powerful. Controlling everything in its reach, moving, shifting.

It stops as quickly as it started, and it's like all my senses have just been switched back on with full force, and I just know. I know what Zeff is.

All the blood drains from my head. Dropping the knife, I stumble backwards, stunned. I feel like I've just been punched in the face.

"H-how did you hide this from me? How did I not know?"

"I know you've got questions," he placates, raising his hands in that way he does.

I've got questions? No fucking kidding.

"Just tell me who are you – really?" I cry at him, breathless.

He sighs a slight sound, then takes a step forward, lifting his chin, his dark eyes meet with mine. "My real name is Matthias Demetrius Vélez. But you'd know me better as an Original."

Chapter 18: Broken

I come alert to the sound of an engine and being in a car.

The night's events smash into my head with full brunt force. My eyes flick open.

I'm in Zeff's car and he's driving.

Well, Zeff or Matthias, or whatever the hell he's called. He's kidnapping me. He knocked me out and he's kidnapping me.

Fuck!

This is it.

My worst nightmare has finally happened. I'm trapped in a car with an Original and he's going to force me to have sex with him and make evil babies and … oh God, oh God, I can't breathe.

"Are you okay?" he asks in a low voice, sensing I'm awake.

I sit myself up, straighter.

"You're asking me if I'm okay?" my voice comes out reedy.

"Yes. I'm asking you if you're okay." He makes it sound like a dumb question.

Shifting sideways in my seat, I push my hair roughly off my face, putting my back flush with the car door, basically putting as much space between him and me as possible.

"I've been attacked by vampires for the second time in a week, and then–" I catch my breath, disbelieving the words I'm about to say. "Find out you are one half of the–the …"

I can barely even bring myself to say it. " … *Original's* – and then you knock me out and kidnap me!"

I'm panting for breath, my voice hitched up in pitch. "So I'd say – no! I'm not fucking okay!"

Well if I'm going down, I'm going down fighting, just like he taught me.

Taking his eyes off the road he casts a glance at me, "I didn't knock you out."

He's laughing. He finds this funny. I clench my hands into fists in my lap. His laugh ceases the second he sees my look of contempt and complete and utter hatred.

He clears his throat. "You fainted, right after I told you who I was. So rather than leave you lying there in the alley, I thought the gentlemanly thing to do would be to pick you up and bring you to my car."

"But you're not a gentleman, are you?" I bite.

"I've never given you any reason to think other, Bunny."

"Stop calling me that!" I cry. "You have no right to call me that!"

He stares at me for a long moment. I hold his stare. My chest, heaving up and down.

Finally, he looks back to the road ahead. I see his grip tighten on the steering wheel.

"I'm sorry you had to find out that way." His voice is low.

"Sorry I found out at all more like! Before you got to have your wicked way with me under the guise of being someone else!"

I feel cheated and betrayed. Humiliation burns through me. I can't believe I let myself feel that way for him for more than a second. I'm a complete fool.

He looks at me again, his eyes harder now. "I said I'm sorry you had to find out the way you did and I mean it. That aside, I wasn't trying to trick you into anything."

I wrap my arms tight, around my cold chest. "Yeah, sure you weren't."

"So you did want to kiss me then, back at the club when we were dancing?"

"What?! No!" I look at him, flabbergasted.

Rage and embarrassment are burning up my cheeks. He stares back at me steadily.

What I really want him to do is stop looking at me and put his eyes back on the road. But it doesn't seem to be of any consequence to him. Then, he is a powerful creature.

His powers go way and above mine. He could probably drive this car with his eyes closed.

"I wanted to kiss you … " He pauses. "I *want* to kiss you." His voice is steady.

"Are you bloody insane! Stop talking to me and look at the fucking road!"

I don't want his burning eyes on me. I feel confused and flustered every single time he looks at me. And right now I just need balance, and to see logic. Tons and tons of logic.

He pulls his eyes from mine to the road. I hear a slight chuckle escape him. "God, I love you."

My head whips around. I stare at him, dumbfounded.

I don't know if that was one of those things he didn't mean to say, but did. Well whatever it was, he said it and now it's out there.

"Love me?! You don't even know me!"

"Yes I do. Better than you care to admit." That's it, end of, apparently. Well not for me.

"Have you lost your mind completely?!" I yell at him.

"Over you, yes." He looks at me steadily again.

My heart drops off the radar.

"We're not talking with about this!"

I grip my head in frustration. I feel like I've stepped out of reality and straight into the fucking Twilight Zone.

"Yes, we are." Pause. "I know you feel the same. I know you love me."

"No!" I cry, rounding on him. "I don't love you! I've only ever loved one person, really and truly, and you are not him and never will be!"

I know I've wounded him. I can see it on his face. Good.

"I'm just sorry I ever fucking met you! Tragically fucking sorry!"

He says nothing.

My heart is raging a storm in my chest. I know I should be panicking right now, but anger is crippling all my other senses, blinding me to anything else. And his declaration of love has done little to help the situation.

I can't believe him. I just can't bloody believe him! What the hell is going on? My mind is reaming with possibilities of what's going to happen to me, but I just can't get it all to configure properly.

He's an Original. The one who is out to hurt me. But he's had ample opportunity to do just that, to do anything to me – a full week's worth. I've slept in his house. But he hasn't once done anything to hurt me. If anything he's helped me. Endlessly. He saved my life. And now he's telling me he loves me.

Nothing about any of this is making sense.

But then he's been around for four hundred years, he's one half of the most powerful creatures on this planet. I'm sure he's learnt a trick or two about deceiving people and getting them to do exactly what he wants.

He could just be saying these things to trick me. Get me to do what he wants in the easiest way possible. No fights. Just a clueless, lonely Alex, so desperate to fill the void that Nathan left in me.

But it doesn't feel like Zeff. It doesn't seem his style. But then really, what do I know about his style. Because he's not Zeff, the guy I thought I knew. He's one of the things that have me running for my life. He's the bad guy. The reason I've lost everything I ever cared about. This isn't any average Vârcolac I'm dealing with here.

And I need to be afraid of him.

Very afraid.

Then it kind of thuds into my head.

He is four hundred years old. Four-bloody-hundred-years-old.

I slide nervous eyes over to him. His face is calm, eyes on the road.

It's so strange; he looks no older than thirty. But to have lived that long … I can't even imagine the things he's seen, or done. Actually, I don't want to imagine any of what he's done; I can't see any of it being good.

Well, apart from helping me that is.

He's Zeff. The nice guy who cooks me dinner and teaches me to fight, and shows me how to shoot guns. He helped me shift. He's helped me to become a better version of what this life had left me with.

No. He's not Zeff.

I have to stop thinking of him that way. That's how he'll trick me into doing what he wants.

He is Matthias. An Original. A monster.

And then all my anger and confusion shrinks as the reality of my situation finally sinks in.

I start to panic.

Complete and utter fear ripples through my blood.

"What are you going to do with me?"

My words are weak, my voice small. I know I sound like a victim but I don't stand a chance against him. I just saw him take out four vampire's single-handed, in a matter of seconds. My life is in his hands now. And whatever he chooses to do with it, will happen, that I know for sure.

He slides me a look. "Are you asking what I want to do with you, or what I am going to do with you?"

Is he joking? I'm not sure. I can't get anything from his even tone or blank expression.

No, he's not joking. He can't be. He means it in the worst way possible. That's the only thing it can be.

Fear ripples through me like a quick shot of adrenaline, straight to the heart.

I need to get out of this car.

Now.

I spin in my seat and pull on the door handle. It's locked. I yank hard, but it won't open. In blind panic, I start banging on the door with my hands, but it won't budge. Is it iron plated or something?

Oh God. I'm trapped in here. I've got no escape.

"Calm down," he says.

I'm not calming down for all the tea in fucking china. I need out of this car. Then I realise my only option is the window. If I smash through it, I can dive out. I'll make the fall, but it'll cut me up pretty badly with the speed he's driving.

The injuries will slow me down until I heal, but I still might be able to outrun him. Anything's better than staying put and enduring what I'm sure he and his brother have planned for me.

And, well, if he catches me, then at the very least I'll know I tried to get away.

I clench my fist and pull my hand back. Closing my eyes for the inevitable shattering of glass. I punch it hard.

"Fuuuuck!!" I cry out, holding my hand to my chest with my other hand. I'm pretty sure it's broken, which is the only thing that is. The glass is still intact.

"It's bulletproof glass, Bunny. You can't break it."

"Arggh!" I cry out in pain and frustration. Tears squeezing out of the corners of my wincing eyes.

"Let me look at your hand." He reaches out to me.

"Don't touch me!" I cry, moving away. "Don't you dare *touch* me. Ever again."

"Bunny…" he placates softly.

"No! I won't be what you want me to be! I won't be your baby maker! I'd rather die than become that – so just fucking kill me now, because if you don't, then I'll do it the second I get a chance!"

He slams the breaks on the car. The force brings my head forward. I have to drive my feet down in the foot well to keep the rest of me on my seat.

Then it's suddenly eerily silent. Only the rumble of the engine ticking over can be heard. That, and the sound of my ragged breath pumping my chest up and down, and my heart that's setting a battering ram against my ribcage.

I'm not sure what is about to happen next. Either way, I know it's not going to be good.

For one, or both, of us.

Chapter 19: The Truth

I lift my heavy head. Keeping a hold of my painful hand against my chest, I try to steady my breathing.

I don't know if my hand is broken or fractured, but I do know I'm going to have to ride the pain out until it heals. Which shouldn't be too long. Hopefully.

"How's your hand?" he asks. His voice sounding ridiculously gentle for his size.

I look at him through my veil of hair. His eyes are set, with complete focus on me.

"Fine," I reply, gruff.

"I don't want to fight with you." He pauses, blowing out a resigned breath. "And I don't want you to be afraid of me. I thought it was plainly obvious what I want from you. And it isn't for you to become my 'baby maker'. I just want to keep you safe. Nothing more."

I open my mouth but nothing comes out. Just the breath I feel like I've been holding forever.

He takes his eyes off me, looking past, he stares out of the window screening the night.

"I'm not here for that. I never was. And I never intended to fall in love with you, either," he adds quietly. "I just—" Shaking his head, he exhales heavily and brings his dark eyes back to my light ones. "I just want to protect you, keep you safe from the ones who do mean you harm. I thought you would see that. I've been with you a week and I haven't touched you, once. I've done nothing to hurt you. All I've done is try to help you become a stronger, more equipped Vârcolac – doesn't *that* tell you everything you need to know?"

Well yes, I did kind of consider it before, but I'm not telling him that.

"But you're an *Original*," I press.

"I'm not that person anymore. I left him behind a very long time ago."

I snort an accusing sound. "Yeah, sure you did."

"And you know me so well, *Alex*?" He highlights my name. I don't like the way it makes me feel.

"Obviously not!" I yell at him. I'm feeling kind of unreasonable here. I like to think it's to be expected. "But you obviously know me – know my real name."

Shifting his body to face forward, he rests his hands on the steering wheel and bows his head. It's a long moment before he moves or speaks.

He glances at me sideways, through his thick lashes. "Of course I do." His voice is intense.

It does a combination of things to me.

I like that he knows me. And I hate that I like the feeling. But mostly it worries me, and that worry grips a tight hold of my stomach and knots it, infinitely.

What if he knows about Nathan and Jack, and the farm? What if they're not all as safe as I'd thought?

"What else do you know?" My voice carries like a whisper.

He lifts his head, but doesn't move his eyes from mine. "If you're asking if I know who you were with and where you were, after the change, then the answer is no."

Relief floods into me. They're still safe.

"But I do know who you were before that." He pauses, deliberation passing over his face. "I know your name is Alexandra Jones. That you went missing after a night out with your friend, Carrie. You had a boyfriend – if you could call him that – Eddie, who you lived with in Scarborough. Your parents died in a car accident when you were sixteen …"

"Okay. Enough." I hold a hand up not needing his reminder of my previous life. "I get you did your homework."

"I just read the newspapers Bunny, that's all. I needed a start in finding you. I needed to get a handle on you as a person. How you lived your life. Your typical behaviour. I didn't get much from the papers, obviously, but just enough to get me started. When I looked back in the news, I knew I was looking for a girl who had recently gone missing in the UK. I figured whoever 'Alex' was, she wouldn't have gone back home after what happened to her. Especially not when she'd been handed over by a shifter."

"Shifter?" My throat closes up. "You know that?"

He raises his eyebrow. "Don't worry. I didn't get his name. Was it him – the boyfriend?" His says the latter part, softer, gentler. But it sounds kind of pitying too.

"No." I give him a sharp look. "Just someone he trusted." I lower my voice, looking away.

He starts to drum his fingers on the steering wheel. I get the impression that wasn't the answer he wanted.

"It took me a long time to find you, Bunny. And a lot of resource. You're good at disappearing, better than you realise. But I'm also good at finding. Then when I found you here two weeks ago–"

I tense up. "Two weeks?"

"Yes. I kept my distance for the first week. I thought it best to take my time before I approached you."

"You don't live here." The truth thuds into me.

He shakes his head, no. "I needed it to appear that way. I wanted you to feel safe with me, so I rented the lodge."

God, I'm so slow.

And then I feel tricked and violated, and stupid and enraged, all over again. But more than anything just confused. So utterly, bloody confused.

"Why have you been keeping me here with you if you're not planning on hurting me? I'm guessing you kept me here by ruining my passport?" I add as the thought occurs to me. And then I start to feel angrier at the realisation.

"I haven't been keeping you anywhere. I've *been* trying to keep you safe – am trying to keep you safe, but recently it's like you're a magnet for trouble."

He doesn't deny ruining my passport though, that doesn't escape me.

"Did you ruin my passport to keep me here with you?" I demand to know.

His eyes meet with mine again. He takes in a deep breath and runs a hand over his black hair. "Yes."

I should have known. I always kept the passport in the zipped pocket, with the picture of Carrie and my money. I just thought the blood had seeped through and ruined them. Stupidly, I trusted his word.

"You ruined the only picture I had of my Carrie! She died and I have nothing left of her! Why would you do that to me? God! If my right hand wasn't broken right now, I'd punch you!"

"I didn't ruin the picture, Bunny. The blood had seeped through; it just hadn't affected the passport." He presses his lips together, looking helplessly at me. It only proves to make me madder. "I only ruined your passport because I needed time; time to gain your trust – that was all. You have to believe me when I tell you I am trying to keep you safe from the one person who does want to hurt you."

I still don't know if I believe his story, but I ask, "Your brother?"

He nods.

"But why? I don't understand any of this. I don't understand you!" Feeling frustrated again, I push my good hand roughly through my tangled hair, trying to grasp hold of a clear thought, any thought, really. "I thought you wanted what he wants?"

Me, for unspeakable things.

That's what I was told to believe. Not just by Nathan, but Albino too. He'd called them. They were both on their way to come and get me from the mansion.

"You were coming for me. When I was been held at that mansion. He said you were coming to take me away."

"Isaiah. Not me. I knew nothing of it at the time. Believe me, if I had I would have been coming there to get you out." He turns, looking away from me, ahead, out of the windscreen and into the night. "I haven't seen my brother in a really long time. I only found out about your existence after you escaped."

"Who told you?"

His shoulders tense. "I still have people I trust, who are, let's say, *around* Isaiah."

"Why haven't you spoken to him in so long? And why do people still think you are."

He stays silent.

"Tell me," I press.

"It's just easier that way."

"I don't understand."

"There's strength in numbers, Bunny. If Elijah knows Isaiah and my relationship has broken down, he'll use it to his advantage. I may not want to be around my brother, or like what he stands for anymore, but I also don't want to see him dead. And, I'd kind of like to keep breathing too."

"Why don't you want to be around him? Did you have a falling out or something?" I probe.

"Yeah, something," he murmurs.

It's obvious he doesn't want to tell me.

"What about?" I ask, softly, using womanly tactics.

He casts a glance at me. There's harshness in his gaze. I don't like it.

"There are things you don't need to know." His tone is final, but I'm not having that.

"That's bullshit! I have a right to know!"

"No, Bunny, you don't." His voice is suddenly rough, affected. I've never heard him sound this way before. He sounds almost, pained, regretful. I can see his jaw working angrily, but somehow I don't think the anger is placed with me.

He looks back at me with those dark eyes of his, intricate darkness in them, as he says, "Look, we just don't share the same vision – I don't think we ever really did. He's my brother." A shrug. "I went along with things until I no longer could." A breath. "Now you're my priority. I need to keep you safe from him. I won't let it happen again."

My body stiffens. "You won't let what happen again?"

I can see it in his face. He didn't mean to tell me that.

"Nothing."

"This has happened before. I'm not the first?" Suddenly I don't feel so lonely. Which is a crazy thing to feel at this time, I know.

He pushes his hands over his hair, hanging them off the back of his neck, exhaling loudly. "No. You are the first of my kind to be female. I just – I failed someone, a long time ago. I won't make that mistake again."

I feel this sudden urge to hug him. It makes me want to slap myself.

"Why didn't you just tell me the truth in the beginning?" It's an accusation, not a question.

He gives me one of his looks. "Would you have believed I didn't mean you any harm? Would you have listened to me? I know what you thought I was, the Matthias me, and I thought the best way was for you to get to know me first before I told you who I am – was. I was going to tell you the truth tomorrow, when I gave you the passport … the vampire's just kind of speeded things up for me."

"That's utter crap!" I say venomously, angry again. "You could – should have told me; trusted me to make my own decisions. But instead you spend a whole week with me, lying to me. Pretending to be my friend. Letting me believe you're someone you are clearly not."

"I never lied to you. I just omitted certain truths." He gives a wry smile. "And I am your friend, believe that if anything."

I let out a sanctimonious laugh. "Friends don't lie to and deceive one another. You said your name was Zeff – Zeff the vampire hunter, not Matthias the Original!" I use air quotes.

Yeah, I know, but I'm not exactly thinking straight at the moment.

"My name is Zeff." His voice is clipped. I can tell he's losing patience. "It's what I go by and have done for the last eighteen years. And I am a vampire hunter. I've been hunting and killing them for the best part of four hundred years, all in the hope of getting close enough to Elijah so I can kill him for what he did to my parents."

I let out another sharp laugh. I know it's cold and cruel but I can't help it. "Yeah you're the real honest kind."

"Don't give me the moral high ground crap, you've hardly been honest yourself, have you?"

I look at him with incredulity. "You and your bloody brother are the reason I wasn't – couldn't be honest! The reason I have to hide myself away, leave behind everyone I care about!" A snarky laugh of disbelief escapes me as I shake my head in disbelief. Disbelief of everything. Of him. "You really are something else."

He drums his fingers against the steering wheel. "I'll try to take that as a compliment."

"Don't." I take a deep breath. "Wait – did you set up that first vampire attack in the woods just as a rouse to get close to me?"

His brows knit together. "Are you not listening to a word I'm saying?! I'm not exactly drinking buddies with vampires if you hadn't noticed – I. Kill. Them." Single and distinct, and I don't like the way his voice sounds when he says it. "It happened exactly as I told you it did."

"You shot him?"

Something flickers over his face. Humour. I'm not feeling so humorous right now. I kind of want to slap it off his face.

"Okay, well not everything happened *exactly* like I said. I didn't shoot him. I … kicked the crap out of him, broke his neck, then silvered him."

Makes sense. I never remembered hearing a gunshot. I was out of it, drained and bleeding, and I guess it didn't seem so relevant at the time. I was just glad to still be alive.

"No one will ever hurt you while I'm still breathing, Bunny."

Then I feel all kinds of breathless myself.

Grasping for air and sanity, I say, "And that's how you got close to him …" I utter, it all just making sense to me. "Because he had no read on you … that thing you did in the alley when you revealed yourself to me … I never had a read on you before, not properly. What is that? How do you do it?"

He lifts his shoulder, lightly. "I shimmered."

I give him a confused look.

"I can do magic. My abuela – grandmother," he explains when I give him a curious look, "She wasn't just a werewolf. She was a very powerful Wiccan. The line goes back for generations. We inherited her magic through our mother, and though we have nothing to the extent of her abilities, I can still conjure up some pretty strong magic. It's not something we have allowed to be common knowledge, you understand. We needed to stay protected and hidden. If Elijah had found us when we were young it would have been a death sentence. So my grandmother spelled us when we were babies, then as we grew up, we just harnessed the power of the magic and continuing protecting ourselves. I live my life under it. It makes things … easier. When I took it off before, for you, that was the first time in as long as I can remember."

"So you just appear just like any other–"

"Regular human being," he finishes for me. "It's just a parlour trick, really, obviously using real magic."

"Well it sure works. You had me fooled." I can't help the bitter tone. "And it's back on now – the spell?"

"Yes."

Something else clicks in my mind. "The magic – would it affect me? You know when I said to you before that I get a shock every time …" I peter off at the look at his face. Anger bursts from me again. "You made me think it was me! That there was something wrong with me! And all that time you knew why it was happening!"

"I'm sorry," he says. But he doesn't sound it. "It doesn't usually affect people so badly. Generally it's just like a tiny static shock, but for some reason it flares up against you." He pauses. "Maybe it's because there's something more between us."

I give him a 'don't start that crap again' look.

He blinks himself free of my annoyance.

I rest back in my seat and look down at my hand. While we've been talking – okay arguing, it's been healing itself. I very carefully stretch my fingers out, flexing them slowly. Not there yet, but almost.

I glance out the window. We're still stationary on the road. Not one single car has passed us by. I sit up, and turning around, looking out of the windows, I try to garner a sense of where we are. All I can see is the dark countryside. "Where are we?"

"About thirty miles out of Sassano."

"And where were you taking me?"

"Somewhere safe."

"Where?" I make my voice harder, insistent. I'm not having him pull this Nathan kind of crap on me.

He sighs. "I have a place, in Vienna. You'll be safe there, until I can move you to my home. Not a sole on earth knows where that is."

"And what if I don't want to go to this safe place?"

He looks at me for a long moment. His eyes are almost intrusive. "Then it changes things."

I swallow down, a hard gulp. "Am I … a prisoner here with you?"

He leans over toward me. I shift back in my seat away from him. With a slight exhalation of breath, he opens the glove box and pulls something out.

Handing me a passport, he says, "I think this should answer your question."

I open the passport to see a small photo of me staring back. The one I gave him for my new passport. This actually looks better than the passport Craig had done for me. Not that I'm a passport expert, obviously, it just looks more authentic. Anyway, I'm guessing Zeff has a disposable amount of money to get the good passports.

I give him a surprised look. "So I'm free. I can leave. Just like that." I open the wallet clasp on my purse, shove it inside and fasten the clasp back down. The click of it closing is oddly loud in the quiet car.

Zeff reaches forward and presses a button on the dash. The doors unlock. "I'd prefer it if you didn't, but you're not a prisoner here with me."

I feel weird. I know I should be out of that door and running from him. Ultimately, he is still the bad guy, irrespective of what he says and claims to want. And a big part of me wants to run, ninety-eight percent of me, but there's two percent which is still curious. And attached to him, I guess.

And that two percent is what is currently keeping me here, stalling.

"I'm sorry for what happened back there," he utters softly. So soft I feel his voice run over my skin like a warm summer's breeze. It only furthers to impale me to this seat. "I didn't know there were any vampires in town, or that they'd be looking for you. I don't know how they found out about you. I killed the one vampire who did know. But I will find out how your existence is now public knowledge. I promise."

He doesn't have to say any more, I get his meaning perfectly, from the dark yet softly spoken implication.

"And you fought really great back there," he adds, giving me a small, even smile. "Your training really paid off. The fighter in you is really starting to come out."

I round on him. I can't help it. I'm swinging between emotions like a monkey in a tree. "You're proud, because you turned me into even more of a monster than I already am!"

I'm angry. No livid. It's his fault I am what I am. And I hate him. I hate him for tricking me and lying to me. But mostly for making me care about him.

"You're not a monster." Zeff looks at me astonished. "You're smart and strong, and beautiful."

"Please, hold my hair back while I vomit."

A smile flickers over his face. I know he's holding back a laugh. "I like this side of you."

"Yeah, well, I hate this side of you." That hurts him. I see it flicker in his eyes. Good.

No, not good. It hurts me to see him hurt.

Oh God!

"I just don't even know who you are!" I cry.

"Yes you do."

"No, I don't! I only know the person you wanted me to know! You tricked me into liking you! You lied and I'm just–" I can't breathe. I need air. I open the car door and fall out into the night.

I hear Zeff's door open. "I know you don't want to hear this right now Bunny, but you need to stay with me. I am the only one who can protect you."

Straightening myself up, I turn, to see he's standing at the other side of the car, his hand on the open door.

"It's you and your brother that I need protecting from!" I cry, slamming my good hand onto the bonnet.

I know I've put a slight dent in the bonnet, but that's the least of my concerns.

Pain furrows his brow. "I would never hurt you."

He rests his hand on the bonnet, mirroring me. I slide mine off, binding it with my other in front of me.

"And now it's not just Isaiah after you," he continues. "Elijah knows, and now that makes you a little pawn in their big game."

He moves around the car, but I inch back away from him. "If Elijah is here Bunny, then you are in serious danger. Just let me get you out of Italy, then you can go it alone if that's what you want. You have my word."

"I'm not going anywhere with you! You're a liar and I don't trust you! All of this could just be lies!"

I throw a hand gesture into the night.

"You heard them," he says in a hard tone.

"No. I heard you ask if he was here. They never answered."

"And you're willing to take that risk?"

"If it means not spending another second around you, then yes!"

He shakes his head, enraging me further so I round it off with, "I hate you! I despise everything about you, everything you are and stand for, and I want you to leave me alone! I want you to get in your car and go! I don't ever want to see you again!"

The angsty teenager in me is appearing, but right now I don't care.

He opens his mouth to say something, then seemingly he changes his mind. He stares at me for a long moment. My whole body is shaking with anger but I don't move my eyes from his depthless ones. Then without another word he turns from me, gets back in his car and drives away.

I stand here on the roadside watching his taillights disappear into the night, trembling and confused.

I feel like I've just lost my best friend. All over again.

I really don't know what to do. Everything has just got blurry and surreal. And more complicated than ever.

I glance down at my purse in my hand. The passport. Then it all just seems so very simple. And I'm running, without reserve, heading for the only place I've ever truly felt safe.

The place to find is within yourself.

Joseph Campbell

Chapter 20: Nathan

Tired, I push my key in the lock and let myself in the front door. I drop my holdall in the hallway. I'll empty it later.

Scarlett's upstairs listening to her annoying Emo music in her bedroom. Alex's old room. I can hear Dad and Craig talking in the kitchen, so I head that way.

"Hey," I mutter as I push the door open.

"Alright mate?" says Craig.

"You should have let me know you were coming back, I'd have picked you up from the airport," dad says as I pull out a chair at the table.

I take my jacket off, hanging it on the back, and drop my knackered arse into it.

"I didn't want to drag you out. I just took a taxi."

"You wouldn't have been dragging me out." There's a notable edge to his voice. After a little silence, dad asks, "How have you been?"

It's been a while since I last spoke to him.

"Fine," I answer. Scratching my beard, I lean back in my chair and stretch my legs out under the table. "How have things been here?"

"Ah, you know, busy."

I nod.

"You're no closer to finding Alex?" asks Craig. But it sounds more like a statement than a question.

I feel a quick irritation at his direct question. I start to drum my fingers on the table top. "No."

"Did you fly in from Spain?" dad questions.

That's his less than subtle way of asking where the hell I've been for the last two weeks, since we last spoke. I don't mean to leave it so long between calls, or visits home for that matter. It's just recently all days seem to bleed into one.

"No. Portugal."

I'm short, I don't mean to be.

I'm just not up for a conversation right now.

All I want is a decent drink and then my own mattress for a few hours.

"Was the flight okay?" asks Craig. An obvious attempt to try and balance things. "Standard class seats are getting smaller I'm sure."

"It was fine," I reply.

They just didn't have enough in-flight drinks.

"Or maybe I'm just getting bigger," he quips, patting his stomach.

I don't respond. I'm too busy glancing around the kitchen looking to see if there's anything to drink on the side. There's usually a bottle of Jack, or something out. But nope, nothing.

Knowing there'll be a bottle in the drinks cupboard, I get up from my seat and meander over. I open the cupboard and heaven stares back at me. A bottle of Gentleman Jack. Dad only gets this is in for special occasions. I wonder what it is. Well, my homecoming counts for sure.

I reach in and pull the bottle out.

"I was saving that for your birthday," dad says from across the room.

My eyes flicker to the calendar on the wall – 1st March.

Fuck, it's my birthday in four days. I didn't even realise what the date was. I'll be turning the grand old age of thirty. I definitely need a drink then.

"I'll get another one in to replace it later," I say. "Anyone want to join me?" I crack the bottle open. The smell hits me, and instantly I start to relax.

"Not for me," says Craig.

"Bit early to be drinking don't you think, son?"

I pour myself a large glass. "It's six p.m. somewhere in the world."

I lift the glass to my lips and take a mouthful of the good stuff, letting it glide down my throat. I take another couple of big gulps, top it back up and make my way back to my seat.

"When did you last sleep?" asks dad.

I know he disapproves of my day drinking, it's written all over his face. What's the difference between drinking in the morning over the evening, anyway? I don't see the big deal. And really I couldn't care less. Whatever gets me through the days.

I take another mouthful and put the glass down on the table.

"I caught a few hours on the plane."

A lie. I only sleep when the alcohol puts me out; hence the drink now. There was no booze on the plane. I'm lying to him because I can't be arsed to get into it.

I can just tell exactly in which direction this conversation is heading. I had this conversation with him a few months ago on the telephone. Or it'll be a similar version of it, depending on the route it takes.

The signs - the way Craig and dad keep casting glances at each other. The weird atmosphere which has been here since I walked through the door. And the way dad keeps having subtle little digs at me.

He's waiting for me to kick off. And right now, I'm totally in the mood for it.

I place my hands palm down on the table.

"Okay, spit it out," I say with an edge.

"What?" dad says, looking over at me innocently.

I give him a fixed look.

He lets out a long sigh. "I guess … well …" Pause. "I think it's time you gave up looking for Alex."

And there it is.

I pick my glass up and take another drink. I roll the liquid around my mouth, warming it before swallowing. "Is that a suggestion or are you telling me?"

He leans forward, hands on the table, picks his Zippo lighter up and starts to turn it over in his hands. "Whichever one would work." He starts to flick the lid on and off.

Click. Click. Click.

He stares at me. "Nate, it's getting to the point of obsession now. You need to let go and stop wasting your life. You need to move forward."

His words hit me square in the jaw. "That's what you think, that I'm wasting my life? You think looking for Alex is a waste of time?"

"No. You're turning my words. I just think you're searching for someone who clearly doesn't want to be found."

"So you're happy to just leave her out there, alone – with those fuckers still looking for her?"

"No. I'm not happy about it. I love Alex like she's one of my own and I want nothing more than to know where she is, and that's she's safe. But we can't force this."

He drops his lighter on the table with a thud. "Okay, let's say you found her - then what? You're gonna force her to come back home. I'm sorry to say it, son, but if she could be here she would be. You know why she left, so for God's sake, respect her wishes and just let her go."

A raw pain deep inside somewhere is starting to fracture. "I can't." I hear the break in my own voice. "Not while I know she's still in danger, I just can't leave her out there alone."

"I know you love her but–"

"That's got nothing to do with it." I glare at him hard.

It has everything to do with it. I know it. He knows it. Hell, even Craig knows it. I can't deal with this right now.

I push my chair back, making to leave, when Craig pitches in, "Look Nate, we're just worried about you."

I drag my cold eyes from dad to him. "Thanks for your concern. It's duly noted."

I love Craig, like family, but fuck I just want to hit him right now. I feel so angry, so frustrated. I clench my fist under the table.

"Why are you even here?"

I'm picking a fight with him. I know it. I just can't seem to stop. I feel like I'm being ganged up on here by the two of them. Like I'm some kid that needs setting on the right path.

"I'm here because I'm your friend," he replies mildly.

"You're out of line, Nate," dad throws at me. "Craig's here more than you are. I needed help on the farm. I needed help with Scarlett. We'd only just buried Sol and you were off searching the world looking for a woman who clearly doesn't want you!"

Fuck that hurts. I take in a sharp breath.

I hear dad sigh. "Sorry, that was out of line. I didn't mean that. I know Alex loves you, she would have left if she didn't."

He rubs his forehead with his fingers. "I'm just–" Another sigh. "I'm just worried about you, son."

But that's the problem. I don't know if she does love me, or if she ever really did. She wouldn't have been able to leave if she did – would she? I know I wouldn't have been able to leave her. No matter what was happening.

I would have given everything up to be with her.

I can't bring myself to look at dad or Craig. The shame is burning like a fire inside. I pick my glass up and drain the contents, needed to douse it out.

"You're driving yourself into the ground, Nate," dad starts up again. "Don't tell me you're sleeping because clearly you're not. You're drinking far too much." He points a finger at the empty glass I've just lowered to the table. "You're searching for answers in there that you're never going to find … you're back to how you were when you got back from Iraq."

Right, I've definitely had enough now. I back my chair out roughly, slamming it back under the table, grabbing my leather jacket off the back of the chair, I make for the door.

"I can't lose another child," he says, low.

I feel sick. My hand is on the door handle, ready to go. I know I should feel guilty for hurting him like this, but I can't seem to. It's like my emotions have just stopped working. And then I start to wonder at which exact moment in my life that it was they stopped working, or actually, if I ever had any to begin with.

"You need to find a way to deal with Sol's death before it kills you too." He's standing now, behind me.

I really can't talk about Sol. Not now. I'm feeling too raw.

Turning angrily, I say, low, "I know he's dead. I don't need fucking reminding."

The raw pain cracks open. It's like all my pain is gushing out. And I can't take anymore. It's like having needles driven into my heart.

He reaches forward, putting his hand on my shoulder. "I'm not trying to hurt you, I just want you to be okay."

His voice is calm, deep. It reminds me of how he would sound when I was a kid and I'd fallen and hurt myself. But I'm not a kid anymore and I haven't just fallen over. This pain is deep, and carved into me.

"Yeah, well, I'll be okay when you all just leave me the fuck alone." My words are deep with meaning. I push his arm from off me just as Scarlett walks in the kitchen.

"Hey, you're home," she says sounding surprised, smiling.

"Yeah, and now I'm leaving." I see the crestfallen look on her face as I turn away, yanking the door open, I slam my way out of the house.

I hear dad come out the door immediately behind me.

"Nate, don't go. Just stay, talk to me."

"No. I've heard enough for one day."

"Where are you going?" I can hear the worried tone in his voice. But it just isn't registering with me at the moment. I just want to get away from him, from Craig. From everything.

"To see my brother."

I've left it far too long already.

*

"Hey kiddo," I murmur, kneeling down on the cold earth. I trace my finger over the writing on the marble headstone.

Solomon Jacob Hargreaves.
April 4th 1992 - August 26th 2011

Forever in our hearts and minds.

As my fingers trace the lettering carved deep into the marble, a pain so intense starts to crush me.

This happens every time I think of him. So I rarely let myself. Aside from searching for Alex it's the other reason why I stay away from home so much, knowing he's out here, all alone. It's unbearable.

"I'm sorry it's been a while since I've been to see you. I'm still looking for Alex, like I know you'd want me to."

I hang my head, feeling ashamed that once again I've let him down. "I haven't found her yet," I lower my voice. "But I will, real soon. I'll make sure she's safe, and I won't give up until I know she is. I promise you."

I let out a breath into the cold morning air, rocking back onto my heels.

"I've fucked everything up. I wish more than anything it was me down there, not you. I'd trade with you in a second if I could."

My emotions break through. I pause, pinching the bridge of my nose, swallowing down. "It should never have been you, it should have been me … I let you go there, and I blamed her for losing you when it was my fault … and–" I catch a sob in my throat.

Clenching my fist, I put it to my mouth. "I'm so sorry, Sol. I just don't know what I'm doing anymore."

I rest my forehead against the cool headstone as tears I have no control over start to run from my eyes. My heart burning a solid pain in my chest. "I miss you so much. And I know I never said it enough, but I love you, and I would give *anything* to have you back here."

I stay silent for a moment, almost willing him to speak back to me. Just to hear his voice one last time.

But all I receive back is the painful silence of his loss.

I take a couple of beats to steady my breathing, then I rub at my eyes roughly, removing any evidence of pain. Taking a deep breath, I get to my feet.

"I'll be back to see you later, kiddo, but for now I've got a date with my lady."

I pat a hand to the headstone and then take off running, heading to the barn, and to the only woman who's never left me.

And here she is, still right where I left her, and looking as beautiful as ever.

My Ducati.

"Hey baby," I croon, as I climb on. "You miss me?"

Getting my helmet off the handlebar, I pull it on, turn the engine over and listen as she purrs to life. The feeling calms me somewhat.

"Come on," I murmur. "Let's go make some noise."

And with that I kick the bike stand away and roar off down the track, heading to nowhere in particular.

I had no intention of coming here, until I find myself riding up to the barrier.

Dalby Forest.

I pay the entrance fee and take a slow ride through the quiet forest. I park up at the lake. The one I brought Alex to all those month ago. I haven't been back here since I came with her that fateful day. Even though she was kidnapped from here, and I had the shit kicked out me, it still is the place where she and I began. The place where I first kissed her.

Dumping my helmet on the bike seat, I walk into the shallow of the lake. The water seeps into my boots, just as I did that day when I was stood in here with her, when I finally let go of holding in my feelings for her. When I realised she felt the same way too. The last time that everything was still okay.

When Sol was still alive. And Cal was still my brother. And Alex was still here, with me.

I let out a sigh into the coming darkness, rubbing my head with my hands.

What the fuck am I doing? Six months looking for Alex and I'm no closer to finding her than I was the day I started. It's like she's just disappeared off the face of the planet.

I don't know where to look anymore. There are no clues. No trace of her anywhere. It's almost as if she never even existed. I run a hand over my ribs, touching where my tattoo is.

The problem is though, I don't know how to stop looking. What will happen to me if I do?

I move on with life, like dad stays. But move on to what? There's nothing left for me anymore. Sol's gone. Cal and I don't speak, granted my choice, but really what choice did he leave me with.

I drive my frustrations with fingers into my scalp, scratching over my head.

From the moment that I woke up in that hotel room to find Alex gone, I've been consumed with finding her. It's all I know now. It's all I have.

I know it was her choice to go, but if I hadn't said what I said, blaming her for Sol's death, if I hadn't treated her the way I did, then maybe she wouldn't have gone. Maybe she would have stayed. Maybe.

I remember the times I would try to convince myself she'd been snatched by the Originals. It was crazy. I knew she hadn't. She took money from me. She took the passport and her clothes.

But the reason I did it was because at that point it was easier to believe that, than to believe she'd left after we'd had sex. That she'd left me right after I told her I loved her.

Now, I just try not to think about any of it. I'm just focussing on finding her and bringing her home. The rest can wait for later.

I just ... I guess I just feel so angry, all the fucking time. I can feel it scratching under my skin, trying to escape.

I sleep angry. I eat angry. I drink angry.

I feel like I'm going insane.

"FUUUUCK!!" I yell into the night, gripping my head in frustration, kicking into the water around me.

The sound of my anger echoes all around the lake. The only real effect it has is driving a flock of settled birds out from the trees.

And I'm still just left here with my anger ripping pieces off me.

Coming out of the water, I tear my clothes off, and then I'm running, shifting, heading straight into the forest.

I'm out here all day, running and hunting. I fall asleep, waking when the sky is night.

I make my way back to the lake, shifting, just before leaving the safety of the trees. I walk over naked and collect my clothes, which are still lying exactly where I left them. My head's a little clearer now and I see how stupid and reckless it was of me to shift like I did, here during the day, just leaving my stuff abandoned.

And I know dad will be getting worried about me. He doesn't deserve this. He's endured more than anyone ever should have to in his life.

I climb back on my bike and head for home.

When I arrive the house is in darkness, everyone sleeping. Except for dad. I hear the light in his bedroom click off the moment I walk through the front door.

I'll talk to him tomorrow. Apologise for my behaviour.

I go straight to the kitchen and grab the bottle of Jack I opened earlier, off the worktop. I don't bother with a glass. Then I head into the living room, peel my T-shirt off, drop it to the floor and sit down in the armchair. I kick my boots off and switch on the TV.

I flick through the channels, there's some Boxing on. I leave that on. I could really do with watching people beat the shit out of each other right now.

Settling back into the chair, I take a long drink from the bottle. Damn, this stuff is good. It courses through me, just the anaesthetic I need at the moment.

My eyes are heavy. My body is trying to force sleep. But I don't want to sleep.

I hate sleeping. Every time I shut my eyes all I see behind them is Sol laid in my arms bleeding to his death. And the look on Alex's face when I told her I blamed her for his death. It's like those two images have burnt themselves into my retinas and are cursed to stay there for the rest of time.

I take another long swig of whiskey and rest my head back against the chair. I just need to numb the pain, even if for a little while.

So, I take another drink, and another …

I wake with a jolt. It's a second before I can grasp my bearings.

Someone's here. Close by the house. Out by the top of the driveway.

Silently, I pick the empty bottle of Jack from off my lap, putting it down to the floor, I quietly get to my feet.

I let my senses go out, trying to get a read on whomever it is that is paying us a very early morning visit. And my heart freezes in my chest.

I'd know that scent anywhere.

Alex.

That's the way things become clear. All of a sudden. And then you realise how obvious they've been all along.

Madeleine L'Engle

Chapter 21: Marked

I let out a long breath into the cold air. Watching as it fogs and then disperses into the night.

I look across the road at the entrance to the driveway. The driveway which will lead me to the farm.

To Nathan.

I know this is the last place I should be, but I couldn't stop myself from coming. There was no more fighting it. I've been looking for a reason to come back here since I left. And Zeff gave me one. Not a rational one I admit. But, a reason, still.

It's taken a long run, two taxis and an aeroplane to get me here. And now I'm almost within reach of him my feet refuse to work.

I literally can't move. Like my feet have been superglued to the floor or something.

My mind keeps coming up with reasons why I shouldn't walk down the driveway and knock on the front door.

I'm putting him – all of them - in danger by coming back.

Just because Zeff claims to not mean me any harm, doesn't mean I'm any safer than I was yesterday. Isaiah is still looking for me, and now I have the added bonus of Elijah searching for me too.

I guess I just want to feel safe. And here is the only place I feel safe. Nathan is the only place I feel safe.

But even still, I shouldn't be here. I know this.

I'm just so confused. I haven't had a straight or coherent thought since I found out about Zeff being an Original. And I can't even bring myself to think about that properly, yet.

The only thing I am clear on, is that my head is pulling me in one direction, my heart another.

It's my heart that's lead me to this point I now find myself at. It's just whether I let it take me the rest of the way is the burning question.

I'm sure Nathan will be sleeping right now. It's late, or early, depending on how you look at it. I don't want to wake him. But then again, he might not even be here. He could be away somewhere. Maybe.

All I have to do is expand my hearing, my senses, and I'll know if he's in there. But I daren't.

Because I'm afraid of what I might discover if I do. Something I hadn't even considered until just now.

He could have someone else.

Nathan could be in there right now with another woman and he'd have every right to be. Just because I've been stuck in the past for the last six months doesn't mean he has.

And now I have this gnarly feeling in the pit of my stomach, running into my veins, turning my blood grey.

He might not want to see me. His life could have moved onto better things. Just like I wanted for him. And me coming back here would only dredge up things for him that he left behind a long time ago.

I turn to leave. Then I stop.

So, I leave and then what? Never know.

I came all this way for a reason. Maybe I need to lay my own ghosts to rest. I left way too much hanging up in the air with Nathan, and if he rejects my return, rejects me, then it's just the way it was meant to be, but at least I'll know.

At least I'll be able to settle the demons in my mind. And currently finding out Nathan has someone else or doesn't want me anywhere in his vicinity is a better prospect than continuing on with the guilt, grief, and longing I've been torturing myself with ever since I left.

I've done the not seeing him for the last six months and it's been agony. Complete and utter agony. And look where it's got me. Found by an Original, and now, right back here.

And if I'm being honest, I never left. Not really.

I see now, that whatever I thought I was feeling for Zeff, was just my way of trying to fill the deep gaping hole Nathan left in my life. The only person I will truly ever want is Nathan.

I'm unequivocally in love with him. It *will* always be him. And that I can't, and don't, want to be away from him for a moment longer. Or ever again. Nathan is everything and all I will ever want.

I turn back to the driveway, looking up, my breath catches in my throat.

Nathan.

He's here, standing at the top of the drive. His face a mixture of emotions, and I can't pick a single one out.

My heart crumbles in my chest.

He looks so different, yet exactly the same. He cut his hair short. It looks like it was shaved off and it's in re-growth. He'd look military if it wasn't for the fact his stubble is something more resembling a beard. He looks leaner than before, like he's lost a bit of weight, and he's wearing his ripped jeans hanging off his hips. His dog tags are around his neck and his feet and chest are bare. And even though he looks tired, his eyes are alert and just as striking as I remember them to be, and they are fixed solely on me.

I've imagined this scenario so many times in my head. What I'd do when I saw him again? What would I say? For that matter, what would he say?

I open my mouth but nothing happens. I can't seem to locate my brain or my voice to find one single word to speak. After everything I rehearsed on my way here, and now I've got nothing.

We haven't taken our eyes off one another, and neither of us has moved. It feels like we've been stood this way for an eternity.

Mentally, I probably have been.

Then propelled forward by sheer longing, I step onto the road and walk toward him, holding my breath the whole way. I can feel myself unravelling inside. I'm so nervous I'm pretty sure I might throw up.

When I reach the other side, I stop a foot away from him.

He still hasn't moved his eyes from mine. He hasn't moved at all. It's unnerving. I need him to do something, say something. And the need to touch him is suddenly so overwhelming, I'm not sure what to do.

I tear my eyes away from his trying to steady myself. Find some form of equilibrium. I feel like I need to come up for air.

I'm gasping for breath like a fish out of water.

I take in a deep breath, but all I manage to do is breathe him in.

His scent rinses through me like sun warmed ocean. It makes me ache inside for all things him.

I look back up to meet his steady gaze. Swallowing past the dryness in my mouth, I force myself to speak.

"Hi."

It's not much, and my small voice sounds eerily loud in the fragile silence, but it's all I've got.

The sound of my voice seems to do something to him, awaken him in some way, and I watch as his eyes rake over me, almost like he's looking for clues as to where I've been for the last six months.

Then wordlessly, he takes a step closer, erasing the gap between us. Lifting a hand slowly to my face, he strokes his thumb across my cheek, barely touching. I feel the hint of his calloused skin on mine. And that one single touch is all it takes to unravel the last thread holding me together. Now all that remains are slippery emotions.

Hot tears, tumble sore, down my cold cheeks. And in this moment I wonder how I ever had the strength to leave him.

Then he grabs my face with both his hands, and kisses me hard. The passion burns up my lips, searing its way down my body. I open up my mouth and he slips his tongue inside, and I just lose all control.

I throw myself into him, letting him fill the empty hollow places being away from him created. I can't get close enough to him. I'm already wrapped around him, but I push myself closer.

He tightens his hold on me. Honestly, if I could fit myself into his skin and rest in-between his bones, right now, I would. I've never needed to be as close to someone as I do him, now. I just need to feel him inside me.

My feelings for him, the ones I've tried so hard to bury for the last six months, are now bursting out of me in a lustful rage.

And it seems so are his. He kisses me harder and harder, his beard rubbing rough against my face, but I don't care. He could be covered in sandpaper and I'd still want him. It's Nathan.

With his hands spanning my hips and my bum, he lifts me up, with no effort whatsoever. I wrap my legs around his waist, with my dress now up and around mine.

Without moving his mouth from mine, he carries me down the driveway, in the house, up the stairs, and in his bedroom within a matter of seconds.

We fall onto his bed, a tangle of mouths and legs.

I'm struggling to maintain any real train of thought. Hands. Hands are everywhere. Remember to breathe.

I kick my shoes off. He tugs at my dress. I incline slightly, allowing him to pull it off over my head.

His hands and mouth are straight back on my body, frantically roaming. It's like he doesn't know which part of me to touch, kiss, first. His practised cool demeanour I know him so well for, gone. I want to tell him to slow down … and I don't. I like that he's so out of control over me. It's doing all kinds of crazy things to me. And right now it's almost like he's never not been touching me.

With my heart pounding out of my chest, I reach down and undo his jeans. Rucking them and his boxer shorts off, I use my foot to shimmy them the rest of the way. Nathan kicks them off. Excitement ripples through me as I feel him against my skin. He slides my bra strap off my shoulder, kissing where it was, then reaches a hand behind me, unclasping my bra, he takes it off. Kissing me still, he reaches down and hooks his thumb under the waistband of my knickers and slides them off too.

It's strange, almost dreamlike. We've not spoken. Done a whole lot of heavy breathing and moaning, but no actual words. It feels wrong, in the right kind of way.

But I want to speak to him.

Need to speak to him. I'm letting the moment carry me away. It's just so hard to focus on anything when he's kissing me this way. A way in which no one has ever kissed me before, or probably ever will again. With just complete and utter need.

Making every single part of me beg, plead, for more from him. I need to feel him inside me more than I've ever needed anything. And I will do anything to have him. I need my fix from him. Like the vampire in me that constantly needs feeding.

But, even still, I know through my cloudy mind, I have to say something, anything …

"Nathan, wait, I …"

He pauses, his mouth on my stomach. Lifting his head, he moves upward until his face is before mine. He looks deep into my eyes and … I see nothing there. No real emotion. No questioning. No feelings. Nothing but his bright green reflective eyes staring down at me.

I feel like I'm looking into the depthless ocean. It's almost like he's switched himself off to everything … everything but the practicality of this moment.

Then I just feel lost. Confused. Needy. And now I can't seem to remember just exactly what it was I wanted to say to him in the first place. It's almost as if while I've laid here beneath him, allowing him to stare into my eyes, he's reached in and stolen the words from right out of my head.

Keeping his empty eyes on me, he reaches over into the drawer in his nightstand, pulling something back out with him.

I hear the crackling of a condom wrapper as he rips it open.

I'm trying not to think why he's got condoms in his nightstand. I want to think they've been in there a long time.

That there's been no one else since me. I can't think anything else.

We hadn't used a condom that one and only time we had sex. But then we hadn't exactly been in the right frame of mind either. The last thing that can happen to me is to get pregnant. So if anything, it's at least smart.

When Nathan is ready, he lifts his hands up to my neck, searing hot, his thumbs pressing into my throat, he tilts my head back and covers my mouth with his. Kissing me deeply, he pushes himself into me without reserve.

It's painful and electric at the same time.

Releasing a moan way down in my throat, I dig my fingers into his hard back. Nathan growls a low guttural sound into my mouth. Excitement and need overtakes everything else. Nothing matters except for this. Nothing matters but him. Everything else can wait.

Taking hold of both my hands, entwining our fingers, he braces them against the mattress, either side of my head, and starts to move inside me, hard, fast, and ruthless.

There's nothing gentle or tender about this. This is sex at its most basic. Animalistic. Nathan is marking me, pure and simple.

Chapter 22: Dawning

Waking, I reach my hand out for Nathan, but instead find a cold empty space where he should be.

Fear creeps over me. Did I dream it?

No, he's here in the room with me. I can feel him, smell him, and his touch is still lingering on my skin too clearly for it to have been a dream.

I blink open my eyes to find him sat on the floor, across the room from me. He's dressed in the same jeans we discarded to the floor, those few lust filled hours earlier. His back rests against the wall, legs bent up, arms resting loosely on his knees, fingers linked together, and his eyes are on me.

Distant eyes. On me, but not on me, if you know what I mean. He doesn't look happy like I want him to. He doesn't look anything, just kind of blank.

All in all, a clear sign something is wrong.

"Hey." I smile lazily over at him.

Resting up on my elbow, I prop my cheek in my palm and desperately try to pretend I don't see the dark shadow of his obvious mood.

He says nothing. Not even a smile. He just keeps those bright green steady eyes of his on me. Exactly as he did when he saw me for the first time earlier, and just right before we had sex.

There's anger and resentment there. And a lot of it.

I let myself ignore it when I first got back, pretended it wasn't there, covered it with unreal emotions. Now, in the harsh light of day it's pretty hard to ignore.

His piercing stare is starting to make me feel empty and alone again. And those hollow places, the ones I naively let myself believe he'd filled to whole, are cracking back open.

It's abundantly clear he's not happy to have me back like I'd hoped he would be. I'm getting that loud and clear. The only other way he could make his feelings more clear, were if he screamed them at me.

Nathan's body may have been doing an awful lot of things to me earlier which were telling me he was overjoyed I was back; really overjoyed in fact, it just seems his mind was elsewhere at that time.

There was an obvious disconnect between the two. A disconnect between the brain in his head and the one in his pants.

He thought with his dick, of course, he's a guy. But now it seems since he's got what he needed to get out of his system with me, the connection has clicked back in, and now all of him is shut off to me.

I can't even be angry, even though I feel it in copious amounts right now. I knew it at the time; I just choose to ignore it. I just needed to be close to him. I wanted him.

But now, he couldn't be further away from me if there were still an ocean between us. I'm just not sure exactly what to do. How to handle this? I feel on edge and uneasy, and completely out of my depth. I don't bode well in situations like this. I get confused, and easily conflicted. And words, the right words, usually fail me.

Knowing I have no choice, this is all on me, as he's apparently got nothing to say, so in a pointless attempt to keep things light, I ask in a warm voice, "What you doing way over there?"

"Thinking," he says, monotone.

Keep it breezy, Alex. Breezy.

"What are you thinking about?"

He looks away. "Things." He looks back. "You."

I'm guessing he isn't replaying fond memories of our reunion over and over in his mind.

I run my tongue around my tacky mouth, readying myself for it. "Any of it good?" I let the warmth slip from my own voice.

His eyes drift down to the carpet. "Some." Silence. "Some, not so much."

He shrugs as his eyes briefly meet with mine, then flicker away again. But I see everything I need to in that one look.

As I guessed, our reunion is well and truly over with. Gone with the night. And now dawn is here, so is reality, and he's pissed.

I left him in that hotel room even though it was with all the best intentions. I left and he's angry about it, and quite possibly about the last six months of zero contact. Six months of nothing from me. Not knowing where I was, if I was okay.

I guess that part of it never occurred to me before. I never thought of it from his point of view.

Nathan likes to be in control. It's who he is. I took that control away from him the moment I left. I know that will have hurt his pride. And gauging by his mood right now, I'm guessing it hurt his pride severely.

Sitting up, I wrap the duvet around myself, get out of bed and go over to him. I sit at his feet. His body tenses, and he shifts position, moving his legs away from me.

It doesn't make me feel great. At all.

"Will you talk to me?" I ask, in attempt to move thing in the right direction. Well, any direction but the one I know this is heading toward. I feel like I'm in a car, with no breaks, careening toward the edge of a cliff.

Head turned away from me, he stares out toward the window, ignoring me.

He's behaving like a child.

Frustrated, I sigh. "Look I get you're angry, so why don't you just say whatever it is you want to say to me–"

"What makes you think I'm *anything* for you?" He turns my way and hard eyes burn into mine.

Ahh shit. That hurts. My eyes sting with unexpected tears.

I see something flicker in his, and if it's regret; it doesn't press him hard enough to take it back.

"Why are you here?" he asks, coldly.

I don't even know how to begin to answer that, and even if I could, I don't think I'd be able to talk right now, my throat is so clogged up with tears.

I feel sick. And stupid. So very stupid that I'd let myself believe everything would be okay by coming back here. Of course it wouldn't be. Everything is different. It's been six months. I don't know what's he's been doing in that time. His world didn't stop turning just because I wasn't with him, even if mine did.

He doesn't want me here. Why would he?

But why have sex with me? I know he's a guy but Jesus, if he's this angry and so turned against me, then why.

To hurt you.

A chill slices straight through me.

I'm dumb, so very fucking dumb. I should have guessed that the second he kissed me. Because prior to that he wasn't exactly jumping for joy, throwing his arms around me.

The sex was hard, raw and angry.

But even still, I can't bring myself to ask him the question. Because I might be right. And I know I won't be able to handle it if I have to hear back the exact words that just echoed in my own mind, from his voice. It will all but kill me.

Withdrawing, I quietly get to my feet, holding the duvet wrapped tight around my body. Numbed, I sit down on the edge of the bed.

I'm not pissed off anymore. I'm hurt. And without my anger I'm simply left naked. No shield for whatever else he has to throw at me.

Reaching down I pick up the discarded underwear and dress up off the floor, and set about dressing myself. I'm tying up the belt on my dress when he speaks again. "Are you ever going to answer my question?" His tone is hard.

I've actually forgotten what he asked me. I search my brain.

"Why are you here?" he says.

I cast a glimmered eye glance in his direction. He looks so closed off, so hard. I can't speak to him about it now, not even if I had it in me to, and especially not while he's in this mood. He wouldn't listen to a word I've got to say. I know

Nathan; he'll only hear the words he wants to hear, not the words I actually say.

He's good at interpreting his own versions of things.

"Not at the moment, no," I utter quietly.

He lets out a sharp laugh. It scratches over my skin.

"I thought you said you wanted to talk?"

I don't think I've ever heard him sound so bitter, not even after Sol died. Things are so much worse than I anticipated.

"I did, then." I shrug. "Now, not so much."

Nathan's mouth opens and I stare at him willing it back shut. Because whatever he says will undoubtedly be covered in barbed wire.

But he ignores my silent pleas and speaks anyway, "So should I take it you're leaving again? Well, at least I'm awake to see you go this time." The sarcasm practically drips off his words and down onto the carpet.

I pull in a breath. Can't say I didn't deserve that one.

"No, I'm not leaving." I try to keep my voice even, calm. I brace my hands on my thighs trying to drum up some inner strength. "Not unless you want me to?"

Holding my breath, I lift my eyes, looking at him, hoping to force something, anything, from him. Well anything except that he wants me to leave.

He looks away, saying nothing.

I exhale. Well, at least he didn't tell me to leave, I guess that's something. A small start.

I slip my shoes on. "There are things we need to talk about," I concede. "But I just don't think now is the right time."

He doesn't argue with me.

I start to walk toward the door. My feet feel like they've got suction cups attached to the soles. Each step, a really huge effort. I actually feel like I'm leaving him all over again. Except this time he's here to witness it.

When I reach the door, I glance down at him.

He's already looking at me. I see his eyes do a quick sweep of my body, up and down. A dark look passes over his face.

"You've changed," he utters.

I'm getting the distinct impression he's not talking about the length of my hair or the style of my clothes.

"Yeah, and you're just exactly the same as you were the day I left." I reach for the door handle, pausing, I turn back, meeting his eyes. "Actually, no scrap that. You're not the same, you're an even bigger arsehole than you were before!"

I slam the door behind me and fall against the wall beside it, heart pounding. The tears I was holding in start to run down my face.

I feel used, and cheap.

Of all the things I ever thought Nathan could make me feel, it wasn't them.

He didn't have sex with me because he missed me, or because he loves me and it's been torture for him all this time without me. He had sex with me to punish me. To hurt me. He knows it would hurt me to do this, because he knows how much I care about him. I've always worn my feelings for him plain for him to see.

And all because I hurt his damn fucking pride. How could he do that to me? I thought he cared about me. Maybe he did, once upon a time, long ago, but not now it seems.

I'd hate him right now if I didn't love him so much.

I want to run away and hide, but I can't. Not again. I'm not going to just up and leave. I'm not giving him the satisfaction of being right. I'm going to stay here until it bugs the shit out of him and drives him to talk to me like a sensible person would, instead of acting like a teenage boy.

I look toward the stairs. It's the only way to get away from Nathan, but I also know down there is the one other person I've been terrified to face for a long time now. But also the one other person I know I have to talk too. I never got the chance to before I left here. The day he buried Sol.

Taking a deep breath I wipe my face dry and very nervously head downstairs.

Jack's in the kitchen with his back to me, making coffee, when I push the door open.

He turns to me. He seems to have aged some while I've been gone. I guess it's to be expected after what he's been through.

"Hiya, Alex, love." His voice is warm.

Everything's the same in here as I remember. The sight of Jack in here making coffee slams open my nostalgia and I feel tears well in my eyes. A long old wound cracks open in my chest, and I suddenly feel like a little kid again. A kid who wants a hug from their dad. Wants them to tell them everything's going to be okay. Except Jack's not my dad. He was the closest thing to one before Sol died. But I am the reason Sol died. I'm the reason he lost his youngest child. He has every right to hate me. But by the way he's looking at me now, I'm not so sure he hates me after all.

"Are you passing through or staying?" he asks. There's no harshness in his words, only kindness and a light smile.

"Depends." I shrug lightly, looking to the floor.

"On?"

My bottom lip quivers. "Nathan ... *you*."

"Me?" He looks surprised.

"Hmm." I bite my lip trying to hold back the tears. I can't cry. It's not fair on him to do so.

"I get the Nathan problem." He shrugs, then a small laugh. "Because, Nathan's well ... Nathan. But me, Alex, love ..." He lets out a light sigh. "I once told you this was your home. That hasn't changed."

I crumble. Tears are running out of my eyes before I can even attempt to stop them. Jack crosses the kitchen in a few strides and wraps his arms around me, enveloping me in a hug.

He smells of everything familiar. Cigars and coffee. Jack is the closest and best thing I'll ever get to having a dad again. He could never replace my own, but he sure comes in at a close second.

"You okay?" he asks after a minute, patting my hair.

I nod into his chest.

Jack loosens his hold on me and rests his hands against my arms. "I've really missed having you here."

"I've missed being here." I notice my tears have soaked through his shirt. "Sorry," I gesture.

He looks down and rubs a hand over the wet patch. "Don't worry," he says kindly. "I brought up three boys. I've had worse on me." A grin.

I can't help but smile back.

Leaving me, Jack gets some kitchen roll off the side and hands it to me. "So Nathan's being his usual self I take it?"

I gulp down and twist the kitchen roll in my hands. "He's angry."

"He's always angry." Jack smiles lightly.

"He's got a right to be angry with me though." I hate to admit it but leaving him like I did was never going to illicit anything but anger. Seeing a slight sense of reason, he has a right to be angry. Not to do what he did; sleeping with me to hurt me, that was a bastard's trick, but the anger, I can't deny him.

"Has he?" Jacks response throws me. I give him a surprised look. "From where I'm standing, he's got no reason to be pissed at you. You did what you thought was right at the time. You did what he couldn't. You let go. That makes you strong in my books."

I feel a swell of emotion inside. Jack thinks I'm strong. There's no higher compliment in my books.

"And to be honest, love," he continues, "He's not angry with you. He's angry with himself … and a little bit pissed off with me at the moment too. But that's nothing your coming home won't help clear up."

I furrow my brows, confused by his last sentence.

"A lot of ears here." He tugs on his ear lobe and I immediately catch his drift. "I was just getting ready to go visit with Sol, you want to come and keep me company?"

He holds out his hand to me in offering.

I have a knot twisting my stomach. Visiting Sol's grave will undoubtedly mean a conversation I've never had with Jack. One I'm afraid to have. Fearful of what he'll say.

He smiles at me, seeing my hesitation. "Come on we can *talk* on the way." He gives me a knowing wink, trying to lighten the obvious tension I'm creating.

"Sure," I nod. "I would love to keep you company."

I follow behind Jack, pausing as he retrieves a bunch of tied flowers off the work top, and then I follow him out of the back door and into the fresh crisp English morning.

Chapter 23: Ghosts

As we walk across the field toward the woods, Jack and me make idle chatter. I can smell the scent of home so clearly now.

I didn't really pay attention last night. I was too nervous about seeing Nathan. But now I can smell my home. It warms and soothes me. Funny, I'd spent so much time missing the people here I'd not realised just how much I missed my home.

"So Erin had a girl," I say, smiling, at the happy news Jack just shared with me. I hide the little drop of sadness I feel deep inside that I wasn't around when she was born.

Jack nods, beaming proudly. "Ahh she is beautiful, Alex. Looks just like Erin."

Good thing, I think to myself. Let's just hope she's all parts Erin and no parts Cal.

"What did they call her?" I ask.

"Rose."

"Beautiful name. I'd love to see her," I say more out of politeness, even though I know that's probably not a good idea. I do miss Erin and I would love to see little Rose, but Cal, not so much.

"Oh, they're not here at the moment love. They all went to stay with Erin's sister after – you know … Sol."

The temperature suddenly drops by about a thousand degrees.

"Oh."

"When they come back, then for sure, I know Erin would love to see you," he says, trying to ease the situation.

I offer a smile. "And how is Cal?" I have to ask. It's kind of hard to care after what he did to me, but he is Jack's son. I wrap my arms around myself, more for something to do with them.

A pause. "He's ahh … you know." A shrug.

Silence hits us. Cal, not a great topic of conversation. Maybe I shouldn't have mentioned him.

"So, Scarlett's still living here. That's great. And Craig's here too." I could sense them both in the house. They were still sleeping when we left, thankfully. I don't think I can face them just yet.

"Yeah." Jack sounds happy to talk about them. "Scarlett's a great kid. She's had a rough life, never knew her parents, in and out of foster care all her life – then onto the streets, where those fuckers picked her up from." The hairs on the back of my neck prickle and a shiver slides down my back. "It took a while, you know it was a big shock to her, finding out the world wasn't exactly as she believed it to be, but she coped well, and she's good now. She helps me here on the farm. Craig does too. He's back and forth from his law practice in Leeds, helping me out. He's a good kid. And I've appreciated his help, both their help to be honest. It's been tough you know – Sol's passing, Cal leaving, and Nathan's never here…"

"Wait." I stop walking. Jack stops too; turning back he looks at me. "What do you mean Nathan's never here?"

He gives me an uneasy look. "Alex love … he's been looking for you ever since the day you left."

I feel like I've just been hit by a freight train. Twice.

"He's been looking for me?" I can barely get the words out.

Jack nods.

"And … when exactly did he stop?" I have a feeling I already know the answer.

Jack gives an unnecessary look at his watch. "As of about four o'clock this morning."

"Oh."

I don't know what else to say. What can I say? I think I may have actually gone into shock.

"He's been home, maybe, what, two weeks in total out of the last six months you've been gone. Just a couple of days at a time he stays home, before he takes off again. He literally just got back yesterday morning. Luckily really that he had, you coming home 'an all."

My mouth forms an 'O' again, but nothing comes out this time.

He's been looking for me for all this time. Why? He's clearly pissed off with me for leaving and then coming back, but yet he's been searching for me. I get in the beginning why he'd look for me. Nathan's got a lot of pride and he's stubborn, it would have hurt his control freak side that I'd taken charge and left. But to look for me for six months ... I just don't even know what to think about that. Or feel to be honest.

I don't think I'll ever understand him, or his motives.

"Are you okay?" Jack asks concerned, at my clearly odd behaviour.

I haven't moved, or blinked, or spoken, for several minutes now.

Blinking, I say, "Yeah, I'm fine. Just a little confused, I guess."

"Welcome to life with Nathan," he murmurs, a little chuckle, and he's carries on walking to the woods.

Finding my feet, I catch pace beside him.

We enter in through the trees. I feel the temperature drop at the loss of sunlight. It's not long before I see Sol's grave.

A feel the inevitable lump in my throat. There's a beautiful headstone on his grave now. I wonder when they got it.

Jack walks over and kneels down at his grave. I sit beside Jack.

Turning to me, he gives me a sad smile. "Nathan blames himself for Sol's death."

I look at him.

"Just like you do you," he adds.

I look to the floor. My guilt is etched all over my face.

"There's not a single day that passes where I don't wish I'd made Sol stay home that night," he says.

"You couldn't have stopped him," I say quietly. I bite my lip wondering if I should have said that at all. Maybe I overstepped my mark.

"You're right. Doesn't make me think it any less though." He exhales deeply. "I guess we all blame ourselves for Sol's death." He looks directly at me. "But it was none of our faults. We couldn't have prevented it. And I never blamed you, Alex. Never. Or Nathan. Or Cal for that matter. I just wish Nathan didn't blame himself." Another heavy sigh. "I've lost Sol. I've as near as good lost Cal. I can't lose Nathan too. He's all I have left." There's real desperation in his voice.

I feel panic rising in my chest. "Why would you ever lose him?"

"He's broken, Alex. Completely. Worse than when he came back from Iraq. Broken over Sol. Over you. I don't mean to lay any guilt on you. I get why you left, I really do. And I admired you for it. I'm just praying you coming back fixes this a bit. Fixes him."

"He's broken, how?" The fear is tightening across my chest.

"The drinking's bad – no it's worse," he highlights. "He doesn't sleep. Barely eats. He's lost weight. Basically he's driving himself into the ground."

"And you think my being here will help him? I'm sorry Jack but I'm not sure about that. I think I'm the last person who can help him. He's beyond angry with me right now."

"You're the only person that can help him. I've never seen him the way he is over you. If you could just talk to him, make him listen, see reason. He won't listen to me or Craig. But I know he'll listen to you."

I'm not so sure about that. He's got way more confidence in me than I have.

"I was going to talk to him anyway," I say. "There are some things he needs to know, but I can try and talk some sense into him if you think that will help." I don't want Nathan to hurt in any way. Just the thought of the pain he's been in is suffocating the hell out of me.

I reach over and pick a wildflower from out of the ground. Putting it to my nose I smell it. I hold it to my chest and stare straight ahead at Sol's headstone.

"I do think it'll help." Jack nods, then reaches out and dusts some dirt off Sol's headstone with his hand.

I was expecting Jack to ask me what else I need to talk to Nathan about, actually I've been wondering when he was going to ask why I came back home. But he hasn't.

I know I should tell Nathan first. But I also should tell Jack; it's the least I owe him.

Taking a deep breath, I wrap my arms around myself.

"You're probably wondering why I came back home after all this time."

He casts me a glance. "Once or twice." A little smile.

I take a deep breath. "An Original found me."

"Which one?" he asks calmly, no hesitation at all.

I glance at him, surprised. I expected him to be shocked, stunned. But he's looking at me like he was expecting it all along.

"I knew it would have to be big for you to come back. I know how much you love Nathan and why you were staying away."

"I haven't brought the danger with me," I say quickly. I need him to know I would never bring danger to them again.

He looks at me steady. "Like I just said, I know how much you love Nathan."

I let out a breath.

"Does Nathan know?" he asks.

I shake my head. "We didn't get that far."

"You need to tell him. In fact you need to talk to him more about that than the other stuff right now."

"I know," I sigh. "I was going to tell him this morning, it just didn't work out that way. He wasn't in the best mood."

Jack runs his hand over his hair. "He spends all that time looking for you, and the moment he's got you back, he's pushing you away. I know he's my son, and I will love him until the day I die, but I will never understand that boy."

I bring my knees up to my chest and wrap my arms around them. "You and me both."

There's a small silence between us.

"So the Original, he cares for you?"

I look at him curious. "What do you mean?"

He gives me a look. A look which tells me exactly what he means.

I want to kiss you ... I love you. Zeff's words echo in my mind.

I shrug, pointlessly. Jack already knows the answer.

"He said he was trying to help keep me safe, that he wants to continue doing so. He said he isn't like Isaiah–"

"So it's Matthias then."

I nod, releasing I hadn't told him which of the two. "He said he doesn't want the same things as his brother and hasn't for a long time. That he wants to protect me from him."

"Do you believe him?"

"He hasn't given me any reason not to."

"But you left him and came back here."

"Yeah," I nod. "I was scared and confused, and I just wanted to see Nathan. And you." I rub my tired eyes. "I guess it was the excuse I'd been looking for to bring me back home."

"So if Matthias isn't out to hurt you, that leaves only one. Makes things a bit easier in a strange kind of way." He shrugs, probably as confused as I am by it all.

"Not exactly." I turn to face him. "The vampires know I exist. Elijah knows."

"Ah." Pause. "Then you definitely need to tell Nathan."

"I know. I'm just worried over how he'll react."

"He might surprise you."

"You believe that about as much as I do." I give him a tight smile.

"He's difficult, but he's also smart and resourceful. He'll know what the best thing for you to do is. And it'll give him something else to focus on instead of his own grief.

Give him something to fight for. Nathan works best when he has a cause."

I lean over and kiss him on the cheek and get to my feet. This is what I love about Jack. You don't need to have a big conversation with him, resulting in an argument, because he just seems to know the right thing to say, he understands. Sol was so much like Jack. I just wish Nathan had the same trait.

I dust the dirt off my legs. "I really missed you, Jack."

He smiles up at me and gives me that wink of his.

"I missed you too."

Chapter 24: Warzone

I find Nathan at Honor's stable, leant up against the stable door, faced away from me. I feel guilty that I haven't been to see her and Hope yet. I'll spend time with them soon, but for now, this is more important.

"Hi," I say a bit louder than necessary.

The muscles in his shoulders and back tense. His head tilts back slightly, but he doesn't respond.

I hate this. I really hate this.

Taking a deep breath I wrap my arms around myself.

"How are they both doing?" I tilt my head in the direction of Honor and Hope's stable; I can't see them as Nathan's blocking my view, but I needn't have bothered as he's still yet to look at me.

"They're fine," he replies curtly. "Why are you here?"

His words slice into the quiet air with the intention he means.

Dropping my arms to my sides I curl my fingers into my hands. "Because we need to talk."

He turns his head and looks at me. "Do we?"

"Yes." I take a fortifying breath. "Not about me and you. We need to talk about the Originals."

I opt to go with this first, like Jack said. We can get to us, and Sol, later.

He moves around, wipes his hands on the front of his jeans and leans his back against the wall next to the stable door. He folds his arms over his chest.

"So that's why you're here." I get nothing from his even tone, or blank expression. "What's changed to bring you back? I'm guessing it's not great if you felt forced back here."

I look at him bewildered. "I didn't feel forced to come back."

"Yeah, sure you didn't," his reply is blunt.

I'm not even going to argue the toss with him. He'll believe what he wants to believe irrespective of what I say.

Trying to ward off the chill his steady cold gaze is giving me, I hug myself, and say, "Matthias found me."

"What?" His eyes flare in surprise and he stands bolt upright, scanning the area like he expects Matthias to jump out on us any second now.

I don't know what he was expecting me to say, but obviously that wasn't it. Looks like I've got his attention for now though, at least.

"You're safe. Everyone is safe," I placate. "I wouldn't have come back if it wasn't. It's fine, really."

"Fine how?" His brow furrows and he looks suspiciously at me.

"It's complicated."

"Complicated?" he echoes.

I take a deep breath. "When I first met him – Matthias - in Italy a week ago, I didn't know who he really was."

"You were in Italy?" he says.

"Yes. Why?"

"No reason. It was just one of my many stop offs in the chase Alex around the world jaunt." There's no humour in his voice.

A pain sears, deep into my chest. I look down at my feet.

"Jack said you'd been looking for me, for all this time." I glance at him. "I'm sorry."

He leans back against the stable and folds his arms over his chest, casting his gaze to the floor. "It doesn't matter."

He shrugs.

What doesn't matter – me or the search? I want to ask. I don't, obviously.

"How did the Original find you?"

I swallow past the dryness. Not because I'm afraid to answer, but because I'm back to struggling to get past the fact that he's been searching for me, for all this time. Does it mean he cares about me, or is it just because it's who he is?

Someone who has to save everyone. Or just because his stubborn pride wouldn't let him stop searching?

Judging from the way he's currently behaving, I'll have to go for the latter.

Shoving my feelings aside I answer his question. "He saved me from a vampire who attacked me when I was hunting one night in the forest. He told me his name was Zeff. That he was a vampire hunter."

Nathan laughs again. It's hollow. Patronising. And really starting to wind me up, like only he can.

Ignoring him, I continue, "My passport got ruined in the attack and he said he could get me a new one."

I don't tell him the truth that Zeff ruined it. It's all too complicated enough as it is.

"And you trusted him? A complete stranger?"

"You were once a stranger and I trusted you."

He sighs, looking away from me and rakes his fingers over his short hair, scratching his scalp. I still can't believe he cut his hair off.

"How did you not know who he was? You must have sensed he was a Vârcolac. I mean this one of the Originals I'm talking about here." His tone is condescending.

"He has abilities," I respond sharply. "His grandmother wasn't just a werewolf, she was also a witch. He and Isaiah both have the power. He can cast spells … one that conceals his true identity. He can make a supernatural being believe he's human."

Caution and deliberation pass over his visage.

"Explains how they've both stayed hidden for so long I suppose," he says, shrugging. Then his eyes snap up at me, like something significant has just dawned. "So just exactly why was the Original helping you get a new passport? Why wasn't he taking you back to Isaiah and getting started on their breeding programme?"

He's such a callous bastard at times.

Shaking my head, I gulp down and work my hands together nervously. "I don't understand it fully myself."

'*I love you.*' Zeff words keep echoing, haunting my mind.

"He pretended to be someone else … Zeff. That he was a vampire hunter. That vampire's had killed his parents. But he never hurt me not once … " I feel like I'm just now myself sorting through the sequence of events in my head. "He helped me – a lot." I nervously pull at the hem on my dress. "He trained me how to fight. How to defend myself. He saved me – twice, from vampires. He seemed like a good guy."

A strange expression crosses over Nathan's face, freezing in place and hardening his features. "Is there something I don't know?"

I stop fidgeting. "Like what?"

A flicker of emotion washes his features as it comes to light in his eyes. "Did something *happen* with him?"

Shit. I know where this is going.

"Such as?" I keep my tone as short.

"Have you had sex with him?"

"No!" I say aghast.

He gives me a look. "Yeah, sure you haven't."

He's dismissing me. It burns me to the core.

"You know, you really should have said last night before you climbed into my bed that you'd been in his. It would have changed things for sure," he says.

"I haven't had sex with him!"

"Kissed him?"

"No!" *Almost, nearly.*

He gives me another disbelieving look.

I hate the way it makes me feel.

Cheap, dirty, a liar. And that's because he's closer to the truth than I would care to admit right now. I might not have kissed Zeff, but at one point I wanted to. And that's just as bad. But Nathan would never understand if I told him. I would only end up pushing him further away than he already is.

"So you're telling me the Original just decided to take care of you – get you a new passport, turn you into some –

fighting machine, and then let you go – just like that, out of the goodness of his heart?"

"There's more to it than just that. You're oversimplifying things."

"Forgive me."

I hate it when he's sarcastic. I fire a look at him.

There are millions of things about the whole situation that I don't even understand. Not fully. One thing more than others. Zeff telling me he loves me.

But I also don't think the best idea is to tell Nathan that Zeff told me he's in love with me. That'd be just adding fuel to his already well lit fire. He already thinks I've had sex with Zeff, me telling him that would only cement his assumption. I know what he's like. And in the grand scheme of things it's irrelevant anyway, because I don't have any feelings for Zeff.

"Look, Nathan, I don't understand much of what happened myself. All I do know is he said he wanted to help me – help keep me safe." Turning to the side, not wanting to see his face when I tell him this. I wrap my arms around my chest and swallow down. "And not just from Isaiah. He's not my only problem now." Deep breath. "Elijah knows I exist. And before you ask – no, I don't know how he knows, and no, he doesn't know where I am."

I'm feeling pretty pissed off now.

"Are you sure?"

I cast a glance in his direction. "I think if he did we'd know about it by now – don't you?"

He rubs his face with his hand and lets out a sigh.

"I know I made a mistake by coming back here, Nathan." My voice is quiet. "And I'm sorry for that. But as far as Elijah knows, I am still in Italy."

Well, I hope he does.

His brow furrows. "I never said you'd made a mistake coming here."

"You didn't have to." I look away.

I hear the light sigh he lets out. "Does the Original know you came back here?"

I shake my head, holding back the tears eager to show. "No. He doesn't know anything about you. I never talked about *you*, specifically."

Then I feel the shift in the air again. A sudden charge of anger comes out from him. I've no idea what's kicked him off, but I'm pretty sure it's because of something I just said.

"So you're telling me the Original just let you go." His voice is hard again, angry. "Just like that. With nothing owing, no come back whatsoever, nothing from you in return. Just a passport and a see you later." He's obviously unwilling to let it go.

And now, I'm left wondering if it's because he's jealous.

I stare steely back, "That's what I'm telling you."

"I don't believe you."

It hurts.

The hurt quickly shifts to anger. "You're angry with me because I left you in that hotel room in Scotland – I get that Nathan – honestly I get *that*. But that doesn't give you the right to call me a liar! I have only slept with you! *You* – and no one else since that night! You can't just treat me this way – have sex with me, ignore me, then accuse me of lying about having sex with Zeff, basically being a complete and utter bastard to me!"

His eyes ignite. Like a match has just been struck behind them. And God they are on fire, practically spitting out flames. He drops his folded arms and stands tall.

"But you can have sex with me and then disappear for six months without so much as a word."

Ahh. Shit.

"B-but t-that was different." I can't control the stammer.

"Really? How so?" There's a crass irony in his voice which is unmistakable.

"I was trying to protect you by leaving. I thought I was doing the right thing – I didn't want to leave you and I've missed you for every single second I've been away."

I lay my heart out to him without meaning to.

He doesn't say a thing. So I look at face, his eyes, searching for something, anything to tell me there are still some feelings for me buried deep down inside of him.

I see nothing.

Then something inside me shatters. And I no longer care if I sound weak. "I know that's why you had sex with me before – for revenge. You wanted to hurt me. It worked. Trust me, I'm hurt."

My voice wobbles in time with my bottom lip.

He visibly flinches. "Is that what you think of me? That I'd have sex with you to hurt you."

"Isn't that exactly what you're did?!" I cry at him.

He shakes his head, disappointed. "You obviously don't know me as well as I thought you did."

He starts to walk away from me.

"Arghhh!" I scream, clutching my head. "You're fucking impossible – you will never talk to me reasonably – ever!"

He stops, turning abruptly, and marches back to me. His face is so angry, he is absolutely steaming. He stops an arm's reach away.

The last time I saw him this angry, a television took the brunt of it. I have to stop myself from stepping back.

"You wanna talk, Alex – fine let's talk. Let's talk about how I gave everything up, left right after my brother died, left my family behind, all to keep you safe, and you just fucked off! Disappeared in the middle of the night without a word! And I don't see you for six months – six fucking months! And then you turn up because you've been found by an Original – who happens to be actually a nice guy."

He air quotes the nice guy. There's not a shred of humour there.

"That he's been helping you – that you've spent a week in Italy with him for fucks sake, all the while I've been searching the world for you like a fucking idiot! And then you have the blatant cheek to accuse me of using you! FUCK!" he roars out, gripping his head with his hands, taking in a hard breath, pacing around before me.

Then he suddenly stops. Turned away from me. He covers his face with his hands. I can hear his ragged breaths. Then he moves his hands away and turns to face me. His eyes look so sad.

It cripples me to see.

"We had sex, Alex. I told you I was in love with you ... and … you just left."

Something like pure hard emotion crackles in the air between us.

"I–" my mouth is open but I'm struggling to find any words to follow through with.

I know he told me he loved me, but he didn't really mean it. Well, I didn't think he did. Now I kind of do. Fuck.

I know I meant it when I said it to him. But honestly I really didn't think he did. We were having sex, he'd been drinking, there was a lot of emotion being thrown around. I thought he'd said it in the heat of the moment – I wanted to believe – but I couldn't. If I had, then I would never have left.

"I know you told me you loved me." My voice is weak and apologetic. "But I didn't think you actually meant it."

I know it's the wrong thing to say the instant the words are out of my mouth. But it's too late to take back.

He laughs, hard. His eyes narrow onto mine and I see something flicker behind them. Pain, I realise. And I couldn't feel any worse if I tried.

"So you didn't mean it?"

"What?"

"That you loved me, Alex. When you told me you loved me, you're saying you didn't mean it?"

"Of course I meant it!"

"Then why wouldn't I?"

"I don't know ... I thought maybe you just said it in the heat of the moment."

He laughs, crass this time. It makes me feel stupid.

"I'm not a fucking teenager! I don't tell a girl I love her to get in her pants! Jesus Christ Alex, that's just utter fucking bullshit and you know it! Don't make excuses!"

"I'm not!"

"Yes you are!"

"I thought I was doing the right thing leaving–"

"To keep me safe – yeah I got it," he snaps.

"I was driving you crazy! You blamed me – rightly so – for everything – for Sol. You were miserable – I think you can see why I wouldn't think you were in love with me for real! I mean why the hell would you love me?!"

"What?" He takes a surprised step back.

"I have absolutely nothing to offer you! I'm not your kind. I'm not a shifter and I never will be. I'm a blood drinking monster for fucks sake! A danger to you – to anyone who gets close to me! And I can never have children!"

I don't know why I just said that last bit. I clutch a hand to my chest, to catch hold of my erratic heart that's trying to force its way out of my chest.

Something in his face breaks, but then I see his mask fall back into place. "Well, unfortunately for me, I didn't get to choose who I fell in love with. If I had, then trust me, it would never have been you."

I feel like he's just punched a fist into my chest and has pulled my heart right back out with it.

With tears blurring my vision, I push my way past him. I need to get out here.

Now.

Chapter 25: Shards

Nathan catches hold of my arm from behind as I'm racing past the barn, yanking me to an abrupt stop.

Tears are streaming down my face. I don't hide the fact. I want him to see how much that hurt.

"Let me go!"

But he doesn't let go.

"I'm sorry, I didn't mean that." His tone is urgent. And then the next thing I know his mouth is on mine, fast and hard, kissing me with an almost dependency.

I fight him for all of a second. Then I'm rendered powerless.

Nathan backs me into the barn until I'm up against the door of a truck parked in there. His hands are everywhere, mouth roaming, clothes being lifted, unbuttoned. I can barely keep up.

No one but Nathan can make me feel so utterly out of control like this. Any anger I had toward him disappeared the second he put his lips on mine.

Nathan pulls on the door handle. Locked.

"Shit," he utters breathless.

His focus scans the barn. "Wait a sec."

Untangling himself from me, leaving me wanting and breathless, he goes over to the tool bench and returns with a hammer. Shifting me aside, I watch wide eyed as he smashes the driver's window out, puts his arm in and unlocks the door.

"What?" he asks innocently, desire still stoking his eyes.

"Is this yours?"

He shakes his head, "Craig's."

"Are you crazy? He's gonna go mad!"

An almost smile. "I'm all kinds of crazy." He drops the hammer to the floor with a clatter, and stalks closer. "But mostly, I'm just crazy about you."

His eyes are blazing with need.

Something in my stomach drops, then coils lower.

The little space there was left between us he eliminates, and his mouth is on mine again. I wrap my arms around his neck.

He reaches behind me and opens the door to the back seat. He lifts me in. I shuffle back as he climbs in, straddling me, he shuts the door with a clunk.

And then it's just us. Alone. On the back seat of a truck.

The blood in my body rushes to every part but my head. And I know the self-preservation half of my brain, the part that would be telling me this isn't a good idea, that I'm here again repeating this cycle with him... we'll sleep together, we'll fight, one or both of us will get hurt - unfortunately seems to have abandoned me again at the very point when I need it.

But right now I can't find the will to care. All I care about is him. Wanting him. Nathan is the anaesthesia for all of my pains. Even the ones he creates. Mainly, the ones he creates. He's an addiction I can't deny myself.

So I let my eyes roam his hard firm chest, indulging in him as he pulls his T-shirt off over his head. Then I notice his tattoo is different. He's had something added to it. I didn't notice this morning, we were too busy fighting, of course.

I sit up to get a closer look. It's above the other names, at the top near his chest. I know what these tattoos are, what they mean to him. A reminder of the people's lives he's saved in Iraq. I'm confused.

"You had another tattoo done?"

Tracing my finger over the lettering, I look up at him.

His body stiffens under my touch. He doesn't meet my eyes. Running a hand over his hair, he nods slightly.

A thought trickles into my brain, making my heart skip over.

"What does it say?" I try to keep my tone even, light, but my mouth suddenly feels gluey.

There's a beat of silence between us.

"Alex," he mutters. "It says, Alex."

Nathan finally meets my eyes and when he does I see something there I never thought I'd see – vulnerability.

My heart starts to beat uncomfortably hard.

He rests back onto his heels with a sigh, a subdued air all around him. "I guess I just needed something to remind me you were real, because after you left, there was nothing ... nothing to say you'd ever been here."

I'm blindsided. And then all the fighting and hard words just become as irrelevant as they truly are.

An unexpected tear sneaks out of my eye. I wipe it away.

"I'm so sorry I left you like I did," I whisper, choked up.

He looks down at me, there's brooding in his eyes.

"You were right to leave. You did the right thing ... just for the wrong reason. You should have left for yourself, not for me." He rubs his face, hard. "I wasn't in a good place before you left and I was even worse after you went. I haven't seen straight for a long time."

He looks so broken. Just like Jack said he is. It's unbearable to see. I open my mouth to speak but he holds a hand up, stopping me. "Just let me get this out please."

I close my mouth, allowing him the time and space he needs.

"What I said to you in that hotel room about Sol. That it was your fault he died. It was unforgivable. And I'm so sorry. If I could take those words back I would."

I can feel a sob welling deep within me, but I hold it back. I don't want to cry anymore.

"I blamed a lot of people for his death, mainly myself – and Cal, but never you. I don't even know why I said it." A sigh. "I spent a long time looking for you, to tell you this, and then when I had the chance to, I screwed it up. I let my anger get the better of me, *again*. I guess ... I don't know, just when you turned up, out of the blue ... it threw me."

He rubs his face with his hand and lets out a sigh. "I was angry that I'd spent so long looking for you, and then there you were, just standing right before me. I didn't handle it well, I know. Trust me, I know what a fuck up I am." He gives me a sad smile. "I'm impulsive, hot tempered, and I drink way too much. But worst of all – I don't do *this* well." He points a finger between us. "Well, I pretty much suck at it. And as it seems for some reason, I do it even worse with you."

My stomach does a nervous flip.

"I suck at this too you know." I give a small smile. "But we could help each other to not … suck."

Raising his eyebrow, he gives a short laugh. It runs in smooth electric waves over my skin.

"I hope you don't mean that literally." His smile is all fox.

God, I love him.

Leaning forward, I slide my hands around his back and kiss my name that's forever branded into his skin. "I missed you," I murmur.

He presses his lips to the top of my head, his dog tags rest cool against my cheek. He doesn't say anything. He doesn't say he missed me too. Not that he has to, there's no prerequisite, but now I just feel awkward for saying it.

"So were you drunk when you had it done?" I lift my head to look at him, running my index finger over his, *my*, tattoo, trying to change the subject.

He tucks my hair behind my ear, a smile creeping onto his lips. "A little."

I arch an eyebrow.

"Okay, a lot." He laughs.

And there he is, my Nathan. "You do a lot of crazy things when you're drunk."

"I do a lot of crazy things when I'm not drunk." He indicates the glass on the front seat.

I let my eyes flicker to the broken shards.

Our relationship is a lot like that broken window. One tap and we break easily, and we can be cutting, but melt us down and we meld straight back together.

"Nathan?"

"Mmm."

"The drinking ... will it stop?"

He hooks my chin with his finger, bringing my face to his. "It already has."

I see that look in his eyes again, the one where I'm pretty sure he's considering all the ways he can devour me. A white hot thrill shoots through me, spiralling me out of control again.

I bite down seductively on my lip. His eyes flicker to them, then back to my eyes. And then he's kissing me.

He wraps his arms around me and kisses me with so much passion and fervour that it sets my whole body alight. As his lips grow impatient, I fall back against the seat and he crashes into me. He starts to pull my dress up. I lift my hips. He slides his hand under my back lifting me up off the seat and pulls my dress over my head with his other. He kisses the skin on my neck and shoulder as he unclasps my bra. I run my hands over his hard sculpted chest. He is perfection in every sense of the word.

Kissing a delicious trail back up my neck, he whispers in my ear, "You are so beautiful. You have no idea what you do to me."

A feeling of complete ecstasy engulfs me. A few choice words from Nathan and I'm left practically immobile.

Unbuttoning his jeans, I slide down the zipper and putting my hand inside, between skin and boxer shorts, I take him in my hand. He groans and closes his eyes.

Turning my head to him, I tease, "I've got a pretty good idea."

He opens his eyes, chuckling, deep and throaty, he presses his lips to mine again, slipping his tongue into my mouth.

Another wave of intense pleasure ripples through me, a moan escaping from deep within.

Nathan shucks out of his jeans and boxer shorts, and then we're skin on skin. Nothing left between us.

"Shit," he says, through ragged breaths, sounding frustrated. "I don't have a condom. They're in my room."

I hadn't even thought to be honest, shows how far gone I am.

His head falls heavily against my own panting chest.

"Nathan the condoms …"

He lifts his head to look at me. "Are really old. There's been no one else, if that's what you're asking." His tone is as intense as his eyes.

"So they probably won't work anyway." I let out a little laugh. The laugh – because I'm relieved there has been no one else. But still we have no condoms, and I want him. Now. That fact – not so funny.

We look at each other for a long moment. Just staring into each other's eyes. Electricity firing between us. I see the question appear there in his eyes. I nod slightly. Just once.

And then there's no stopping if we tried.

"I'll pull out," he breathes into my mouth.

"No. It'll be fine." I can hear the words, but it's like it isn't even me saying them. I can't believe how reckless I'm being.

But my mind is lost in this moment as much as my body is. Lost to Nathan. And right now I don't care about anything, but having him.

He grabs my hands, bringing them up above my head, resting them against the door of the truck, his mouth fixed on mine.

"You're all I want," he groans, as he moves inside me.

"Oh God, Nathan," I sigh, my own breath staggered.

His movements start to become harder as his need overtakes, a sheen of sweat slick between us. I dig my nails into his rough hands with each move he makes.

And then when his body tenses and his movements become rigid, I can feel myself shifting to a whole other place with him. Then as my own body starts to shake and quiver, Nathan growls deep in his throat, pressing into me one last time, groaning and quivering above me.

Staying inside me, he kisses me again, slowly. Then finally moving, he lays beside me, wrapping his arms tight around me, holding me to him as I rest my head on his chest.

He reaches up and grabs the blanket off the back shelf, laying it over our entwined naked bodies.

I snuggle closer to him and he tightens his hold on me. "Are you happy?"

"I'm happy," he says, and I can feel his smile.

After a while I feel his breaths start to labour.

"You're tired?" I smooth my hand over his chest, fingers tracing over my tattoo. I still can't believe he did this.

"Yeah." He sighs. "I haven't had much sleep."

"You didn't sleep last night?" I glance up at him.

"I haven't slept properly since you left."

I look away, pressing my lips together, holding back a painful breath.

"Just don't leave this time, okay?" he says, gripping me with his fingers, his voice sounding so very tired.

Nuzzling his neck, I press a kiss to skin, feeling sick that he even has to ask, "I'm not going anywhere. I'll be here when you wake up, I promise."

I'm never, ever, leaving you again.

Chapter 26: Hunger

I wake in Nathan's bed with him beside me, awake and watching me.

This is so much better than when I woke yesterday morning, or any other morning for the last six months when I've woken without him, for that matter.

"Hey," I mumble, groggily.

"Hey, yourself." His deep voice strokes over my senses, like a feather on my skin.

He leans in and kisses me. It's a long, slow kiss. No tongues though, thankfully. Morning breath, not so pretty. Not that I imagine I look any shade of pretty at the moment. Bed hair and all.

I'm fully aware of how bad I can look in a morning. But then again, since yesterday afternoon he's seen, and had me, in pretty much all of the hair ruffling sexual positions known to man, sweating and near to depletion. The guy is a walking encyclopaedia of sexual positions, and how best to do them.

Not that I'm complaining. Far from it.

Memories of yesterday flood my mind, sending shivers running through me and raising a blush in my cheeks.

Yesterday, Nathan sleep a short while in the truck, I laid awake with him the whole time, just happy to be in his arms. Then when he woke, he seemed better, refreshed. We dressed and came back to the house; me with the intention of him getting some more sleep. It didn't quite work out that way. We've only left to use the bathroom, and Nathan once when he went downstairs to get us sustenance. Apart from that we've not left his bed.

As I've discovered, Nathan has a lot of stamina. A heck of a lot. Well, so do I for that matter. But he has way, way, *way* more.

We've used condoms the whole time. Neither of us has mentioned the fact we didn't in the truck. I'm sure I'll be fine, but even still I'll ask Nathan to go pick the morning after pill up for me later.

But we both finally passed out a few hours ago from sheer exhaustion. As it seems though, my body has a hard time sleeping in close proximity to Nathan, hence why I'm awake now.

"You slept?" I check.

"I did." He smiles.

"Have you been awake long?" I ask, stroking my fingers over his hard chest.

"No." He traces my lower lip with his fingertip. "I woke a few minutes before you did."

Seems our bodies are in sync too. I like that. A lot.

"Nice hair by the way." He flicks his eyes up cheekily, to my hair.

A self-conscious hand flies up to my current bird's nest. It's all stuck up at the back.

"Screw you," I say, grinning, trying to smooth it down to presentable. "You're not looking so hot yourself."

That's a complete lie. I don't think there is ever a moment Nathan doesn't look gorgeous.

"Promises, promises," he murmurs.

I grunt a response at him and run my fingers over his shoulder, up the back of his neck and into his own short presentable hair as he leans in and starts to kiss my neck.

"Speaking of hair, when did you cut yours?" I ask, loving the feel of his lips on my skin, but realising I haven't even mentioned it until now.

He stops kissing and moves back. I groan inwardly at the loss of contact. Resting his head on the pillow, he stares at me.

"When, or why?"

Hmm.

I go for when.

"A while ago. I've been keeping it short. Less hassle."

Okay. "Why?"

"Why, am I keeping it short?" He queries, knowing full well what I mean. He only prolongs things when he doesn't want to answer a question. And now I'm curious.

"No. Why did you cut it in the first place?"

I see emotion flicker through his eyes. There's a noticeable pause before he speaks.

"I was angry." Deep breath. "At you."

And now I wish I'd never asked. I try, unsuccessfully, to quell the pain it causes me.

Looking away, I whisper, "I'm sorry." My voice is hoarse and apologetic.

He cups my chin with his hand, forcing my eyes up to his.

"Don't be."

His gaze is warm, soft. It eases my pain right away.

"I like it," I say softly, running my finger over his cropped hair, and curving it around his ear.

"No you don't." He smiles.

"Okay, I don't," I grin.

"I'll grow it back."

"Do that." Moving closer to him, I wrap my leg around his, put my arm over his waist, rest my face against his chest, and hug him.

Putting his arm around me, he hugs me right back, firmly, holding me tight to him.

"Did I tell you I missed you?" I say, my words muffled by his chest.

"A couple of times." I can hear the smile in his voice. But still, he doesn't tell me he missed me.

Just as he didn't in the truck or on the couple of other occasions I've told him. Neither has he reciprocated when I've told him I love him over the last twelve hours, and yes, mostly I said it when I was reaching climax, but that's not the point, it doesn't make it any less true.

He's said a couple of choice words, 'I need you', 'You're all I want', but for someone who claims to have been in love with me before I left; which he's only ever said once, mid-argument in past tense, has said nothing to the contrary since.

I get that he's not the caring, sharing, emotional type; it takes a lot to get that side out of him, but sometimes a girl just needs to hear it. Needs to know where she stands.

Or maybe that's just it. He did love me, now it's not love anymore. Maybe he lost that while I was away.

I shift back out of his embrace, putting a gap between us.

It's his turn to not look happy about the loss of contact, but then he doesn't make a move to touch me again either.

Okay, so now my mind is cranking up gear and working on its usual overtime, and I'm starting to worry that maybe this whole thing is mostly … just about sex for him.

The control Nathan needs to have is one part of this equation, especially when it comes to me. The incessant idea he has that he has to take care of me. That it's his responsibility to keep me safe because he saved my life.

Well, my life's been saved again since by Zeff, so that kind of null and voids that argument, if he raises it. Actually thinking about it, it's probably best I don't say that to him.

"So …" I say.

"So …" he mirrors, curiously, leaving the obvious 'what' off the end.

I brace myself to ask the question I have to ask. The one where I'm basically laying all my cards out the table to him, but I don't care, I have to know what this is we doing here, aside from the obvious.

I know a lot of things have been said between us in the last twenty-four hours. Mostly coming from me, a small amount from him, which could be interpreted as to what I want us to be, of how he feels about me. About us, if there is an us.

But that doesn't necessarily mean I'm right. I've been wrong about Nathan a lot of times in the past and he hasn't exactly been forthcoming with his words since we woke.

Basically since the sex is currently sitting at score nil.

I have to ask so I make no error in where I stand with him. And I know for a fact I'll regret it if I don't ask him.

I take a deep breath. "Nathan."

"Alex." A smile starts to play on his lips.

"Stop it." I playfully punch him in the arm. "I'm trying to be serious here."

"Sorry. Go on." He gestures, but I can still see the trace of humour in his eyes, sparkling away at me.

Fighting the reddening I can feel rising up through the skin on my face, the one set to cover my whole body to a shade of inferno, I ask, after inhaling another deep breath, "So what exactly are we doing here? What I mean is, are we just having sex —"

"Not currently we're not." His smile widens. "But that can be rectified." He moves in closer and reaches his hand down between my legs.

I clamp my thighs on his hand, trapping it. "I'm trying to talk to you here."

His eyes widen at my serious tone. Slowly, he retracts his hand and shifts back to his side of the bed.

Okay, so that action hasn't exactly bolstered my confidence. And now I'm feeling kind of cold.

Fuck it. All or nothing.

"Nathan, are we doing this? What I mean is - are we together?"

Raising an eyebrow, he says, "Together?"

"Yeah, you know … me and you … like, together, together."

So far this isn't going well and I'm very quickly getting embarrassed, but more so irritated, with myself and him.

He rubs his finger over his lips. I know he's trying to hide a smile. "Like, together, together," he echoes, dryly.

He's taking the piss.

"Fuck off," I say, hitting him again, this time in the chest, and not so much playfully this time, but still I grin.

He catches hold of me by my wrist. My grin fades the second his expression changes from amused to intense.

Keeping his large hand encircling my wrist, he places his other palm flat against mine. My mouth dries. He slides his fingers, slowly down, in-between mine. My heart starts to beat an unsteady rhythm in my chest.

He stares at our entwined hands for a long moment, then, slowly lowering them, he rests our hands on the space on the bed between us.

He brings his eyes to meet mine. I see depth in them, the depth which he doesn't show often. "If that's the Alex way of asking, would I like us to be in a relationship, then I'd say that's pretty obvious."

I'm getting nothing from his even tone. I swallow. "Obvious … how?"

His face turns from intense to serious in a second, his eyes darkening. "Obvious, as in, I've spent the last six months searching the world for you. That good enough?"

He doesn't give me chance to respond before he starts up again. "Or, obvious, because I smash my buddy's car window out – the car that is the current and *only* love of his life – which he's gonna make me pay dearly for, so I could have sex in it, with you, because I couldn't think past anything but being inside you, right there and then."

Okay, so I'm getting the distinct impression he's pissed off by my question. But Nathan, and more than two sentences in a row, especially in this context, is not something I'm going to interrupt. Especially not since his words are making my whole body quiver in the best kind of way.

"Or because I haven't been able to think of anything but you, for the last six months … fuck … since you came into my life for that matter! About being with you, having a life with you, kissing you, holding you, tasting you – basically doing everything we've done over the last twelve hours together. Making love, fucking, or however you want to phrase it, all over my bedroom, because I'm so desperate for you, so desperate to make up for the time we lost. Or how about, because I look at you and everything just makes sense. And I can't see another day in my future without you in it. But if that's not enough to show it, then …" He pauses, breathless, his gaze even harder on me, bewilderment shrouding it. "How do you not even know?"

I feel out of breath just listening to him. "Know what?" The nerves show in my voice.

He shakes his head lightly, not moving his eyes from mine. "That I'm crazy in love with you, and I have been from the day I sat here with you, praying for you to live."

An intense heat fires up in my belly, shaking my core. I blink rapidly, my eyelids matching my current heart rate.

"You were? I mean, you are?" I don't know which question to address first.

"Yes."

"You're crazy in love with me?"

I have to ask again, etching it out, because I don't know if or when I'll ever hear a speech like that from him again.

But I like that I can fire him up so much. It's doing plenty for my confidence right now.

He brings our hands to his mouth and brushes his lips over my knuckles, his eyes not leaving mine. "Completely and utterly."

I can't contain my feelings anymore, and I move, with no hesitation, ensuring my mouth meets with his, clamping myself to him, kissing him firmly. Any prior worries of my morning breath, gone. Nathan's mouth opens under mine, his tongue roaming my mouth, taking me into him. His hand moves to my back, holding me to him and I start to lose all my senses in him.

"I'm crazy in love with you too," I gasp, coming up for air.

He groans, a delicious sound. Then his tongue delves back into my mouth, making me dizzy with want. My hand goes lower, wrapping around him.

He sighs into my mouth. It's not a positive sigh. It's more of a, 'I'm not going to ravage you right here and now', kind of sigh.

"Right now there is nothing more I want to do – than you," he murmurs. "Believe me … but you're hungry and you need to feed."

How does he do that? How does he know when I'm hungry?

I sigh out my disappointment, knowing full well he's not going to let me wait to feed and have my wicked way with him beforehand. Nathan is practical, if anything.

I'm going to have to tear myself away from him to go hunting. I highly doubt they've got any blood stocked up for me here, and it has been way too long since my last feed. I just haven't wanted to be away from him to do so.

He starts to move away from me. "You stay here and I'll go get you some blood. I'll be real quick, then we'll pick this straight back up."

I stop him, taking hold of his arm. "No. It's okay, I can go myself."

He looks back at me.

"I've fed myself for the last six months, remember?"

I see a flicker of pain in his eyes. Well done for reminding him, Alex. Really, well done.

"I remember," he says, low.

"Sorry," I cringe. "Hey, look I've got an idea," I say brightly, as it suddenly appears in my mind.

This I know he will definitely like.

Climbing over him I get out of bed, and go over to his wardrobe. I can feel him watching me, with interest, and unmistakable lust in his eyes. I love that the sight of me naked has him feeling the way I think he is feeling right now. Because I know one million percent that the sight of him does exactly the same to me.

"Care to share?" he asks as I open the wardrobe doors wide.

"No. It's a surprise."

"What are you doing?" he questions, as I start rummaging through his wardrobe.

"Getting us both some clothes." I pull out a pair of his jeans and his Jim Morrison T-shirt. I love him in that. I toss them over onto the bed where he's still laid.

"So, you're dressing me nowadays too?" he quips.

Pushing the duvet and clothes aside, he sits up, putting his feet to the floor.

I grin at him over my shoulder and gain an involuntary shudder at the sight of him. I have had my hands and mouth all over that body. I mentally shake my head clear.

"You could do with the help," I say dryly.

"Well, can I get a shower first, ma'am?"

Still grinning, I say, "Sure thing. I'll jump in after you." I turn my attention back to the wardrobe. "Once I find something of yours to wear that'll fit me that is. I've had that dress on for the best part of two days now. I really need to get some new clothes."

I feel him come up behind me. Wrapping his arms around my chest, he nuzzles his face into my neck.

"How about you jump in the shower with me? Then afterwards I'll get some clothes from Scarlett for you to borrow."

Heat sizzles through me, cranking my body temperature up by about fifty degrees, almost melting me down into a puddle. And then I feel an unexpected but familiar pang in my mouth.

Oh crap. Well, this is new.

I inhale, trying to find a trace of blood anywhere on him. Nothing but what's under his skin.

Turning in his arms, I glance up at him, "Okay, but just a shower. And preferably a cold one."

I kink my lip showing him a fang.

I see the look of surprise in his eyes, and oddly very quickly followed by lust.

"That ever happened before when you've been turned on?"

"Who said I was turned on?"

He grins, quirking his eyebrow.

"Okay, well considering this is the first time I've been stood naked in a man's bedroom after about sixty orgasms and still find myself able to be turned on, then I'm gonna say – no."

"Has it happened at all while we've been making love?"

He just said making love, not sex. I feel all warm and fuzzy inside. I stop the grin that licks across my face.

"Not that I've noticed, and I'm pretty sure I would have noticed."

His eyes keep flicking to my mouth. But he doesn't look nervous, he looks kind of hungry, and I don't mean for food. He looks lusty and turned on.

"Do I need to be worried about this?"

"No."

I don't think he's actually listening to me right now.

And I am worried, but I don't tell him that. Yes, I have control, but hell, he wants me to shower with him, and Nathan and me showering together... Christ, just thinking about it is doing all kinds of crazy things to me, obviously, one of them being, bringing my fangs out for a show.

What will happen when I'm in there with him?

"I don't know, I think, maybe we shouldn't shower together while I'm like this. I mean I don't know how I'll react if I'm out of control." I shrug. "And I feel pretty much out of control when I'm around you, especially like this." I'm starting to flush again. "I just don't want to end up doing something stupid ... like biting you."

"Hmm," he murmurs, bringing his lips down to mine. "You're probably right ... we shouldn't shower together ... it's the smart thing to do."

He runs the tip of his tongue along the bottom of my fangs, one by one, and I almost lose all my self-control right here and now. "But then again, I never said I was smart."

And taking me by the hand, he pulls me toward the bathroom.

Oh God, what happened to practical Nathan?

Self-control, Alex.

Self. Control.

Chapter 27: Paradise

Nathan turns the engine off and we both climb out of the Range Rover.

"You sure you want to do this?" he asks again, taking me by the hand as we meet in front of the car.

"Sure I do. I have done it before you know."

"But you never wanted to do it before with me–"

"And now I do." I cut him off before he can say any more. I don't want this to lead into a conversation tied to Zeff. "I want to shift with you. I want to hunt with you. I want to be with *you*."

A grin commands his face, nearly melting me into yet another puddle right before him. He pulls his T-shirt off, sealing the deal. "Then your wish is my command."

Good, God. What did he have to go and say that for? It was hard enough being naked with him in the shower without doing anything. It turns out that I do actually possess some form of restraint, Nathan, not so much, but he did once I hammered my point home. Figuratively speaking of course.

Every fibre of me is singing in his view. His body is ridiculous. And I mean that in the greatest sense of the word.

It takes everything in me to tear my eyes away from him so I can undress. I'm literally like a dog in heat. Ironic, since I'm about to turn into one. Well, not a dog as such, but you know what I mean.

Taking off the last remaining item of clothing, I drop my undies onto the car bonnet.

Nathan raises an eyebrow. "Okay, so I was good in the shower. Great in fact. Actually, I was on my absolute fucking best behaviour considering how crazy hot you are, without even adding in the fact you were all soapy and wet. But shit, Alex, seriously, you naked out here in my territory … well, it's kind of getting hard to abstain." He looks down. I follow his gaze. "In the literal sense."

He smiles sexily and starts to move toward me. "If you need to bite me, seriously bite away. Whatever. I'll live." He grins, joking. Well, I hope he's joking.

Glancing at his dog tags resting on his perfect chest, then moving my eyes lower. I tuck my hair behind my ear, bite down on my bottom lip and look at him through my lowered lashes.

Good God, he's hot.

"We can't." I put a hand flat to his chest as he reaches me.

I watch him watching me.

"We can." He leans in against my hand.

Drawing me to him, his hands find my waist and he rubs circles into my skin with his thumbs, distracting the hell out of me. He's good, I'll give him that.

"Don't you ever get tired?" I ask, dryly, running my fingers over his dog tags.

His fingers stroke down my sides over my hips and he looks at me seriously. "Of you? Never." Another foxy grin. "You've turned me into a walking hard-on."

I let out a laugh. I love this side of Nathan. The side only I get to see, the one when he's happy and relaxed. I got a brief glimpse of it before everything went to shit. I missed it.

But things are great now between us, fantastic in fact, and I couldn't be more grateful for that. I haven't forgotten there is bad stuff out there waiting for me. I know I still have Isaiah the loon searching for me, and now Elijah the equal lunatic.

And I'll deal with those thoughts real soon.

But not now. I want to enjoy this, enjoy him, and some normality; well as normal as we can get, for as long as I can.

He's kissing my neck now and his hands are starting to wander away from my hips.

I wonder if Nathan behaved like this with his other girlfriends – hot and horny all the time. Okay, scrap that thought. It's making me feel sick. Actually, no think about it, it'll stop me from letting him get his way with me.

Nathan with other women. Ugh. It hurts more than distracts. Try again. Nathan mucking out the stables. Okay, here we go, I'm getting there.

His mouth fixed on mine, kissing me, his hands wandering everywhere. We're going to end up having sex here if he gets his way. What was that all about earlier, stopping us having sex so I could feed? It's like he's forgotten all about that.

But he was right. I do need to feed. And I need to stop this, but my mind isn't responding, it's just going along with the amazing feelings I'm having. But I could lose control and hurt him. Keep thinking yucky things, Alex.

Nathan milking a cow. Yep, that'll do it. Nathan milking, milk from a cow's udder. Oh God, gross.

There we go.

And somehow I manage to extract myself from him, using a great deal of self-restraint, and say, "Well, horny boy. You're just going to have to wait a while longer, because I'm not risking it. I'm not risking you."

Pushing him back gently, I give him a soft smile.

"Killjoy." He pouts, which only makes me want to kiss him.

Manure. Think manure, Alex, and cow udders.

"What happened to practical Nathan, you know the one from earlier? Who are you and what have you done with him?"

He lets out a low chuckle.

It does all kinds of evil things to me.

"Seriously, since when did I turn into the sensible one of the two of us?" I ask, bemused.

"Since you came back on fire."

I raise an eyebrow at him. "What do you mean?"

He cups my face with his hand. The contact drives me crazy.

"You're different Alex, but still the same, if that makes sense. You're just so independent and strong. You're full of determination and it's as hot as fucking hell."

He lets out a small laugh. "You used to need me, before … now, not so much – and it's okay." He says at my expression. "I like it."

"I need you," I say fervently, meeting my blue eyes to his green ones, ignoring the little voice in my head, saying I'm like this because of Zeff.

I'm stronger and more independent because he helped me to become a better version of myself. Better than the one that left Nathan sleeping in that hotel room that night.

I sweep my Jiminy Cricket to the back of my mind and watch as Nathan's smile turns into a slippery grin.

"You turned me on before, no doubt about that, but now, well you can see for yourself." He looks down and I follow his gaze.

We both look back up at the same time. I feel a strong frisson of energy; electricity and arousal flow between us.

Will it always be like this with him?

God, I hope so.

I bite down on a smile, which I think would have become a lusty smile had I not stopped it, and move away from him before he can try and get his way with me, again.

Then without looking at him, I shift into my other self.

I look up at him. He's smiling down at me. He looks impressed. He pulls his dog tags off over his head, dropping then on our pile of clothes, and then he shifts too. I've never seen him turn before. His fur is dark brown. He nuzzles into my own fur with his nose, sniffing me. Looks at me for a long moment and I see an almost smile in his eyes, then he takes off running.

I dart off after him, very quickly catching up.

We hunt together, and it's the most exciting and exhilarating feeling ever. After we've finished we lay together in the woods, sated.

I watch with my wolf eyes Nathan changing back to his human form. Then I let my body shift back too.

I lay on my front, propped up on my elbows, looking at him laid there on his back, staring over at me.

"You're amazing, you know that?" he says in a low voice.

"That a compliment, Hargreaves?" I tease. Nathan doesn't issue compliments often or freely. But he sure is throwing quite a few around today. "Because I could seriously get used to them."

"Maybe … Jones." He turns onto his side, facing me, and runs his fingertip lightly down my back. It sends a shiver rushing down my spine.

I can't believe I'm laid here in the woods, naked, and I actually feel comfortable.

And it's because I'm with him. He makes me feel so utterly safe and comfortable.

I rest my chin on my shoulder and stare at him.

He stares back.

"What are you thinking?" he asks, his voice warm.

"Nothing." I smile. "I'm just happy."

"And fed."

"Well, yeah, that too."

He leans closer and gives me a delicious kiss. Moving a breath away from my lips, he says, "Are you happy, here with me?"

I feel a sudden ache deep within my chest that he even has to ask. It knocks the wind out of me.

"Of course I am," I say emphatically.

He says nothing more, just stares into my eyes, piercing straight into my soul. But something tells me there's more to come. That there's more he wants to say … ask.

But he doesn't.

Do I think this because I keep expecting him to ask me about Zeff, and he doesn't? Not once has he mentioned his name, or anything Original wise, since I told him about Zeff yesterday at the stables.

I guess I just thought he'd be curious. I know I would be. He knows I spent a week with Zeff in Italy, I thought he would question the contents of that week. Have questions about Zeff, knowing exactly who and what he is. But so far, nothing.

Not a nada.

If it were me, I'd be more jealous of the thought of Nathan spending a serious amount of time with another woman, irrespective of who they were.

And part of me is glad he doesn't ask, don't get me wrong. But another part of me is bothered as to why he doesn't.

The rational side of me is saying, maybe he just doesn't want to know, that's simply it. The irrational side is saying … well you can probably guess what my irrational side is conjuring up.

But then ultimately there is nothing to know. Not really. A fleeting almost moment, that he doesn't need to know about, because it was nothing.

So it's a moot point.

I know that whatever I thought I might have been feeling for Zeff at that time was just me projecting my feelings for Nathan onto him.

My loneliness was looking for a substitute, and Zeff fit the bill.

Nathan starts to stroke the skin on my shoulder with his rough finger, removing all traces of thoughts over Zeff from my mind with it, trailing it down my arm, his eyes following. I watch him, watching me. He moves his attention back to my face, my mouth. I wet my dry lips. His gaze softens, and the way he's touching me and looking at me has my skin fizzing, tingling. The feeling rushing over me, taking complete hold.

You know that feeling, the one when you know you've finally got it. Got the one person you're meant to spend your whole life with, right here in front of you. Someone so truly amazing they beggar belief. And he wants you right back, as you are, asking for nothing in return.

Nathan is mine. My one.

The sensation makes me dizzy, heady.

"I want you in the worst kind of way," he murmurs.

And with his words, all my thoughts slide south of dirty.

Wearing nothing but a smile, he leans closer, his hard body pressed up against my side, he kisses me gently, lips barely touching. A little moan of pleasure escapes me.

That's all it takes for him.

I feel him harden against my leg, then shifting me up and onto my side, he rolls onto his back, pulling me on top of him in one fluid movement. He kisses me deeply, intensely, in only the way he can, making me feel like only he can. Unknowingly lifting me out of my jaded past, taking me far *far* away from all the pain and hurt I've carried around for so long, and he lands me into paradise.

Our paradise.

And I swear to all the gods, I'm never coming up for air again. I am never losing this feeling that I have right now, here, with him.

Chapter 28: Birthday Boy

"Careful, watch the door," I say, as I manoeuvre Nathan through into the dining room, my hands covering his eyes.

Jack, Craig, and Scarlett, are standing around the table in silent anticipation.

Today is the 5th of March. The day Nathan turns thirty.

I couldn't believe it when he told me that it was going to be his birthday today – such a coincidence. I only realised it was March when he told me.

My birthday is March 6th. I didn't tell him though. It's not important and I don't really feel like celebrating it.

I shopped online for Nathan's present, he hadn't exactly left me with much time. He was insistent he didn't want a present or to celebrate, but I told him to put a sock in it.

He's turning thirty, it's a big deal.

Borrowing Craig's laptop I searched online for ages, finally stumbling across something … well the only think I could think of to buy him really.

He's not so easy to buy for, I've discovered.

Well I ordered the gift, and Craig collected it first thing this morning for me, as I still can't go out in public around here. I'm just praying Nathan will like it.

I also ordered clothes, shoes, and underwear too, and had them delivered on express delivery. I'm wearing dark blue skinny jeans and a black strappy top. Simple yet, sexy. Oh and my new underwear of course. No more basic white bras and undies for me. Sexy, all the way from now on.

God bless the internet is all I can say.

I did have to borrow Craig's credit card though to pay online, but I gave him the cash straight away. His credit card bill will look interesting that's for sure … La Perla, Victoria's Secret, Topshop, H&M. I hate been trapped on the farm like this, having to rely on delivery and them to get things I need. Hopefully it won't be for too long.

I used the money that I should have given Zeff to pay for my passport to pay for Nathan's birthday present and my new stuff. I should feel guilty, I know I should, but right now I'm too mad with him to care. I've still got plenty of money left over, but I'm going to work here on the farm in exchange for my room and board. Jack didn't want me to pay him rent, but I was insistent.

I pay my own way from now on. No relying on anyone else.

Jack has cooked an amazing lobster dinner. He even let me and Scarlett help him cook, which is a first for Jack. It was awesome. I had a real blast in the kitchen with them both. It was really good to spend time with Scarlett, getting to know her better.

The table is all set up for dinner, candles lining the centre, and a pile of presents and cards at the end from us all.

Champagne is chilling in the cooler. Birthday cake at the ready. I really hope he likes it.

I'm so nervous I've got butterflies swooping circles in my stomach. We spent the morning together, but he went out this afternoon Carting with Craig, giving us time to surprise him with this meal tonight.

I position him in front of the table.

Sliding my hands away from his eyes, I say, "Happy birthday!"

Jack, Craig, and Scarlett, all chorus in too.

Moving around, I see the smile on his face. But I also know he's so uncomfortable right now. He really doesn't do the centre of attention thing. But I don't care. It's his birthday. And he's turned thirty. It's an important day, even if he says it isn't.

"Thank you," he murmurs, leaning down to kiss me on the cheek, just skimming shy of my lips. I still get spine tingles every single time he kisses me.

"It wasn't just me, it was a team effort." I smile around at everyone.

"Cheers guys," says Nathan.

"You're welcome, son," Jack pats him on the back. "And happy birthday."

I can see how happy Jack is that Nathan's happy.

And it makes me happy. That's a lot of happy's but rather that than going back to where we all were before.

"Happy birthday," chirps Scarlett.

"Yeah, happy birthday mate," Craig chips in.

"Food smells great, what're we having?" Nathan asks me.

"Lobster with garlic sauce."

His face lights up.

"It's all on Jack. He said lobster is your favourite." There's so much I still don't know about him. But I'm loving learning.

"It's ready to dish up now," says Jack, heading for the kitchen.

"You need a hand?" I ask, turning to him.

He shakes his head, "No. You all just sit yourselves down."

Jack loves having people to cook for and take care of. It's his thing for sure. I pull my chair out and sit down, Nathan sits beside me. Craig is opposite Nathan, Scarlett across from me.

"So I get presents too?" says Nathan, eyeing the little pile of gifts.

"Of course you do, silly," I nudge him with my elbow.

"Yours in there?" he nudges me back.

I shake my head. Mine is in my pocket, hidden from view.

Craig smiles at me over the table. A little conspiratorial smile.

Jeez, you'd think it was something big I've got him. Because it's not. Not really. Or maybe it is. I don't know.

I start to feel nervous and a little nauseous. My hand is resting on the table. I drum my fingers on it. I think Nathan senses my nerves because he reaches over and takes my hand in his, entwining our fingers. That one simple act from him calms me and sends shivers running all over my skin.

No one has ever been able to make me feel like he does. Or ever will again.

Jack starts to bring the food over, laying the platters in the centre of the table, and everyone quickly tucks in, presents momentarily forgotten.

There is no clean way to eat lobster, it's ridiculous. I'm making a real mess. But it's also delicious which makes it hard to care.

Nathan looks at me, a smile forming on his lips. He reaches over and wipes a dribble of garlic sauce from my chin, then licks it off his thumb. Heat flushes through me, intimately.

He leans over and gives me a soft kiss on the lips. I'm left feeling disappointed when he moves away and continues on eating.

Coming to, I glance around the table, wondering if anyone just saw our exchange. They are all too busy tearing into their lobster to have noticed. Then I just sit for a moment watching them all, eating, drinking, the odd exchange of idle chatter.

And it feels just like old times.

Except there's a few faces missing from around the table. A feel a pang for Sol and Erin. Carrie too, even though she was never here, I always wished she was.

But no, tonight is not about sadness of any kind, or discussing the Original's or vampires or anything. It's just about Nathan.

I filled Craig in, yesterday, about Zeff, and learnt a few things myself …

"So let me get this straight. You've met Matthias," Craig said, a puzzled expression on his face.

"Yes."

"And you thought he was someone else, because that's what he told wanted you to believe?"

"Yes."

"And he helped you? Wants to protect you from Isaiah?"

"Yep."

"And they haven't seen each other for eighteen years?"

"Nope."

"Wow. Shit. I know they cast me out, but hell, I thought I was still in the loop to a certain extent. But fuck, there's been a lot going on I didn't know about."

"Cast you out?"

Pause. "I'm kind of related to the Originals."

"What?!"

"It's not common knowledge, we have to keep it secret, obviously, but as you – know him, well then, I guess it's not such a big deal now."

My mouth opened forming an 'O'.

"Their aunt, Genevieve, she was my paternal, great great and beyond grandmother."

"Oh." I wondered if Craig has the magic gene at all. I didn't ask though.

"And my family. We the ones who are charged with protecting and keeping them both safe. Have done for generations. I didn't want in. I wanted a semblance of a normal life. Hence the cast out."

Apparently, that's why I felt that weird pull to Craig when I first met him. The bloodline. His bloodline is what in effect swims through my veins.

So I'm guessing that was part of the allure with Zeff too.

Anyway, enough Original talk. I don't want to think about Zeff. It's coming close to a week since I watched him drive away from me in Italy. And not a murmur.

I hope for it to stay that way. With all of them. No one knows I'm here. Still, I know I can't stay here permanently. But I'm in a bubble at the moment with Nathan and I don't want to burst it.

The real world is out there waiting to destroy me. So for now, I'm hiding in here with him.

I've noticed Nathan isn't really drinking much tonight, he's still on his first glass of champagne. I want him to have fun on his birthday, but still, I'm glad he's eased back on the drinking.

We get to the presents and cards before having the birthday cake. Jack didn't make it, he didn't have the time, so he bought one and it looks delicious.

"There's a card from Erin, Rose and ... Cal," Jack says, holding a card out to Nathan.

The temperature in the room drops to sub-zero.

Nathan's eyes flick to it. He stares at the card for a long moment but makes no attempt to pick it up.

Jack puts it down on the table.

"Get to it later," he says.

"And of course there's mine," Craig says, breaking the tense moment, handing him over a card and what looks to be a CD."

"I got you something too," Scarlett says, sounding nervous.

He opens the presents. Craig has got him the Coldplay album, and when he opens it, two tickets to go see them in concert at Wembley later this year falls out.

"Shit man," says Nathan. "This is awesome! Thanks!"

"Ah," Craig waves him off. "No probs. It's your thirtieth. It should have been more really."

"No mate, this is great," Nathan enthuses, eyes scanning the text on the tickets.

"I got you two, so you and Alex could go together."

"No," I say to Nathan, raising my hand in resistance. "You should go with Craig."

"Already got myself a ticket to go to," he grins. "Scarlett too." She smiles, seemingly already aware of this. "I thought we could make a weekend of it."

"Sounds great," Nathan beams, squeezing my leg under the table. "Don't you think?"

I nod, smiling.

I'm worried about going out in public like that here. But then the gig is in November which is ages away. And it is in London. I don't think anyone would recognise me down there. But, then, will I still even be here to go. I shove the thought from my head. Either way I'll be with Nathan. I'm never leaving him again.

"You not down for it?" I ask, Jack trying to stay upbeat for Nathan's sake.

He rumbles out a laugh. "Not my scene love. Give me Cat Stevens any day."

"My turn," Scarlett jumps in eagerly, holding her gift out for Nathan to take.

I helped her pick his present. I know how much Nathan likes his vintage T-shirts, so she ordered him a vintage Rolling Stones T-shirt online. We got it on express delivery so it would be here in time.

"Cool, thanks," he says pulling it out of the wrapping paper, holding it out to look at.

Putting it on the table he pulls the Metallica T-shirt off he's currently wearing and pulls his new T-shirt on.

"Fits perfect," he says to Scarlett, smiling.

I think that was his way of letting her know he loves her gift. What he fails to realise is he's just left the poor girl rigid in her seat and blushing at the sight of his bare chest. I know for sure I am and I get to see it regularly.

He sees her as a little sister I think, which is sweet. I think she might have the teeniest tiniest crush on him. Not that I'd ever say anything. It's understandable, though. Nathan has that closed off bad boy way about him that women just love, especially teenage girls, and he is really beautiful to look at. Sometimes I don't think he realises the effect he has on women.

And I love that he's mine.

I smile at Scarlett over the table, widening my eyes and lifting my eyebrows, giving her a 'what are men like' look. Returning my smile, she seemingly relaxes

It's Jack's turn next. He suddenly looks anxious. Not like Jack at all. He picks his present up off the table and hands it to Nathan.

"Happy birthday, son."

Nathan opens the box and inside is a watch. It looks really old and antique. "It was your Granddad's," Jack says.

"Your Nan bought it for him as a wedding present. I've had it for so long and it's just been gathering dust, so I took it to the jewellers and had it fixed up and back to working."

A truly genuine smile is on Nathan's face. I feel a lump in my throat.

"Thanks, dad." I can hear deep emotion in Nathan's voice. It's not something you hear often from him, so you know when you do he means it. Nathan puts the watch on, looking at it for a long moment.

And now it's my turn. I really didn't think this present through now faced with having it to give him. I feel stupid.

I don't want it to give him now, in front of everyone. Craig knows what it is of course. It's just Nathan is not easy to buy for, and he did brand himself with my name in Arabic. But one of the main reasons I got him this gift is because Nathan has abandonment issues.

Not that he'd ever admit it. But it goes back to his mum leaving. Stupidly, I'd never really taken it into consideration until talking to Jack. And me leaving him like I did, at that time, so soon after Sol – well even though for the right reasons, it wasn't great for Nathan. So I got him this gift, because I want him to know how much he means to me, and that I am committed to him, everything else aside.

Everyone is looking at me expectantly. Oh God. My face is starting to heat.

Hell, why am I so nervous? I mean it's not like I'm asking him to marry me or anything.

Craig gives me a look of encouragement.

Okay, here goes. If he hates it, thinks it's stupid, well, it's no big deal. I won't be gutted at all.

Okay, well maybe just a little bit.

I reach into my jeans pocket and pull the little box out. I see his eyes widen when he sees it.

"Don't worry," I say hastily. "I'm not asking you to marry me or anything. It's just – it's a promise ring," I explain as I hand it to him.

My face is bright red, and I can't bring myself to look at anyone. It's that quiet you could hear a bloody spider drop in here.

He opens the box.

There are two rings in there. One for him. One for me. Stainless steel, both engraved inside with, 'Forever'.

Okay, I know it's corny, but have you seen him, and I'm in love. Like never before.

"One for you and one for me," I explain, as he sees the two rings. I was going to take mine out, but I thought it better to leave them together, so he'd get the meaning.

"I guessed," he says smiling. A real smile. A huge smile in fact.

Does this mean he likes it?

He takes his ring, the larger of the two, out of the box, and looks at it. Looking at the engraving inside.

"You wear it on your right hand," I say. "I mean of course you wouldn't wear it on your left, that's what people do when they get married. And you don't have to wear it if you don't want to – of course." I'm babbling.

Shit, this embarrassing.

He looks at me. Then without hesitation he slides the ring onto the ring finger on his right hand. He takes the smaller ring, my ring, out of the box, all the while, staring at me intensely, for a long moment, and my heart starts to cartwheel. He takes hold of my right hand and gently pushes it onto my ring finger.

Is this what people feel like when they are getting engaged? Because if it's anywhere near as intense as this, I think I would actually explode if Nathan did ever see crazy and ask me to marry him.

I gulp down.

I feel like the world has shrunk down to just us two. He leans forward and presses his lips to mine, murmuring quietly, "I love it, and I love you. Thank you."

"Get a room!" jests Craig.

We break apart, smiling. My face is still a shade of beetroot.

"So, time for birthday cake," says Jacks, clapping his hands together he stands.

I notice his voice is a little gruff. Then I see a sheen in his eyes as he turns. I feel a tug on my heartstrings once again.

Nathan takes my right hand in his, entwining our fingers, he stares down at our rings side by side.

Then he looks up, meeting my eyes, and smiles at me again, intimately. And I know at this moment I did the right thing getting the rings.

Chapter 29: Close Shave

It's late when they start filtering off to bed. Jack's the last left, but I usher him off to bed making him a hot chocolate to take with him, telling him I'll load the dishwasher and finish up cleaning the kitchen.

One, because he looks knackered. And two, because I'm dying for some alone time with Nathan.

Nathan thanks Jack again for the watch just as he's retreating. Then seemingly out of the blue, he hugs Jack. I see the flicker of surprise, then genuine emotion on Jack's face as he hugs Nathan back, and I nearly burst out crying.

I have to turn away to clear my eyes of the welling tears. I get the distinct impression hugs from Nathan to Jack happen, rarely, if ever.

Then it's just the two of us.

Nathan goes over to the table, where I'd purposefully left Cal's card. I might hate the guy but he is Nathan's brother, and the card was from Erin and Rose too. He loves them, if anything.

He stares down at the blue envelope for a long moment, I pretend to not be paying any attention as I wipe the countertop clean.

Finally he picks it up and opens it. He screws the envelope into a ball and tosses it onto the table. Opening the card, I watch his eyes as they read, looking for any hint of emotion. He presses his lips together, concealing whatever emotion was trying to escape. Then he folds the card over and shoves it in his back pocket.

"Okay?" I ask, as he walks over to me.

"Yep. You need a hand?" he touches the small of my back.

"No. Just the dishwasher left to load. You go and relax."

"I'll help."

"It's your birthday. Go sit down." I put on my best commanding voice.

"I'm helping." He nudges me with his hip. Smiling up at him, I shake my head and nudge him back.

"I'll rinse. You load."

I can hardly keep my eyes off him while we work in comfortable silence. Every time he bends down to put a plate in the dishwasher his new T-shirt rides up and I get a show of his toned abs, and a bolt of lust shoots through me, and I just want to take his new T-shirt off for him again.

I'm set on lust twenty-four-seven. Being away from Nathan for so long was so incredibly hard, and now that I'm here with him it's hard to stay away, and to not touch him incessantly.

I've had quite a few glasses of champagne tonight so my emotions are slightly heightened, but even still it wouldn't matter. I just have to be near him. Touching him constantly. He doesn't seem to mind though, and if anything he's just as bad. He has his hands on me plenty.

We're in the early stage of our relationship; a relationship neither of us thought we'd ever have, so whereas it's normally all lust and sex, yeah well times it by about ten thousand and you'll be about where we are right now.

I know it will at some point wear off, not anytime soon I hope, but while it's here I'm going to make the most of it and enjoy it to the max. After not having him in my life for so long I don't want to take a single thing about him for granted.

I hand him the last plate and dry my hands on the towel. As he leans over putting it in the dishwasher rack I move behind him and put my water cooled hands under his T-shirt and slide them around his waist. I hear his sharp intake of breath.

"So, it's just me and you," I murmur.

I can practically feel his smile. I don't need to see his smile to feel it, I know it like it's my own and it spreads over my skin like the warm evening air.

He straightens up and turns in my arms. Placing his hands on my shoulders, he smoothes them down my arms in a very slow deliberate movement. "Just the way I like it."

"Is it selfish that I want you to myself all the time?"

"Not at all." He leans down and kisses the side of my mouth, ever so gently. "I'd call us even on that score."

His lips graze over mine as he moves central, his breath caressing my skin.

I make a noise somewhere between a gasp and a moan.

It seems to have an effect on him because without taking his mouth off mine, he reaches his hand back, shoves the dishwasher door shut, then picks me up and turns with me, depositing me onto the counter.

I love it when he takes control like this.

He presses his face into the curve where my neck and shoulder meet and runs his tongue over my skin. I entwine my legs around his, keeping him held tight against me.

"Mmm," he murmurs. "You taste sweet."

"I reek of garlic."

"So do I." He presses his lips softly to mine. His hands go to the small of my back. "But even garlicky you're still incredibly sexy … so is this the rest of my birthday present? You, I mean."

Biting the grin on my lips, I say, "I'm a sure thing for you every day, not just on your birthday you know."

He grins back at me, then moves a hand to my thigh, rubbing over my jeans with his thumb, moving higher and higher.

"We should go upstairs," I mutter, feeling all kinds of breathless the higher his hand goes, tremors rolling from my head to my toes.

"We should," he murmurs, moving his hand up toward the button on my jeans.

"I don't think I could ever look Jack in the eye again if we defile his kitchen."

Nathan stops and he raises his eyebrow. "Defile?"

I laugh, softly.

"Come on, we'll go up to our bedroom. I'll defile you there instead," he chuckles.

Pausing, with my hands pressed against his chest, I utter surprised, "*Our* bedroom?"

My heart without warning starts to thud in my chest.

He shifts on his feet, looking at the floor. "It doesn't have to be – I just thought–"

I put my hand to his cheek, and he looks up at me. "I want it to be *ours*. More than anything."

He grins and my stomach fills with fairies fluttering about.

Then he lifts me down off the counter and takes me by the hand, leading me upstairs.

When we're heading down the hall toward our room, I suggest a detour to the bathroom to freshen up, basically rid myself of the smell of garlic.

We stand side by side at the sink brushing our teeth. I stare at him in the mirror.

"Is the beard a keeper?" I ask.

He spits out in the sink and rinses his toothbrush.

"You don't like it?" He rubs his hand over his beard. "I thought you liked me with stubble?" The twinkle in his eye is unmistakable.

I spit out too and clean my toothbrush.

"Stubble, I like." I turn to his side to touch is face. "With the full beard I can't see your face properly." I reach up on my tiptoes and kiss the hair free smooth part of his cheek. "I like seeing your face."

"So the beard goes." His voice is suddenly gravelly.

He slides a hand around my waist and pulls me in front of him, leaning me back against the sink. Bracing a hand either side of me, gripping hold of the sink, he leans down and he lowers his mouth to mine, kissing me, gently, slowly. He tastes all fresh and minty and yummy.

When he drifts his mouth away from mine, his eyes aglow with desire, I take the opportunity to reach over and grab a razor off the shelf, waggling it before him.

"Now?" he says.

"As good a time as any."

"You're going to make me shave my beard off on my birthday?"

"Call it a birthday present."

He looks at me confused. "How is me shaving my beard off a present for me? I am kind of attached to it, you know. It keeps me warm in the cold weather." He puts a mock-dramatic hand to his beard.

I have a flashback to being in his car with him … him telling me I had to cut my hair off … me covering my hair with my hands … Nathan yelling at me …

"You've got me to keep you warm now," I say, feeling irked by the memory, and also a little frustrated. "Just call it an early birthday present for me then."

"When is it your birthday?" he inquires, raising an eyebrow.

Okay, so I walked straight into that one. "Oh … um … *tomorrow,*" I raise a little smile.

"Shit," he sighs, dramatically. "I should have known this. How did I not know this?"

"Because I didn't tell you."

"Why?"

"Because I'm not really that bothered about it, I don't want any fuss, and it's your birthday today – your *thirtieth* birthday," I highlight the point. "It's more important than mine. I'm only turning twenty-seven."

"*Nothing* is more important than you." He traces my jaw with his fingertips. Butterflies swarm my stomach. "And you're saying me having a shave is what you want for your birthday?" he reaffirms.

Smiling, I nod vigorously. Really all I want is him period.

"You're easy to please." A grin. He reaches a hand up to take the razor from me, but I pull it back.

He looks at me confused.

"Do you trust me?" I ask, provocatively.

His eyes pool. "With my life."

"Let me shave you?"

He closes his eyes briefly in agreement. Side-stepping him, I put the lid down on the toilet, instructing Nathan to sit down on it. I fill the sink with warm water and get the shaving foam off the shelf. I wet my hands, then kneeling down before him, I squirt foam into my hands, lathering it up, I rub it all over his beard.

"It's kind of cool our birthdays are right next to each other," he says, face covered in foam.

I chuckle. "Means we won't forget them."

"I'd never forget yours," he says. "How could I ever forget the day you landed on this planet, destination my way."

Call it corny, but I think that is the most romantic thing anyone has ever said to me. "I'd kiss you right now if you weren't covered in foam."

He grins, "Save it for later?"

"Deal."

I pick the razor up from the edge of the sink. Nathan tilts his head to the side and I very carefully start to shave his beard off.

When I've removed all trace of the hair from his beautiful face, Nathan surveys my work in the mirror while I rinse the sink clean and put the razor back.

I did a pretty good job if I do say so myself. No nicks or cuts at all.

Getting the aftershave lotion off the shelf I squeeze a small amount on my hand, spreading it between my palms by rubbing them together.

"Here," I say, holding up my hands to him.

Turning to me, Nathan bends at the knees, coming down to my height. I press my hands softly against his cheeks and gently rub the lotion into his skin using my fingers.

"So, do I look better for you?" he asks, his still minty breath blowing over me as he speaks.

Keeping my fingertips resting lightly against his cheeks, I reply in a low voice, "You always look good to me."

I lean in and press a soft kiss to his lips.

Nathan scoops me up into his arms, emitting a little squeal from me, and carries me across the hall to our bedroom.

He pushes the door closed with his foot and deposits me on the bed. Climbing on top of me he starts kissing my neck, the skin on his face so soft and smooth against mine, he feels like heaven. He slides his hand up my top.

Moving back, he eases it up. I lift, allowing him to pull it over my head, then I lay back down.

His eyes appraise me. "Nice bra." He trails a finger over the black lace.

"Glad you approve."

"Oh, I more than approve," he murmurs, leaning down to kiss the exposed skin on my breast, lips drifting over the fabric of my bra.

Wild desire drives through me. I'm just about to grab him and get straight down to business when he sits up, pulls his T-shirt off, and tosses it to the floor. He returns straight back to me though. I wrap my arms around his neck as he kisses mine. He moves, kissing a path down my chest, working his way around my bra.

I push my fingers into his short hair, lifting my stomach, when his lips reach it. I miss his hair; I can't wait until it grows back.

"So did you have a good birthday?" I ask, in a murmur.

His trails his tongue around my belly button. "I had a great birthday."

He moves to kiss my scar. I don't make any attempt to hide it from him now. It's a part of who I am. He accepted me for that a long time ago. I shiver deep within and my legs start to tremble. He peels my skinny jeans off, then gives my lacy knickers an approving grin before removing them too.

"How's your birthday going so far," he asks, as he pushes himself into me.

"It's not my birthday yet," I breathe, lifting my hips. My whole body shivering in reaction to him.

His eyes flick to the clock. "It's past midnight."

"Oh, well in that case, it's going awesome."

He rests down on his elbows and kisses me gently on the lips. He stills inside me for a moment.

"Happy birthday." His lips brush over mine. "And you know I'm getting you a birthday present right?" he says, moving again, ever so slightly.

"I don't need one. I have everything I need right here."

"I love you," he whispers, kissing me.

"I love you too."

He moves out of me, again, then pushes deeper inside. "And I'm buying you a present, end of."

"Okay," I gasp.

Chapter 30: Never Tear Us Apart

"You can come out now!" Nathan hollers from the back door.

Why he's shouting I have no clue. He knows I can hear him talking at a normal level, from way across the garden.

Chuckling, I get up from the sofa and make my way into the kitchen.

Nathan's had me sat waiting in here while he sets up for my birthday meal. I told him I didn't want any fuss. He told me neither did he, but I didn't listen to him – did I.

I had no come back.

Who would have thought all those months ago, eight months to be exact, that mean hard Nathan who I argued with all the time, would be making me a birthday meal. Or that I'd be crazy in love with him.

I'm trying not to think about how I celebrated my birthday last year. With Carrie, Eddie, Angie, and Tom. A different lifetime ago. Sometimes it's hard to believe how much my life has changed since then.

I walk through the open back door to see Nathan standing in the garden. Behind him is a small table set up for two. The garden adorned with fairy lights, all twinkling away, and there's a heater lamp by the table to keep the chill at bay. Also a little table set up with his iPod docking station, his new Coldplay album playing in the background.

It's amazing. The most amazing thing I have ever seen. I can't help the big smile that forms on my face.

"You like?" he asks, smiling nervously.

"I love," I say, walking over to him.

He wraps his arms around me as I reach up on my tiptoes, kissing him lightly on the lips.

"I know you didn't want to do anything but I couldn't not celebrate your birthday."

"Two parties in two days. We are spoilt."

"I think after the year we've had we more than deserve it."

I wrap my arms tight around him, holding him close.

"Come on," he says. "Dinner will be getting cold."

"Ooh, what are we having?" I ask, as he helps me into my seat. He's being very attentive and very gentlemanly tonight. I could get used to this side of him.

"Homemade ravioli in tomato and chilli sauce."

"Wow," I say, impressed. "I thought the extent of your cooking was a fry up."

He looks sheepish. "It is. Dad made it earlier. I just reheated it."

Talking of Jack, he, Scarlett, and Craig, are noticeably absent tonight. Probably gone to the pub to give us some time alone.

I reach across the table and squeeze his hand. "I don't care who made it, I just care who I'm eating it with."

He gives a gentle smile. Then loosening his hand from mine he pulls a bottle of champagne out of the cooler beside his seat, takes the foil off, and pops the cork.

"I could seriously get used to this drinking champagne all the time, you know."

"Hey, stable drinker here if you don't mind," he chuckles.

Nathan really has cut back on his drinking. Not stopped entirely, but he's not relying on it to get him through the day. I know that it has a lot to do with me being here. I worry what would happen if I'm not, again.

"I never said I was going to share it with you," I nudge his leg under the table with my foot.

Grinning, he pours the champagne into my glass, then his own. I take a sip, loving the feel of the bubbles down the back of my throat. We get tucked into dinner and it's wonderful. Jack is an amazingly good cook.

We talk through dinner about anything and everything. Nathan even talks a little about Sol, without once shutting down. It's progress in the biggest sense of the word.

Everything is so perfect right now. I can hardly believe it. I'm just waiting for our bubble to burst.

When we've finished our ravioli Nathan goes inside, telling me he'll be back out in a minute.

He returns in just that, with a mint chocolate cheesecake, which I'm hazarding a guess Jack also made.

There's a lit candle in the middle.

Setting it down on the table between us, he says, "Make a wish."

I close my eyes, making a wish. A wish that … well if I tell you then it won't come true, will it.

I lean forward and blow the candle out.

Nathan takes the candle out of the cake and cuts me a piece. Putting it onto a small plate, he hands it to me.

I pick up the spoon and slice a piece off, putting it in my mouth. "Oh my God," I murmur, closing my eyes, savouring the taste which is exploding in my mouth right now. "This is amazing."

He chuckles. "I remember you told me once that mint choc-chip ice-cream was your favourite dessert, but I thought the ice-cream might melt with the candle so this was the next best thing."

I'm surprised and touched he remembered such a small detail. I wonder what else he remembers. I open my eyes to find he's already watching me.

"It's way better than the next best thing."

When I've finished stuffing my face with cheesecake and have drained my champagne glass empty, twice, Nathan gets up from the table and goes over to the iPod.

'Never Tear Us Apart' by Inxs, starts to drift out of the speakers.

I haven't heard this song in forever.

He turns and looks at me. "Dance with me."

I have a vivid flashback to being with Zeff in the club. Dancing with Zeff. Almost kissing him.

I blink myself free.

Wordlessly, and feeling oddly nervous, I get to my feet and walk toward him. My heart is swimming around my chest.

Nathan pulls me close and slides his arms around me. I put my arms around his neck as we start to move to the music.

He starts to hum, slipping into the words, his voice surprisingly lovely.

I have an intense rush of love for him. And I know, unequivocally, that whenever I hear this song I will always think of him and this moment.

Tears, surprisingly, fill my eyes. Briefly closing them, forcing them back, I take a deep breath in.

"I didn't know you could sing."

"There's a lot you don't know about me." He smiles down at me, and I remember the first time he said that to me, here in this very garden.

I stare into his vivid green eyes. "This really is a perfect night."

"You're perfect."

"You know you're turning into a walking cliché, right?" I grin, mischievously.

"A walking hard-on – a walking cliché – whatever next?"

"I don't know, but I'm looking forward to finding out," I say quietly, laying my head against his chest. I move my hands around his back and hold him tight.

I feel his deep intake of breath, almost with an air of hesitation, like he's going to say something. Then after what seems to be a long moment, he holds me tighter, but he doesn't speak. And we stay here dancing long after Michael Hutchence sings his last word.

We're laid in bed together, my head on Nathan's chest listening to his heart beating while he strokes my hair, when he gives me my birthday present.

Reaching down he picks his jeans up off the floor, retrieving something out of the pocket. He sets a jewellery box on his chest, before me. The type of box which necklaces usually come in.

"Don't worry, I'm not asking you to marry me," he laughs, taking the piss out of me over last night.

He could ask me to marry him and I'd say yes, no hesitation. Seriously. I can hardly believe I'm thinking these things, but I am. I would marry Nathan tomorrow if I could.

"I meant to give you it earlier," he says. "But we got a little carried away while we were dancing."

I can't help but smile at the memory.

Kissing, the kissing getting heated, us stumbling back into the house and barely making it upstairs to bed. You can guess the rest.

I incline myself up to rest on my elbow and pick the box up. Nervously, I open it.

There's a key inside. I look at him, confused.

"It's for the front door." He takes a deep breath and I realise he's nervous.

I have a swell of love for him, so big, it almost engulfs me whole.

"I want you to know this is your home and you can always come back here, no matter what. If you ever have to leave again, for whatever reason, that key is me telling you, you can come back whenever and I will always be here waiting for you."

I have the biggest lump in my throat. I reach up and gently kiss his lips. "I love it. Thank you. But I'm never leaving again. You know that right?"

"Yes," he says. But I can hear in his tone that he doesn't entirely believe me.

And I'm not sure if I do. Not that I would ever leave him voluntarily. But that choice could very easily be taken away from me. As it has been done so in the past.

I lay my cheek against his chest again, holding the box in my hand. Then I see something sparkly dangling before my eyes. A necklace, white gold with a diamond set heart pendant.

I sit up, looking at him shocked.

"You didn't think I was just going to get you a key for your birthday, did you?" He's grinning.

"I'd have been happy with just the key."

"Mmm."

"But the diamonds totally work too."

"I can imagine." He chuckles as he sits up and lays it around my neck, fastening the clasp at the back.

"How does it look?" I ask, touching the cool metal against my neck as he lays back down.

"Beautiful."

I rest back down on his chest. "I can't believe you bought me diamonds."

I never figured Nathan for a diamond buying type of guy. I like that he can surprise me.

"Only the best, for the best," he exhales.

"Another cliché?" I giggle.

"Yep."

We lay here in comfortable silence for a while, Nathan stroking my hair again, but I've been feeling tension rising in him

So I'm not at all surprised when he says, "Would you have ever come back to me if the Original hadn't found you?"

His voice is so quiet in the dark.

This question has been a long time coming.

I lift my head up off his chest, resting my forearms there.

"Yes, I would have," I say resolutely. I don't want him to ever think anything different. "When, I don't know? But one day I would have found my way back here to you. Because I'm meant to be with you."

Pressing his lips together, he drifts into a long blink, then he cups my face with his hands and guides me to his lips. He kisses me, hard. And before I know it we're making love again.

He stares down at me intently in the darkness. "I know what I said about the key and that I would always be here waiting for you, but … the truth is, I don't want to be without you again – I can't be without you."

"Me either," I touch his face. He kisses my wrist.

"Promise me something?" he whispers.

"Anything."

I'd promise him my soul right now if it would keep him moving inside me like this. Every nerve ending in me is singing. I've never felt a need like it before. It's not a physical need; it's a pure, unadulterated, emotional need.

"You'll never leave me."

"I promise."

"Say it."

"I'll never leave you," I breathe.

He seals his mouth over mine, kissing me deeply, passionately, emotionally. And we end my birthday just like we did his, making love. Except this time it's intense and emotional. And afterwards I have the strong urge to cry, but I don't.

It's almost as if I know our happiness will soon be over. And I think Nathan knows it too.

Chapter 31: From Good to Worse

I roll over, smoothing a hand over the empty space in our bed where Nathan was sleeping a short while ago, smiling to myself.

He got up early to do some work on the farm, leaving me to have a lie in.

Life is good. Simple.

During the day I work on the farm. We all eat dinner together. Or Nathan takes me out for an early evening picnic.

Late night walks. Hunting together. Watching movies. Nathan reads to me. Another thing I didn't know about him, he likes to read. A lot. I like to sit curled up with him while he reads to me. We do what normal couples do together, except for the shifting, hunting and drinking of blood for me. But that's normal for us.

I've been back home for almost two weeks. We don't talk about the future. We talk about today. Maybe that's because neither of us wants to tempt fate by talking about the future, in case something turns up to take it away. Take me away.

I shower, then come back into our bedroom and get dressed. Taking my still dry hair out its ponytail from the shower, I brush it, leaving it down. Just how Nathan likes it.

Opening the curtains to the day, I see Nathan is in the garden watering the plants. Probably sounds stupid but I kind of miss him. I hate not being around him. I feel like a part of me is missing when I'm not with him.

Going downstairs, I don't bother with breakfast. Instead I go straight outside to see him. He turns, lowering the hose, puts the clip down, halting the water. He smiles at me. It melts me to the ground.

"Hey," he murmurs. "You enjoy your lie in?"

He holds his arm out for me and I move into his embrace. I reach up on my tiptoes and kiss him.

His deliciousness warms right through me. "It was okay. Would have been better if you'd been there."

"Work to be done," he says.

"You need a hand?" I offer.

"Sure." He smiles. "Go have your feed and I'll find a job for you." A wink.

"Okay," I sigh, mock-drama, and reluctantly move out of his hold.

As I turn, I hear before I see, Craig in the tractor at the far side of the field, driving along singing to himself. He's a funny guy. I like him a lot. Then I see Jack and Scarlett coming out of the woods, heading in the direction of the barn. She must have gone with him to visit with Sol. I'll go later. I'm sure Nathan will be ready to visit again.

We went a few days ago to visit Sol's grave. It was hard for Nathan. It was hard for me to see him so broken up. But this time he let me be there for him. He didn't cry. I could tell he was holding back, but we talked about Sol for a long time.

I tried to make him see that Sol's death was not his fault. Just like Carrie's wasn't mine. He said he could see that Sol's death wasn't his fault. I know he was lying to me, telling me what he thought he should be saying. Nathan will always blame himself. Like a small part of me with always blame myself for Carrie. Even though I know events are out of our control, the rational side doesn't connect with the guilty side.

Just these last few days I'm already seeing the heavy burden of Nathan's guilt lifting just a tad, allowing him to finally grieve for Sol, and he's slowly finding a way to cope with it.

I'm just walking back through the garden toward the house when I feel the squirt of water on my back, soaking through my T-shirt.

I spin around to Nathan, who is wearing a big playful mischievous look on his face. He raises the hose again, aiming it straight for me.

"You bloody better not!" I warn, putting a hand to the damp patch on my back.

His eyes are alight with a wicked glint. "Call it long overdue payback for the time you soaked me at the lake."

I put my hand up protectively. "I never soaked you! I just wet you a little."

Mischief sparkles in his eyes.

Aim … fire…

"Arghh! You shit!" I screech as he squirts me again, this time drenching me. "I'm bloody soaked!"

Right, now it's game on. And with nothing to lose, I run at him – my sole aim to get that hose off him and give him a good soaking.

He moves quickly, laughing, dodging me at each turn, but I finally catch him from behind and try to wrestle the hose from him, but he's not letting go, squirting it under at me, soaking me through. I manage to grab a hold of the hose in his hand and twist it around and spray it up in his face, soaking him.

Laughing, breathless, and both ending up drenched, we flop down on the grass side by side. My breaths are coming in fast and heavy, and it's not because I'm worn out – it's because I am exhilarated. And happy. So very happy.

I turn my head to the side to look at him. He stares back at me. I can read Nathan's eyes like they are his thoughts. He's so clear for me to see. And then I desperately, urgently, want him to kiss me. He rolls on top of me, taking my face in his hands and kisses me, deeply, passionately. I kiss him back with fervour. We stay like that for a long time.

"I'm soaked," I grumble, pouting, as I start to become aware of the dampness all around me.

"You look beautiful," he says. "But we should really get you out of these wet clothes." He tugs at my soppy T-shirt, which is clinging to my skin like a second skin. "I don't want you to catch cold."

"Hmm, no we wouldn't want that, would we?"

"Well if you get sick, I won't be able to do this." He leans down to my neck and ever so gently licks a running drop of water off my skin. Every particle of me is sent into frenzy from that one single action.

"No. We definitely don't want you to stop doing that." I turn my face to his, "I love you."

Pressing a gentle kiss to my lips, he whispers, "I love you too."

Lifting off me, he gets up and pulls me to me feet. I look up at him, feeling all shades of pink ridiculous happiness. A movie kind of happiness. The kind of happiness that not so long ago I didn't think I deserved, let alone would ever have the chance to feel. And I feel it, right now, because of him.

He might be hard work at times. Rough and damaged. Harsh and callous. He has demons. So do I. Mine are quite possibly worse. I have the potential to be a killer. One drop of pure human blood past my lips, and I know I'll be changed for good. For the worst. There's kind of no topping that.

He is so gentle and tender with me. So utterly sweet and loving. And boy is he good in bed. Really good. Am I grinning? Yes. Damn bloody right I am.

He's mine and I am his. And nothing else will ever come between us again. I wrap my arms around his soggy waist, resting my head against his chest and holding him tight. He puts strong arms around me and presses his lips to my wet hair.

And then it's this exact moment that I know, all those words, all this happiness is lost. For now at least. Or maybe forever.

They are here. And there is not another second to think.

I break away from Nathan wide eyed. He looks back at me equally taken by surprise. Then we are both moving into action.

Is that all these guys ever do – surprise attacks? I guess so because I'd sense them, well, if I was listening out for them.

Silver, I need silver.

Thinking fast, I run for the house, I manage to dodge a vampire coming straight for me, striking him with an elbow jab to his ribs, temporarily winding him.

Nathan is yelling my name, telling me to run, but I'm not running away. I just need to get in the house and get a gun. There's one in every room. Nathan made sure of that since I came back. Ever the cautious. I guess we just didn't plan for an outside attack. Not an attack at all really. How do these fuckers keep finding me?

Focus Alex.

I fly into the house, yanking open the kitchen drawer, I pull the gun out, safety off, and I fire straight for the bastard who is still hot on my tail. I hit him in the chest, but not the heart, so as he advances quickly, I hold my breath, aim, and fire. He dusts before my eyes.

I grab the pack of silver bullets out the drawer, ram them in my pocket, grabbing one of Jack's large sharp silver cooking knives. I head for the back door.

I'm grabbed from behind. Spinning, I'm just about to drive the knife into the heart of my attacker when his voice comes in my ear.

"Bunny."

"Zeff?!" I spin around, wild and wide eyed.

Surprising to me, I actually feel an overwhelming rush of affection for him, and I also kind of want to punch him too. But knowing he is here gives me a huge sense of relief. He's an Original. A one man ninja bad ass kicking band. Or something less dorky sounding. I've seen him in action. He fears nothing.

"I need to get you out of here."

He grabs my arm and tries to tug me toward him.

"NO!" I yell, yanking my arm free. "I'M NOT LEAVING THEM OUT THERE!"

Is he fucking insane.

I'm moving quickly toward the open back door. Then Zeff is in front of me. For a second I think he's trying to block my path, then I realise he's protecting me.

Another vampire appears through the doorway in an instant, this one armed with a gun. But he's not expecting Zeff, and Zeff drives a silver blade which appeared from out of nowhere straight into his heart, dusting him. Does he keep them up his sleeve or something?

He glances at the gun on the floor. Picking it up, he says, "Tranquilliser gun. They came prepared."

Not caring about the gun, just needing to get to Nathan, and knowing there's no more vampires lurking outside the house, I push past Zeff, searching for Nathan.

I see him. He's fighting two vampires. My heart thuds with a dull thump, down into my feet.

I see him throw one off him, and then with one hard swing Nathan knocks the other one off his feet.

That's it baby, kick his arse!

I start to run toward him, shoving the knife into my back pocket as I move. I raise the gun. My aim is going to be shit while running, but I have to do something. Nathan might be holding his own, but he's unarmed. And both of them are already back and up on their feet.

For a split second, I catch Nathan's eye as he turns in my direction. A silent communication passes between us. A second later he drops to the floor and I start to fire at the vampires. Bullets hit them – arms, legs, shoulder.

I'm all over the place, because I'm still moving. Then my gun clicks empty. And they're still standing. And not looking pleased at all by the fact I just emptied my clip into them.

I'm not going to have enough time to reload before they come for me. I am, after all the one they're here for. I pull the knife out of my back pocket, readying myself.

As they make a move to come for me, Nathan jumps one of them, taking him down to the floor. Then I see Zeff blur past me. The first one is dusted in less than a few seconds. Nathan's knelt on one pounding his face in.

I stare as Nathan's pushed backwards and Zeff moves in, allowing him the space he needs to drive his knife into the vampire's heart.

As he turns to dust beneath Nathan, he sags to the floor.

I run to him, sitting at his side. Putting my gun and knife down, I roll him onto his back.

That when I see the blood, oozing out of his left side.

"Oh God!" I say, instantly panicked, my hands on him. "Did I shoot you?!"

"No," he groans. "One of the vamps got me. Sliced me with his fucking blade."

My insides freeze. "Silver?!"

He can tell from my tone what my worry is.

"Silver doesn't hurt me like it does you. Don't worry baby, I'm fine. I'm cut but it's nothing that won't heal."

Putting a hand to his ribcage, he starts to sit himself up. I take his arm, helping him.

I look at the blood seeping out of his side from in-between his fingers, and my natural instinct takes over. I feel that familiar pang in my mouth. I stop it from happening.

That's how disgusting I am.

The love of my life is cut and bleeding and my natural reaction is to want to feed. I hate myself in this moment.

Nathan gets to his knees, then his feet. Zeff is just stood here to the side of us, eyes on me and Nathan.

I'm trying to pretend he's not here. Nathan isn't. He turns to face him.

"You're the Original?"

"Zeff," he nods.

Nathan turns to me. Apparently that's the extent of their conversation. Can't say I'm not relieved.

"There's more of them. I saw two of them make for the barn where dad and Scarlett were."

His hand is still gripping his side. He's in obvious pain, though he'll never admit just how much. I'm worried over how deep that cut goes.

"Where's Craig?" I ask, in the same instance as I reach my senses out. But Zeff speaks before I even get a read.

"There's a human, a werewolf, and a shifter, in the barn over there. No vampires."

The relief I feel is astronomical.

"We should get to them," I say with urgency.

Much to his protest, I put Nathan's arm around my shoulder, giving him some support. Then me, Nathan, and Zeff, make our way to the barn. Now there's a sentence I never thought I'd say.

Jack, Craig, and Scarlett, walk out of the barn, meeting us on the track.

Craig looks pretty beat up. Jack's bleeding from the nose. Scarlett looks unharmed, but terrified. Making sure Nathan can stand on his own, I go straight over to Scarlett.

"Are you okay?" I ask her, putting my arm around her shoulders, pulling her close.

She's shivering with fear.

"Um … yeah … I think so…" she says quietly.

This is all my bloody fault. I'm so fucking stupid. Of course they would find me here. I've almost just let happen again the very reason I left the last time. One of them could have died.

What, I thought Zeff finding me made it okay for me to come back here? In what fucking warped world do I live? I'm so unbelievably selfish. I just can't see past my own love for Nathan at times.

I glance at Zeff. He's standing back. His eyes on me.

He knew this would happen. He warned me. And I didn't listen.

"Thank you," I say with sincerity. If he hadn't have been here who knows what would have happened.

He nods, eyes still scribed to mine.

I guess the question is, what was he doing here? Actually, no. I think I already know the answer to that.

"How did you know they were coming?"

"I was nearby."

"Oh," I say. His face tells me the rest. I was right in my thinking. He's been here the whole time.

I don't know whether to be freaked out or grateful. Both, I think. I can feel Nathan's unease and anger emanating from my left, but I can't look at him. Not yet.

Eyes still set on me, Zeff says, "You need to get out of here, and soon. More will be coming for you. A bounty has gone on your head."

A chill slivers through me. I can feel Nathan's stare on me, but I daren't look at him. Not yet anyway.

"A bounty?" my mouth barely forms the words.

"After we killed those vampires … well, let's put it this way – Elijah doesn't know I was here - so his assumption is you have help or you took them out alone, either one will scare the hell out of him. He doesn't do scared, or losing, so basically he's taking no chances now when it comes to you. He wants you dead. And he's paying big."

I slide my arm from around Scarlett and wrap them around myself. I feel like it's only me and Zeff here right now. How does he do that?

"Every supernatural being you wouldn't want coming after you, now is," Zeff continues. "Which means Isaiah will also pick up pace to find you before anyone else does. It didn't take those ones long to find you. It won't take the others."

"Why is it always the bloody vampires that find me?!"I cry at Zeff. Not that I want any of them to find me.

"Because they're excellent trackers. Vârcolac's are blood driven, lazy, and mostly stupid. Out for themselves and what they can get. There is no loyalty in my off-breeds."

"Wow. You must be so proud," I say, snarky.

He gives me a look. I feel a pang, and realise I've actually missed those looks of his. I don't like the feeling one little bit.

"Not really." He shakes his head, dragging my eyes in movement with his. "For me they could all be eradicated. I don't care for any of it – I told you."

I slide a glance in Nathan's direction. He's still holding his wound. I meet his eyes. There's no real connection in our gaze. I want him to come over to me, to put his arms around me, but he doesn't. I don't think I want to know why not.

"Vampires are dangerous because they're smart and loyal to their makers requests. If they are on a hunt, tracking a mark, that's all that counts to them, and they will find it without a doubt. You need to leave here, yes, and you can keep running, but running will only be effective if they have no read on you. No way to track you."

I almost know what's coming.

"There is something we could try to keep you hidden." Pause. "I could spell you. I've never done it to another before, but it's worth a try."

"What's the catch?" I ask.

He stares at me for a long moment. Almost as if he's forgetting there are others here. I know I keep forgetting there are.

What is that all about? Is he somehow doing that to me with his magic?

I start to feel uncomfortable under his heavy stare, and I'm about to look away when he says, "You have to stay with the power source."

Nathan strides over to me, putting a protective arm around my shoulders. Fingers gripping a tight hold of me, staring a hard look at Zeff, he says, "You? No way is Alex leaving here with you."

I look up at Nathan. I see it all in his eyes.

"Promise me something?" he said
"Anything."
"You'll never leave me."
"I promise."
"Say it."
"I'll never leave you."

I promised him. I can't break that promise.

I drag my eyes from Nathan, back to Zeff. "You want to help me. Okay, that's great. Thank you. But if you spell me and I go with you–"

"Alex–" Nathan butts in.

"Nathan has to come too. You want to help me like you say you do, he comes too. If not, thank you for your offer, but we'll take our chances alone." I emphasise the *we'll* to let Zeff know that's how I see things. It's not just me anymore. It's me and Nathan.

Nathan visibly relaxes next to me.

I see it in Zeff eyes, the discourse. I know I'm risking a lot. I need his help. And by the looks of things after today, I won't survive five minutes out there without his protection.

I'm just praying on the fact it's not in him to walk away. If I'm guessing right, he's been here since I left Italy. He followed me here. It wasn't exactly a coincidence he was here at just the exact right time, was it. And that tells me all I need to know.

"Okay," he nods. "The more bodies, the better you are protected."

He doesn't mean that for one second. Zeff could protect me fine alone. He could probably take down a small army of vampires single-handed if he wanted to.

"Well, if you and Nate are going, then I'm coming too," Jack pipes up. I swivel to look at him. "Well, I can't stay here now, can I? With a shit load of vampires and God knows what else readying to swoop in … so where else am I going to go?"

"Somewhere safe?" I pipe up.

"I'm in too," Craig says, obviously ignoring me.

"Me too," Scarlett says from beside me. I give her a confused look. "Well where else am I gonna go?" She shrugs. "It's either brave the streets, or stay with you guys and go on the run with one of the most powerful creatures on earth who can protect us. Hands down, it's an easy choice from where I'm stood."

I hear Zeff's little snuffle of laughter. I fire him a sharp look. He lets out a cough.

"Okay," he says, composing his features to neutral. "We need to get moving, and now. So grab what you need and be quick about it."

Chapter 32: Family

I'm in the passenger seat of the Range Rover. Nathan next to me, driving. Our bags in the back.

A horse box is attached to the back containing Honor. There was no way we were leaving them there. Zeff assured us, where we're going there would be a place for them to stay.

In front of us is Zeff in his car. Behind us, Craig, Jack and Scarlett, in Craig's truck, the other horse box with Hope attached to it. Nathan's Ducati is in there too. He wasn't leaving without her, apparently.

Zeff gave us directions, but we're still following close behind him. He spelled me before we left the farm. It worked. I think he always knew it would. It was the oddest sensation I've ever felt.

Like I was showering in electricity. Now I don't feel anything. Just back to normal. Well, except for the fact that I'm tied to Zeff by a powerful magical force.

Zeff wanted me to ride with him in his car, because I need to stay within decent proximity to keep the spell active. If I break it he has to respell me.

Not a massive effort, but not something I fancy having done on a regular basis. But still I said no. As long as Nathan stays close to his car, then we're fine. I wanted this time alone with Nathan because who knows when we'll be alone properly together, or how long I really have left.

One of two things will happen.

I'll be taken by Isaiah and they'll never find me again.

Or, I'm going to die.

The latter is looking most likely considering it's the vampires who seem to be the best at finding me, and they want me dead. I haven't really considered the fact Elijah wanted me dead until now. It's not personal, I know that, but still it's hard to know that my existence is so pernicious to someone that they've put a bounty on my head.

I guess that's one thing I have in common with both Zeff and Isaiah. Elijah wanted … well still, wants them dead. They've managed to stay alive for four hundred years. Maybe I have a chance of surviving the next fifty or so.

Maybe.

Hopefully.

A life lived in the shadows. But a life in the shadows with Nathan is better than no life at all.

I reach my hand out to his side, fingers gently touching the area just outside his knife wound. I hear his sharp intake of breath.

"Sorry," I say.

A soft smile. The sweet kind which makes me want to reach over and kiss him. So I do. A light kiss on his cheek.

It wins me another smile.

Nathan wouldn't let me have Jack or anyone stitch his wound up. He said there was no time, and it would heal soon enough. I'm just worried it'll get infected. He said it wouldn't, but I think he would have said anything to get me out of the house and moving. I did manage to get to put some gauze on it.

"Is it healing okay?" I ask.

"Yes."

"Is that a yes to shut me up and stop me worrying, or a real yes?"

He slides his eyes off the road to me, momentarily. "A real yes." He reaches over and takes hold of my hand, bringing to his mouth, he kisses it.

"You feel a little funny," he says.

"Funny how?"

"Like … I keep getting tiny static shocks from you every time I touch you. I just thought it was static at first, but it's every time."

"Oh." Pause. "It's the magic."

"Ah … okay." But he doesn't let go off my hand, which makes me feel better.

I inhale a deep breath. "Nathan, is this the right thing to do?"

He looks at me again. "It's your call. You just say the word and I'll swing this car around now, and we'll take our chances alone."

I can see the glimmer of hope in his eyes. I know he wants to keep me safe, and safe is under Zeff's spell. But he doesn't want to be in this with Zeff. I know Nathan, he's the in charge guy, so I figure this can't be easy for him. In more ways than one.

We'd just found one another, had settled into something, and here we are again on the run. But this time, we've lost the sanctuary of home. And I've lost the one remaining place I could run to for safety.

"I know keeping me hidden is the right thing to do," I say slowly. "What I meant when I said it is, you all coming with me."

I see the hope in his eyes fade, quickly replaced by hurt.

"And don't take that as I don't want you with me. Because I do, more than anything. I just feel like you're all being dragged, yet again, into my fight."

"Obviously there was no stopping me. Even if you didn't want me here, I'd have still come." He gives me a warm smile. "And seriously, do you really think you would have been able to stop my dad from coming?"

"I guess not." I shake my head. "It's just pulling them away from their lives. Your dad leaving behind the farm. It must be killing him; I know how much that place means to him."

"But that's what you do for family. You drop everything to help them."

"I know your dad's doing it for you, I get that, but you're doing this for me and that's makes me feel like utter crap for creating the domino effect."

He casts me a surprised look. "I didn't mean just me. You're his family too. Craig and Scarlett. We're all a family."

A sudden rise of tears, warn the backs of my eyes. "We are?"

"You remember back when I was being a bastard in Scotland, and I said you didn't have any family left? Well I was talking shit, as usual. I said it to hurt you because you were trying to leave me, and I was scared. I didn't want you to go."

He lets out a small laugh. "You know, because back then I thought being a complete and utter shit to you would make you want to stay." He raises his brows at me. I actually have to let out a little laugh at that one. "You have family Alex, the same as you did back then. You have me. Us."

He thumbs behind him.

"Family isn't always blood. It comes from friendships. When people care for one another. That's what makes family. Just like Carrie and Angie and Tom were. And well, those lot in that car back there, are doing this because they care about you, because they love you. Just like I do," he says.

"Maybe not Scarlett," I say, trying to lighten my own heart. "I think she's pretty much confused half the time about what's going on. Living in her own world. Which is probably a good place to be right now. I might ask her if she fancies a trade."

Nathan laughs, "Yeah, we're a pretty fucked up weird kind of family – two shifters, the only female Vârcolac in existence, an outcast werewolf, and an ex-street girl. But we are family. I guarantee you that."

I laugh again. But inside I'm all types of fuzzy feelings, because the word 'family' has coated me, wrapping around me like a life-jacket, helping me bob up to the water's surface I keep feeling like I'm been pulled under, with the ever strong current, and Nathan has just resurfaced me.

Kissing my hand one last time, he releases it, and says, "I need to make a call."

He pulls his phone out of his pocket. "I promised dad I'd make sure the animals left on the farm are sorted and cared for," he says when he sees my puzzled expression.

"Oh okay, sure."

Scrolling through his phone book, he dials a number, then clicks the phone into his hands-free kit on the dashboard.

It rings a few times, before answering.

"Nate?" comes the female voice down the line. I noticed how surprised she sounds to be hearing from him.

"Hi Beth."

I notice the change in his voice. For some reason it bothers me.

"It's been a long time," she says. "How are you?"

Her voice is lovely. Soft and nice sounding. I don't like it.

"I'm good, thanks. You?"

I feel like I'm listening in on a conversation I really shouldn't be listening to.

"I'm well, thanks," she sounds distracted. "Look Nate, I'm really glad you called. I've wanted to speak to you for a while now, I mean the last time we spoke, and well, what I said, I just want you to know–"

"You're on speaker," he cuts in. "And I'm not alone."

Silence.

I don't know if he said that to spare me, or her.

And now all I want to know is who the hell Beth is, and what did she say to him the last time they spoke?

I'm guessing she was more than a friend once upon a time. Just how long ago was she his 'non-friend'? Was it in the six months I was gone? I mean, we've never discussed what, or who, he did while I was away. I never wanted to ask in case I didn't like the answer.

Also I hate the way she calls him Nate. Only his family and close friends call him Nate, but to me he's Nathan. I hate the ways she's so familiar with him. And more to the point why couldn't he wait to ring her when I'm not here listening. I know this is something to do with the animals and the farm but Jesus Christ. And now I'm just really irritated.

"I need you to do me a favour," he says.

"Okay," Beth says. "What is it?"

"We've had to leave the farm unexpectedly."

"Is everything okay?"

She sounds concerned, worried. I actually want to punch the phone to silent. I never knew I had such a jealous streak.

"Yeah. Kind of. Nothing to worry about, it's just there's no one there to take care of the animals. Would you be able to move them off the farm and find them a good home?"

"You going to be gone a while?" she inquires.

"Yeah. So can you make sure they get good homes? Another farmer, give them away, it's no problem."

"I can take them in. I've got the space, and then you can get them back when you come home."

"Thanks. I'll reimburse you for any cost."

"Don't be silly," she says. "What about Honor?"

"She's with me."

"Ah. Okay."

"You're sure you're fine with doing this?" he confirms.

"Of course."

"Will you let me know when you've got the animals?"

"Sure."

"And Beth, don't go there yourself. Send one of the collection guys to get the animals – actually send a few of them, and tell them to not go anywhere near the house. And when they get there, if there are any cars parked on the drive, tell them to turn around and drive away, and not to go back – ever. Okay?"

"Okay," she says tentatively. "Nate." Pause. "Are you sure you're okay?"

I can hear the worry in her voice. Again, I don't like it. It tells me more than I think I want to know.

"I'm fine." His tone is soft with her. I hate that even more.

I really wish this phone call would end. I can feel my heart pumping hard against my chest.

"Okay," she says. "I'll go now and call you later when I've moved them."

"Thanks."

He clicks off.

There is absolute silence in the car, except for the sound of my pumping heart. I know she's doing him a favour, and I have no clue who she is, but I'm feeling kind of irrational at the moment. And I've got a thousand questions reaming through my mind, I'm just not sure which one to start with.

Eventually, I have to ask, "Who's Beth?" Before I bite my tongue off.

"An old friend."

"Oh." I start to fiddle with my necklace, holding the pendant, sliding it around the chain. "She an old friend, of the old girlfriend variety?"

"Yes."

"Is she the last girlfriend? The serious one?" I remember him telling me there was one serious girlfriend that time in the Dalby Forest, the one who left him because she didn't like who he'd become after leaving the army.

He looks at me. "Yes."

"And why did you just call her exactly?"

He gives me a 'were you actually listening to the conversation' look.

"Because she's a vet, and she is the only person I know who can take the animals, and more to the point won't ask too many questions."

"Oh – wait, is she the one who you got Honor from?"

"Yeah, she works at the RSPCA, well she volunteers actually."

Great, so his ex-girlfriend is a saint. She volunteers her free time to sick and injured animals. I drink blood from animals, and kill them.

And I'm on the run from some of the world's most dangerous supernatural creatures, and have dragged pretty much the remainder of his family into running with me, and they've all lost their home because of me. And his ex-girlfriend, Beth, who clearly, if I'm reading her tone right, still has feelings for him, is doing the good Samaritan bit.

Brilliant. Just bloody fucking brilliant.

Okay, I know this is probably the worst time to start feeling jealous, but honestly I can't seem to help it. I'm putting it down to recent events absconding with any sense there was in me.

"Have you seen her recently?" I finger the lapel of my jacket.

"No."

"In the last six months?"

He gives me another slow look. "No."

"So what was she trying to apologise for?"

"I don't know"

"You must do."

He grips the steering wheel, harder. "No, Alex, I don't."

"So why did you stop her from talking then?"

"Because the reason I called her was not to rehash the past."

"So you did know what she was going to say?"

"No!" He's getting frustrated.

So am I. Jealous and frustrated. I didn't know it was in me to feel this level of envy. I guess it shows how much he means to me.

"Did you call her to punish me?"

He looks at me surprised.

"For Zeff turning up," I add, like he didn't already catch my meaning.

His face hardens. "Are we really going to do this now?"

I shrug, feigning indifference, but clearly I'm up for it.

"You're pissed off because of a two minute phone call to an ex-girlfriend so I can get the animals safely off the farm and cared for, because we are now, yet again, on the run for your life. Hmm…" He drums his fingers against his lips. "Yeah, sure I get why you're pissed off," he says sarcastically.

"Fuck off!" I curse at him. "You're such an arsehole at times!"

"And you're irrational. Come on, it's hardly the time to have a conversation like this. I mean, how do you think I'm feeling right now? Not so fucking great. But I cast it aside because there are bigger things to worry about at the moment."

I turn to him, feeling a wave of guilt.

"I'm sorry you've had to leave the farm again because of me," I say quietly.

"That's not what I meant." A sigh. "I'd leave there in a heartbeat for you. I did leave there in a heartbeat for you. None of that matters if I don't have you, Alex … it's just."

He sighs again. "Don't you think I don't hate this." He jabs a finger ahead in Zeff's car's direction. "Don't you see it's hard for me to accept that we are going to be with *him* for an infinite amount of time, because we have to be, because I can't protect you enough, not in the way he can. You think that I don't feel completely fucking useless?"

"You're not useless," I say emphatically. "You're the strongest, bravest person, I've ever known."

"Aside from superman there in front us."

"He might be strong, but he's no hero."

He snorts a really pissed off sound. "Yeah and neither am I, Alex. You just like to think I am. And you think I don't see that he's got feelings for you."

"He hasn't got feelings for me," I laugh.

I hear the break in my voice, so I know he does too. I don't want to lie to him. But I also don't want to upset and piss him off more than he is right now. And the fact Zeff made a declaration of love to me a few weeks ago is of little consequence to me.

"Don't treat me like an idiot. The guy's clearly in love with you. I spotted that the second he put his eyes on you. And he wouldn't be doing this if he wasn't. Remember who he is."

"Whatever reason he is doing this is nothing to do with me. He's doing it for his own reasons from the past, between him and his brother – whatever they are." I'm not sure if even I believe that statement fully, so I know he's not going to. "Whether he's in love with me or not, is irrelevant."

"Is it?" He looks at me, a mixture of fear and anger in his eyes.

"Yes."

He looks away. "The irrelevance depends on whether you have feelings for him or not." His voice has dropped a few decibels lower.

"I don't have feelings for him. I'm not having this fight with you again."

"Alex, I know you feel connected to him. I see it in you. I have from the moment you got back. And I get it – I do. It's taken me a while, but I've accepted it. He's your maker. God, I saw how you reacted to Craig the first time you met him." He releases a humourless laugh.

"I didn't react to Craig in any way at all!"

I'm angry now.

"And so fucking what if he's–" I jab a thumb at Zeff's car in front of us. "My 'maker'." I air quote. "I am not in love with him!" I hold my breath for a moment, tears in my eyes again. "He's not you."

I can hear Nathan's own breathing. It's ragged. He glances steady eyes at me.

The cracks are starting to set in between us again, and we've only been driving for half-an hour. We're going to end up right back where we were six months ago.

Our honeymoon period sure is over.

"Are we going back there, already?"

His steady gaze slides to confused, but softens in transition too. "Back to where?"

"To the people we were together six months ago. To the people who fought in that hotel room that night."

His eyes flick back to the road, then back to me. Reaching his arm over, he slides it behind my neck, around my shoulder, pulling me over to him.

I rest my head on his shoulder. His presses his lips to the top of my head.

"No," he murmurs, muffled by my hair. The heat from his breath warms and soothes me. "We're not going back. It's just me and you now, and we're good. We'll always be good."

He presses another, firmer, kiss to my head again. "And whomever happens to have to join along for the ride – if it means keeping you alive and safe – well then fine, but they're not getting in the front seat with us, okay? We're a two seat ride."

I laugh, lifting my head. "I think those shocks are effecting you worse than you're letting on. That analogy sounded like the kind of shit I would come up with. You're spending way too much time around me, Hargreaves. I'm starting to rub off on you."

He laughs again, louder this time, but quickly quietens, putting his hand to his sore wound.

"Rub away," he says, managing a cheeky glint.

Pressing a quick, soft kiss to my lips, he looks back to the road ahead.

And I know, no matter what, we'll get through it together. Whatever is out there waiting for me. Whatever they choose to throw at me, I'll get through it, because I've got Nathan by my side, in front of me, and covering my back, watching out for me, always taking care of me.

Zeff might be able to work his magic and kick ass to the end of time, but Nathan is the one who will always keep me safe. The one who I'll always feel safe with.

I glance back at my makeshift family in the car behind us, then up at Nathan again. I press a kiss to his cheek, then snuggle in under his arm, moving in closer. He welcomes me gladly.

He takes hold of my hand, entwining our fingers he kisses my ring, holding it to his mouth, his breath warm on my skin, heating my heart.

I may have the world's two most evil creatures after me. One wanting me dead. The other as his sex slave. Their part equivalents hot on my heels - thanks to Elijah's bounty. And the added complication of Zeff as a now permanent part of my foreseeable future.

But I couldn't feel more loved and more protected than I am right now, here with Nathan – and with them behind me in the truck; Jack, Craig, and Scarlett.

And I know whatever comes at us. It does just that. It comes at *us*.

I'm no longer alone.

I have a family again.

Acknowledgements

First and foremost, I want to say a humongous thank you to Poppet. You're not just my friend; you're my guide, my light when I'm lost. I adore you!

A huge thank you to my family. The important ones. You know who you are.

And also my online family – Jess, LilyCat, Reg, Rob, Shalini, Suzy, Mandy, Johanna, Heather, Mike, John, Janus and Hannah – I love you guys!

Thank you to Tim Roux and Kathleen McKenna for all your support.

Mum, as always, thank you for everything you do for me.

Thank you to my gorgeous husband, Craig, and my two beautiful children, Riley and Isabella. This is it now. This is where it begins. I love you three, beyond any words I could ever write.

And lastly, I want to say a massive thank you to all my readers. Thank you for living Alex and Nathan's story with me. Thank you for loving them as much as I do. The support I receive from you guys on a daily basis astounds me. I treasure each and every one of you, and I especially love our man candy days … long may they continue!

3592875R00152

Printed in Great Britain
by Amazon.co.uk, Ltd.,
Marston Gate.